Praise

"Evoking *Breakfast of Champions* in the best possible way, Karl Dehmelt casts a satirical alien's-eye-view on a recent, unfinished history Americans know all too well. It is in part the story of a plague we all (kinda) survive—afflicting heart, mind, and culture—that is revealed in hilarious and heartbreaking detail as only a non-Earth narrator could. It's intense and dizzying, even frightening at times, but then again all the best drugs are."

— Thaddeus Gunn

"... a scathing piece of trenchant brilliance ... an absurd and astonishingly poignant portrait of modern-day America ... with the comedically lyrical lines of Tom Robbins and savage turns of phrase that would make Hunter S. Thompson tip his cap, Dehmelt stands on the shoulders of giants without slipping too far into derivative tropes. The author is right in thanking John Kennedy O'Toole in his introduction, for much of this prose is laced with perfectly visceral wording, while there are also echoes of Pynchon from the more in-depth diatribes... this romp of a political screed will have you hysterical in more ways than one."

— *The Independent Review of Books*

DAFT MEJORA's INFINITE MADNESS
(Or, How to Travel Near America with Friends)

DAFT MEJORA's INFINITE MADNESS
(Or, How to Travel Near America with Friends)

Karl Dehmelt

Apprentice
House Press
Loyola University Maryland

First Edition

Hardover ISBN: 978-1-62720-499-6
Paperback ISBN: 978-1-62720-500-9
Ebook ISBN: 978-1-62720-501-6

Cover by Sienna Whalen
Internal Design by Sienna Whalen & Katie McDonnell
Author photo by Joaquín Floro

Published by Apprentice House Press

Apprentice
House Press
Loyola University Maryland

Loyola University Maryland
4501 N. Charles Street, Baltimore, MD 21210
410.617.5265
www.ApprenticeHouse.com

info@ApprenticeHouse.com

To the more than one million Americans who have lost their lives at least, in part, to COVID-19.

ACKNOWLEDGEMENTS

This work has been inspired by the likes of Hunter S. Thompson, Kurt Vonnegut, Philip Roth (particularly *Portnoy's Complaint* in terms of frankness of language), internet creators such as Cyriak Harris, Anonymoose, and comedians such as George Carlin, Dave Chappelle, Eric Andre, and Sarah Squirm. A huge debt of gratitude to Toni Morrison for her work, Raymond Carver for his, and Denis Johnson and Cormac McCarthy and Robert Olen Butler for theirs, as well. The early films of John Waters (particularly the work of Divine) and Flying Lotus, as well as other universally acclaimed storytellers such as Hayao Miyazaki and classic video games, *Zelda* in particular, all contributed to this work's collective imagination. John Kennedy Toole's *Confederacy of Dunces* has served as a constant reminder of how life works in both its story and its story of publication. Additionally, the works of the Marquis de Sade, the music of Marilyn Manson, and classics such as van Goethe's *Faust* showcase the shortness of the space between love, art, hatred, madness, and what drives people to those places in this world in ways that are, somehow, human, for better and for worse, at times. Eternal credit to Albert Camus for his striking depictions of human absurdity and compassion. Anyone who has ever survived a traumatic time of their life with humor has contributed to this book in some way, because the point of The Daft One's COVID mask design is that the line between tragedy and comedy is as thin as the wires connecting us to one another in a realm far beyond the simply physical: the ones where our emotions meet those we love, no matter where they are (or are no longer).

Eternal gratitude to Dr. Kevin Atticks (current Maryland Secretary of Agriculture!) and the students of Apprentice House Press (especially Sienna Whelan for the cover design and Katie McDonnell for the interior) for believing in me to the zenith, especially over the course of my career and in the face of a lot of dishonesty and disinformation as is common in the world today. Originally, when I published this project as The Daft One, I did not want it to be tied to my true identity due to still believing I needed to be someone other than who I was on the page, and while many circles of the still-remaining, decentralized literary community might not have taken a chance on this book, the fact that its gained the word of mouth recognition that it has along with the responses so far is a testament to how a press committed to good work can do amazing things in a time when reading isn't seen as cool by some people. I'm also grateful for the chance to perform this work in varying forms of media and to engage with an audience who wants to still value the arts along with science in an age where both have been called into deep question thanks to the fractured nature of general American discourse. Gratitude as well to the Loyola University Maryland Writing Department for the enduring lessons I have kept five years after graduation.

For Madrid: I am so thankful to have written this work in the neighborhoods of Prosperidad, Anton Martin, and Carabanchel, and I am most grateful to the Deep Cove, especially Khaled for his insights on life, and the staff and community of that locale for the tremendous creative atmosphere and sense of purpose I found in writing this work in a supportive environment, especially those who were there between September of 2021 and

December of 2021 during the book's writing, and to those who still remain in the city, where people come and go over the course of life, potentially to return. A particular shoutout to my "agent," León David Levy, as well, for his addition to and expansion of my creative processes through exploration of thinking and visual art outside of the written work of this book. Gracias a Madrid por todo, en particular la experiencia he tenido en esa época de tiempo y la vida en general, porque el espíritu de la ciudad es una cosa es posible que tenga cada día allí – es un fenómeno físico y mucho más. In addition to this, thanks to my former school, La Escuela Superior de Hosteleria y Turismo, and the staff who talked with me about this work as I developed it over the academic year, along with fellow Madrid regulars John G., Javier Yusta, Isabella Cruz, Jose Carlos Gaspar, Khaled al-Senussi (as mentioned!), Luca Bonarelli, Sultan Turki, Marta C., Andrea, Juán C., Fernando Palma, Peter Davey, Cósima Ramirez, Terry Craven (and the crew at Desperate Literature, including Charlotte, of course), Elizabeth Jane Woods, Lydia Ellis, and a shoutout to Bollullos par del Condado for the 8 months I spent there in 2018-2019, as well as the city of Granada and the study abroad program through which I was introduced to Spain in 2017.

Staying on the European side of things, huge shoutout to my Berlin family as well, particularly the great Yugo Taguchi, and Felix, plus the rest of the crew at Buy Reggae / Blessed Love Records, and also to Dr. Leif Dehmelt and his family in Essen. Additionally, and on a trans-continental note, a shoutout to Dr. Sofie Verraest for her support, and, of course, to Thaddeus Gunn, Teresa Wilson-Gunn, J.C. Geiger, Flaminia Chiodi, Tom Dean in the U.K., Alina Kotova in San Francisco, Katie Szyszko in Folkestone, and to the man who has somehow not won a

Pulitzer in the United States but who has indeed won the Man Booker, George W. Saunders, for his and the indomitable Mary Karr's absolutely incredible workshop experience on Patmos in 2018 and for George's congratulations and encouragement to me for my voice. Thanks to Mary for her wisdom and her incredible work. Shoutout to George Cossette as well for his and his family's commitment to the arts, and to John Engman, dearly departed but never forgotten, whose poetry I recited to a group of Spanish students to demonstrate the translational beauty of rhythm. Additionally, thanks to my friends Dragan P., Lachlan K., Justin C., Gary G., Luke C., Keith M., Chris C., Ali C., Amber W., Emily C., Jenelle B., Alex A., Steven B., Jeff W., Brian K., Ryan H., James M., Wesley P., Matt B., Kru, Michael B., Reanne and Ros, Natalie K., and Joaquin F., my flatmate and friend in Madrid. I am grateful to my family from the United States of America, specifically my mother (rest in peace as always) and my father and my family on both sides of what was a divorce in 2010, for their continuation of supporting my writing career despite the dramatic change I've undergone as a person and as an artist and as someone with something valuable to say about the current era.

To anyone who read the version of this book posted online or on reddit for the hell of it, originally, simply to have it out there, thanks for believing in the project and let's see where it goes. I am filled with optimism that the work's impact will continuously echo, and by the time the second one comes out, we shall see how much reality catches up to the life and words of those of us who have been forced to live as we have needed to at the speed of reality in 2023.

To anyone who reads this book: thank you for your time, it's precious for us all.

THE CAST OF CHARACTERS

THE THREE FRIENDS:

- The Daft One (Daft Mejora (pronounced Meh-jore-uhhh in English) – interplanetary, undercover leader of the alien expedition to earth; presents himself as a 14 year old white boy.

- The Donger Pony – Mejora's faithful, plastic, 'inanimate' steed, shaped like a strange cross between a horse's body and a suggestive sculpture, AND

- The Wise Owl – an actual, living, anthropomorphic owl who speaks solely in bardic rhymes.

DJ AND HIS FAMILY:

- Dylan James "DJ" Jones – the "New Boy" who becomes Mejora's best friend, senior at Dickson County High School

- Paul "DJ Daddy" Jones – the State Representative who helps catapult Mejora's celebrity career

- Charlene Jones – The woman who sacrifices her own life for her family.

ESTEEMED POLITICIANS AND PUBLIC FIGURES:

- Senator Jim Baetz – Florida's Celebri-Senator

- Justice Britt – Presides over the trial that happens near the end.

- Marlene – Jim's loyal paramour/press secretary

- Ms. America – You'll see.

PART I:
THE DAFT ONE COMES
TO EARTH

ONE

The kid spends more time in his room than any other human we've ever watched through their cameras. He's one of these ones with the palest skin, white already due to genealogy, heritage, but also due to the amount of hours he spends amidst the darkness of his chamber, the sun burning its finite divinity inches from his face behind a set of blinds that have seen a whole lot of things. They've seen victories and losses in the game *Counter-Strike*, the one where you're either a terrorist or someone trying to stop them, a simulator for the kind of shootings they perform on each other every single day. Their rituals are so violent, so depraved – you might think DJ's association with this murderous, virtual puppetry makes him like one of those people who gather at the beach near his house and claim the flag of "traitors" constitutes "heritage." But no, he doesn't wander down there with the shittiest alcohol possible, smelling like how their gums and teeth and lips and cheeks do following a cycle of tobacco through their saliva. Instead, he sits in his room and plays the games, jerks the offs, and wastes as much time as possible not completing simple tasks by doing something else random, like falling too far down the internet into places where they sell and buy people (and do the types of things they'll *arrest* you for if they find you there). A place like that is where we met, where he found us. And now we're due to meet him, my friends and I, having ventured through lights and time and understanding solely to wash up on the shores of the LAND OF OPPORTUNITY, the place where dreams become real and what's real becomes fake depending on exactly where you stand.

These … *people* …

When talking to THE DONGER PONUS, my trusty steed and phallically inclined, porcelain penis-looking horse, I almost had to talk like one of these human travel guides.

"We can go see a wedding at a slave holder's house," I told the Pone one day, as we were surfing through the most recent absurdities on their social media sites. As always, my dongered friend hopped up and down, his plastic-ish hooves click-clacking on the chair excitedly. "No, don't worry, your skin is the right color. You won't be shot by one of the people who protect and serve. We should have no problem finding THE NEW BOY in that family-sized house of his."

And what a house it *is*, Mr. DJ's home base. His father is the type of human who drives a Hummer everywhere he possibly can and imagines himself to be driving across a war zone – to say nothing of the fact he locks the doors while 'patrolling' through certain neighborhoods. He's not quite a neighborhood watchman, but he placed a bid on a gun that one of those men used to shoot an unarmed teenager those few years ago. He was the third runner up and the money he was willing to spend would have been enough to sustain his son's first year of University, but he's not there yet. DJ still has an entire year before he's expected to *make it on his own* in the world, still has the chance to be fastening his own bootstraps by doing menial yardwork amidst the crocodiles and rattlesnakes. With the fancy house in which he spends all his time in only *his* room, the boy's trying to be a competitive electronic sports player, the kind who make hundreds of thousands in South Korea and are seen as celebrities. Their television show currently dominating the streaming services is such a perfect depiction of the species. Humans will watch other humans do anything, truly, especially for the women who spend their time in hot tubs, with or without water, just chatting on Twitch while dozens upon hundreds upon millions of hungry eyes, like DJ's, do whatever it is they want to her in their depraved, perverted dreams. I myself have stared into the eyes of what they bury inside, and while DJ doesn't strike any of us as the type of white boy to go 'postal' like so many like him have, there are some twisted people who drink all of these streamers in, sucking them down like an obsession until their brains and ways of thinking legitimately change due to the presence of an invisible, shared connection.

In short, such is why studying them from the ground level is necessary, thus why DJ would be one of the people *best positioned* to receive the teachings of THE DAFT ONE. Along with our friend, the WISE OLD OWL, small, round, and greenish gray, speaking only in poetic forms, we three voyagers have a mission based upon intergalactic understanding to complete, one which focuses on the power of the human brain underneath the ballistics and bullshit we were just discussing. And oh, DJ's intelligent: he's already started noticing some of the minimal signals we've sent him, since his mother and he himself are the type of people who believe in those types of deities. The shift in energy, the drop in temperature feeling like an encounter with a ghost, a spirit, they say; the superstitious routine DJ has before playing a match, involving the de-greasing of his gamer gloves, the adjustments to his gamer chair, the reminder not to utter any of what they're calling *gamer words* during the parts of the broadcast where the audience will be watching *him*.

This is the same country making entertainment out of war

who also made concussions a necessary sacrifice for their Sunday rituals; they find themselves so far removed from men who sliced each other's throats and coated their steel blades in blood, and yet each one of those modern gladiators puts his pads and jockstrap and pride on in the same order every time. That's how we knew DJ could believe in things; his father's the type of dude who sees Qs in cloud formations. Not exactly, maybe. But from how we seen him behave and the type of shit *he's* been searching for, he's not quite down at the point where the line between truth and fiction blurs and ends up hanging in the center of it; instead, he's the type who believes the most powerful, wealthiest humans on earth are part of a type of ring of other humans who cook children in their own blood, drink the substance, and then put their hard things and soft things together until they're the devil's envy. And that's what makes me so hopelessly addicted to these people, to this country, to everything that makes us seek to understand their barbaric, uncivilized culture as a species: how they could have so much potential in their hands, something they like to call miracles, and use it to waste away in only the presence of one's own acidic scents and the cacophony of one's own mind.

Thus, THE NEW BOY was perfect for us. And he's due to meet us at the beach on Sunday after church.

TWO

I've done the best that I can to look like some sort of boy: I want the first impression DJ has when he sees me to be surprise at how young I seem. So I stole the raggedy goldilocks hairstyle from some fashion images and fused it with the fact I'm wearing open toed sandals over my feet while dressed in preppy jeans and a polo shirt by Ralph Lauren. My *electric blue* eyes, as they call them, feel charged by the ocean itself behind us. At my side, I hold MY TRUSTY STEED close and tightly. People probably think its some kind of bomb, that way they could imagine driving their Jeeps and Fords and Chevies and all this shit through the dunes and believe me to be some kind of "illegal alien." While I indeed have no documentation in my sorta-soaked pockets, my skin, so long as DJ doesn't stand us up and leave us here, will be the color of mayonnaise if we do not burn. However, DJ is the type of kid who will show up to what he wants to show up for; hell, he'll even lead the team at times when he sees they're starting to get down or too far into themselves. Around us, THE WISE OWL on my shoulder balks at the size of some of these contraptions as they smoke their cancers into the clear, blue sky, just like the mouths of the people reclining on the beach around them and their cigarettes.

THE WISE OWL:

Oh Daft One, my savior, my Iris, my lord,
What is the real difference between Chevy and Ford?

For why are there testicles under their axles,
And why are they dressed like they're ready for battle?

"Well, Mr. Owl," I tell him, using an example with three cow-sized humans in the back of the truck near us, with two in confederate flag one pieces and the other with his penis engorged in his swimming shorts. "This is what makes it impossible for us to invade them from the ground. This is why we're meeting DJ."

THE WISE OWL:
My absurd converter, my prophet, my sage-
Is this not why they say America is Great?

"Indeed it is," I tell him. "Look at that one over *there*."

In the slight cancer cloud provided by the perpetually coughing exhaust, amidst the rumbles from the massive engine, there is an elderly couple with skin wrinkled nearly to shrivels, tanner than fresh dirt. They're on a towel with the one leader's orange face painted on it, like the people who make pornographic content in tanning booths. Thankfully, the United States is one of the groups of humans who fear female breasts the most, or else we would be subjected to not only the atrocity known as trumpussy, but we'd have to see the man's Viagra powered punisher. Both of these would have been ruinous to my dongered pony's invisible eyes. He jumps in the sand and hops away from a toddler trying to push him into a waterlogged hole they've dug in the shoreline. He's threatening to trip the child and toss him down there, but thankfully we get saved from the secondhand smoke and accusations of accidental death by DJ, dressed in all-black pants and a shirt with a mean looking skull on it, with his headphones in, walking sheepishly up to us amidst the crashing waves and drunken hollers. He's squinting as though we're the sun.

"Yo," he says, sounding like he's wandered off the set of

Breaking Bad during Spring Break. "Are you The Daft One?" He refers to me by the screenname of my Platinum ranked CS:GO account, the one where I befriended him and we shared in the miracle of their world's small size.

"Hi DJ," I say to him, most of my true voice and tone suppressed by the slightly effeminate charm of the surfer boy we've chosen for me this fine morning. "So glad we can finally meet you!"

"Is that …" he stops short, his sneakers in the wet sand planted flat. "Is that a *real owl?*"

"Indeed it is, Dylan," I tell him. "Would you like to hear it speak?"

"Sure," DJ says, looking around him at some of the bug-eyed stares at us, the odd couple, from these deep frying marshmallows. "It's fuckin' *hot* out here today."

I nod at THE WISE OWL. He shuffles his ancient wings and points his black beak at DJ.

THE WISE OWL:

Pleased to meet you, Sir DJ, the best shot in Florida,
Are you ready to meet the general of absurd Sparta?

"That's *wild*," DJ says, his own double entendre never a flash in his eyes. "It almost sounds like he's saying *words!*"

The owl looks back at me, his little chest sighing and his eyes spinning 360 degrees laterally, from yellow and black to white and back around again. That means he's upset with me.

THE WISE OWL:

I told you this boy did not possess our hearing,
Despite his pension for apathy and his eternal god-fearing;
I fear now that he's not going to understand our goals,
Short of us asking for a golden fiddle to spare his soul.

I ignore my poetically pessimistic, foulish friend, and say to

DJ, "He's the smartest bird in the whole South."

"Seriously," DJ says, the easy laugh fuller than it had been over Discord, despite competing with the waves. "You could make a lot of money with that."

"We should start a Twitch channel." I tell him, allowing my slightly noticeable canines to unsheathe themselves from behind my lips, underneath my mask. DJ's limp, surgical blue one hangs onto one of his nailless digits by a single thin white strand. He nods enthusiastically, checking his phone at the same time and probably texting his realtor cunt of a mother – I'm sorry, I don't like her and you will understand why very shortly, the pony starts screaming whenever she enters into DJ's room during games – that he's safe and not the victim of some strange internet kidnapping scheme. Well, at least not until the rest of us get here, anyway – its telling that they've depicted aliens as being these people obsessed with the human anus, while I can assuredly report we find the entire sexual, digestive, and psychological systems disgusting works of atrocious error; the only thing I'd ever insert into a human anus would be the barrel of one of their own weapons. Like the ones strapped across the backs of some of the people who are standing around a massive bonfire *downrange* on this very beach. It's something we're actually going to be able to watch with our new best friend, because his dad is the one who drove him here and who is somewhere in that crowd, supervising the *cool, trendy gamer meetup* like a shotgun toting papa at a backyard wedding. *Those* videos are the funnest to watch, I swear, but I must admit to DJ that we, as a threesome, now as four, do not want to become fodder for those who spend hours watching the violent truths of life on sites live LiveLeak.

"Don't worry about it at all," DJ says. "I told you my dad's a state rep, right?"

"Indeed you did," I tell him. He's currently locked in a fight, like a bull in another's horns, against the democratic school-board of the affluent, sorta-kinda-private district in which DJ lives. He's dressed like he's selling the best crop, the marijuana, the mary jane, the dank kush that powers three generations of George Bush, on the streets instead of having it delivered to him as artisan edibles so that his hawkish father doesn't think he's converted to the devil's lettuce, as he terms it. And he tells us, of course, that his father is one of the featured speakers who is advocating for the rights of individuals. Remember, dear friends, these are the same species who had their founding fathers lauded as being enlightened figures as well as brutal, practical mathe-maticians. Judging from his internet usage, DJ's Daddy is also extremely familiar with the types of women who would have intercourse with a man like him due to the shape of his jaw for a reason unknown to all three of us, but DJ does not need to know this. It's important to remember, though, because he once had DJ's family pose for a billboard where they were said to be *focused on the family* together. And now here we are walking through the smells of burning wood and male piss, towards a group of people who have assembled with strange signs. These are the people who consider the vaccinations, one of the most important advents in the history of this twisted species, to be filled with a small, mechanical object that not only tracks them, but swims through their blood as though the spider has finally learned how to climb back up the spout, against the force of the drain. They also believe the Five gigabyte service is going to control their brains and infect them with the type of cancers they aren't getting by breathing in or out or at all at this very moment. And they've put their creativity into the pictures they're carrying, flapping like laminated flags in their hands whenever the man on the smallish stage says something that would make it in *Borat*.

UNMASKED, UNVAX'D, UNAFRAID, MENSTRUATING one sign says, held in the hands of a woman whose lips remind me of the sorts of slugs they remove from horses with the most recent treatment they've discovered for the *novel bug*. A picture of their former leader on her shirt has him sitting on one of those smoke-shitting motorcycles, his *exotic* model wife hanging on his back, a bunch of people just like the ones around here gathered behind them with the same reverence they used to reserve only for people who they 'read' about in their books. And yet they've made him into flesh and he's covered their flesh again, right alongside another woman, a concerned parent by any other name, holding up a sign above the already sunburnt back of her neck in a way that's nearly untranslatable:

"THERE IS A TIME TO SEW AND A TIME TO REAP" (ECCLESIASTES 3:2) quoted from one of their best books, with the original verse replaced by a red white and blue Q, the words horribly printed like a shitty rental car service advertisement in the subway in that cheap-ass font, and with pictures of politicians of the opposite party frowning and sniffing other humans' hair, etc. *I have no idea what the fuck she means*, the pony says, hopping in the loose sand.

A man standing near us, his biceps bursting like a pornstar and his testicles probably smaller than pearls, at this point, looks at the donger pony hopping in the sand and his plastic appendage in my hand, along with my proximity to DJ, and says, almost under his breath while turning away to place his ugly fucking lips to the top of his lukewarm Bud-Lite can, "I didn't know f*****s voted for Republicans."

DJ heard him. He looks at me and arches his thin eyebrows like I'm the newest, roundest ass he's ever seen on a lonely night at home. "Did you hear him?" He asks.

The owl digs its talons into my shoulder and flutters its wings. He's *feeling it, dude*. I shall allowl him (LOOL) to tell you the next part of the story, seeing as with DJ's actions it gets quite entertaining.

THE WISE OWL:

All you need to understand hatred in the breeze,
Play a few public games of P versus P.
The n-word, the mongoloid *shouted by tweens*
It's either winning or losing, there's no in-between.
It was said easily as hello or goodbye or good morning
And if the game was going shit, you'd have no warning.
You'd do something small, fall off a ladder or two
And have the worst slurs in their language shouted at you,
So when DJ heard the man call us the slur for gay men,
He was as if a knight sent by a king with the need to defend
His kingdom like when the rivers ran red with Roland's blood,
It seems like DJ's rage dam has started to flood.
So he started talking shit, called the guy a fat fuck
Like he'd just walked up to and keyed his massive-ass truck,
And so the jacket guy turned with his beer belly heaving,
And asked DJ exactly to whom the fuck he thought he was
    speaking.
DJ said, "The guy who just called me and my friend two
    f*****s!"
The jacket man looked us up and down and said, "There you
    have it."
The Daft One explains the sculpture in his hand's a family gift,
And the man says this is why they shouldn't show that shit to
    kids.
At this, DJ's so incensed his neck's as raw red as being rubbed,

12

And he says his father's the speaker after next coming up.
"Oh damn," Jacketguy says, looking DJ up and down to assess
Whether he should be intimidated or just slightly impressed,
Then he says, "Your friend must be fucking retarded, then."
"He's not, he's clearly just a bit on the eccentric end."
Through the entire ordeal, we simply stood there and smiled,
Because we successfully had retained our state as a child.

DJ eventually un-tilts after proving both his manhood and
the ability to navigate these types of situations in a way that feels
like he's won something, stood a little taller. And honestly, for
how long it took us to develop these disguises and try our hand
at navigating this society, now that we've bonded with DJ's trust
and will be sitting right behind his father's watching eyes in the
rearview mirror of their tank tonight when this is done before
what should be an amazingly white family dinner, we've successfully crossed the boundary between our theoretical research and
virtual engagement through this strange, tribal species. We're
standing on their own shores, amongst the best of them, and
learning how hatred shapes their tongues so easily, either when
they type them in crossteam chat while heated or right before
raising their beers up and cheering

THREE

We decided to take a nice afternoon drive with our doors locked through some black neighborhoods down to the local Doorstore to check out the gun section. The second most intriguing peculiarity about these *people*, as they call themselves (or at least some of them), is their fascination with their driving machines. This Hummer in which we are riding was inspired by the same sand terrain vehicles used by their soldiers in war, as I may have mentioned. We could fit nearly 13 donger ponies inside of this thing's interior, and could easily flatten groups of passing protestors while sustaining no damage to the civilian Humvee. However, as this thing shits out smoke at a conversion velocity uncalculatable by my race's arithmetic, the driver, DJ Daddy, has us not only sharing our exhaust with the rest of the city's downtown area, but also the animalistic, assaulting riffs, licks, and chugs of Guns N' "fuckin'" Roses. DJ's back is so flat against the cow-skin backseat that he could be a little soldier, reporting about a confrontation avoided like an averted start to war.

"I'm buying you a *beer* later!" The father says, his designer sunglasses bobbing in the *oppressive* afternoon heat across the dashboard and hot steering wheel.

"Thanks, dad," DJ says, nodding at me like *yes, my penis IS bigger, thanks for asking*. "I'm learning how to *shotgun* tonight!"

"Atta *man*," The dad says, trying to catch my cloudless sky eyes in his shades. "Pretty impressive way to meet somebody, right, little Kurt Cobain?"

I am flattered by the man's ability to recognize our ability to so closely resemble someone who knows how to use a shotgun properly. "Master Jonesman," I say to him.

"Stop it with that *master* crap," The state rep says, frowning and shaking his head like I just defecated on his Humvee's interior. "Just call me Paul."

"Paul, like the apostle," I say, nodding towards the line of rosary beads hanging down from his rearview mirror. The woman in the funeral card must be someone dear to them.

"I don't write letters," The guy says, smiling, turning his eyes back towards the road as its beginning to congest with vehicles. "What were you gonna ask me, son?"

Call him daddy, the pony whispers, clopping its hooves on the leather with little squeaks.

"I wanted to know if it was true that young children are trained in heavy arms."

"Here?" He asks, a lift of interest in his voice now. "Hell yes. This is Florida, young man. We tell our stop signs by their bullet holes."

"I was holding guns at the age of three," DJ says, nodding. "I think my dad showed me how to load a sniper when I was 7?"

"6." The councilman says. "Same year your mother started going to therapy."

"Because of your training of your son in soldiers' arms?"

"They're not *just* for soldiers," the man scolds me, as though I've insulted his intelligence. "Anyone can own an assault rifle if they want to."

"Yeah man," DJ says, slapping me on my upper forearm and winking his eye like this is a porn video. "Hasn't *Counter-Strike* taught you anything?"

"It's taught me we don't negotiate with terrorists." I say.

"Goddamn right!" The father says, with an apologetic glance at the rosary beads. "You should've been here in the early 2000s. If you thought rifles were bad, you would've *loved* the targets at the shooting ranges."

"Were they shaped like children?" I ask, as innocently as possible.

"No!" The father says, turning around in his chair as we're coasting into the turning lane towards the Doorstore parking lot. "They were shaped like Arab terrorists."

"Oh," I say to DJ, speaking beneath the screeching guitar in "Rocket Queen," the one where the woman's getting fucked in the studio. "So the terrorists ground invaded the United States?"

"You're such a fucking troll," DJ says to me. There's one of those weird silences where the dad probably wants to ask us what we said, but we've gotten close enough to the Doorstore that the entire course of our existence is about to change thanks to the wonderous place where they sell *all* the things, where you see people who stretch the limits of publicly acceptable conditions by their very presence in the store. It's past those very people we walk, a couple of them nodding or waving or shouting *Build the Wall Paul!* at our local celebrity chauffeur, him raising a fist back at them like us walking into the air-conditioned doors is akin to him walking into an arena with a sword clutched in his fist and a cheer from a roaring, ready crowd.

We're barely through the second set of sliding glass doors when the bullshit starts. The first thing is the greeter, whose mask hangs beneath his chin and barely covers a third of it due to the accumulated neck fat, saying *hello, welcome to Doorstore! I like your stuffed animal!* at us as we pass by. THE WISE OWL is doing the best he can to maintain his stillness, feeling more like a fluffy, taxidermy trophy on my shoulder than a bird of prey who holds the knowledge of an infinite nation inside his brain. So long as they don't mistake the donger pony for some kind of crazy homemade bomb, we should be able to navigate our way to the gun department safely. Perhaps they'll be offering free samples today, where you get to fire a pistol at one silhouetted target that looks like a young, white man.

They said terrorists! The pony reminds me

Sorry, Saint Dongerus. You're one hundred percent correct. They're supposed to have things wrapped around their heads that scare the people who carry military grade arms with them when they go to the supermarket. Like one of the families who stops to congratulate DJ's dad on his phenomenal, patriotic speech at the conservatard conference earlier today.

The owl, through his protectionary petrification, snaps at me,

THE WISE OWL:

O daft one, I must be the one to urgently remind
You of the need for correct language at all times.
You can't call DJ Daddy's constituents "retarded,"
Or you'll become one of the dearly, canceled departed!

Sorry another time, Pontificus Ponerus the Pentagonal. I was preparing for my next questions to DJ's father, who is taking his sweet ass time getting us to the gun aisles. "Mr. Paul," I ask him. "Do you think any *libtards* shop here?"

"Everybody shops here," he says, still glowing in the aftermath of his own recognition. "You'll see them based on their masks."

This is the first time he's mentioned mine, or made any kind of recognition whatsoever about my own. I'm hoping he and DJ both are going to eventually ask about the cartoonish, artisanal mask painted in the center, the one with the comedy and tragedy masks, orange and blue, merged together to make one face with a gaping mouth and four curved corners. It's the same as my avatar on the Steam platform. He assures me by his most recent comment and glance that he hasn't attempted to imply that *I'm* a libtard. He says that will depend on whether or not he ever sees me cry, or if DJ ever goes over to my house and sees participation trophies on the wall. I'm pretty sure the pony just cringed so hard it damaged its invisible sphincter. We finally get to the fucking gun section, with the shotguns, pistols, glocks, specials, and other glinting glee machines beneath glass thinner than the skin of one of the people the representative's talking shit about. The customer service expert is a pale teenager, in a town of pale teenagers, who has wild hair and the thin, brown moustache of a man who feels at home only when he's away from people, the kind who likens themselves to predatory animals on their hunting trips. Of course, he recognizes the glorious representative and turns on the bit of charm he's got nestled inside that bony chest of his for not only Build the Wall Paul (with the awesome YouTube videos!) but DJ and I, myself, as I'm presented as being someone *who's new to town* and who *needs to see what the state of Florida is really all about!*

"Sure thing," the boy says, jingling his keys and making a beeline for the assault rifle aisle. "I'll show him the best gun we've got to offer any kid his age." He returns quickly with an AR-15 held in his slightly perspiring hands, his face broken by a giddy, curved grin. "You ever loaded one of these before?"

Honestly, our weapons are indeed the envy of some of these machines, but we also don't require such barbaric technology. It's like asking me how to load a musket, if you must know the comparison. Instead, I simply shake my head at him. Before he starts disassembling the thing from its current form, Paul reaches his wedding ring hand over and says, "Wait, can DJ do it?"

"Absolutely," The employee says. Beaming, DJ takes the assault rifle in his hand, makes a crackling in his throat like a radio, and then says, in his best robot voice, *Affirmative!*

"These kids are both gamers," Daddy says, putting his hands in the pockets of his suit jacket and bouncing up and down on the balls of his dress shoes. "My son knows the ropes in the real world, though!"

DJ has the thing unclipped and totally disassembled at a speed only possible from years of practice. The smoothness might be concerning to anyone who didn't teach it to him, but it impresses the employee so much so that he gives a shrill whistle of his chapped lips. "We have a professional in the house." He says it dryly. "For first-timers like our friend who likes stuffed animals here, though, I recommend shotguns."

"Are they easier to aim?" I ask the man.

"Sometimes," he says. "Depending on what you're shooting and how close you are to it."

"Would you like to see?" A different, male voice asks. Looks like another employee has floated over after hearing our discussion on firearms. This one's wearing a beanie over his acne-covered forehead and has holes in his ears the size of small craters. There's a wild look in his eyes, most similar to one of those same apex animals, but one which has gone rabid and is now staring down something already bleeding. At first, our customer associate turning around towards his coworker started with a sense of enthusiasm. However, that enthusiasm drains like a lake into a sinkhole when seeing the very real shotgun now sticking directly into his stomach as held by the feral teenager.

"I am here to share the gospel of the ones whose heads are temples," The aspiring shooter says, his voice trembling, his eyes *free* of something that tethered them to what they're seeing.

"Dalton," our associate says, calm as he's been handed a cup of coffee. "Are you still on the mescaline?"

"The sun will shine back at them the way it does off a mirror!" Dalton screams, shoving the associate back into the glass case of firearms. He turns towards DJ's Dad, whose phone is already raised to his ear calling someone who you probably should during one of these situations, and glares at him with a glassy, disconnected rage accompanied by a scowl. He backs away from the other associate, who is half on the counter display, half sinking towards the floor, and instead points the gun directly at the politician. Shoppers who'd been dawdling around buying whatever random shit they do on Sunday afternoon now gasp, imagining themselves as names in a Wikipedia article made to chronicle these types of things. Daddy Rep raises his hands and says something like *we all need to just take it easy* as the disgruntled gunman keeps sprouting phrases lost to their ideas of logic. Luckily for all of us, there was one little thing that the gunman doesn't know: DJ's got his *personal* gun that his father gave to him on his third birthday, and as soon as the other guy came into view and before he broke his serpentine glaring from his coworker's terrified eyes, DJ grabbed it. He's sitting on this side of the counter, completely out of view of the gunman as he trains the shotgun barrel on his father. If he were to pull that trigger, everyone knows there'd be something happening in the tradition of what killed the Kennedys, some new example of the devil's work held in a place where if people aren't protected, the bad guys win. But even with the gun in his hand, DJ's looking over at me with the fear of a little boy beholding the man who helped form his world now a single fingertip flick away from being gone forever.

"Dude," he says to me, whispering, tears streaking his nose and his upper lip. "You've gotta do it."

"Do what?" I ask him.

"You've gotta do it!" He says. He points the gun's butt at me. "I can't kill somebody."

If the kid's saying this while his own father's about to pay the price for trying to talk down the shooter, it's probably true. So, in one swift motion, I take the gun from him, peak over the counter, and, right as the shooter's backing DJ's Daddy up into a rack of $15 pants, I point the pistol at the guy, safety already disengaged thanks to DJ, level the gun with the guy's beanie covered back of his head, and pull the trigger. The round flies right through his skull, rips through three racks of clothes, and plants itself with a blood-covered thud right into the smiling face of a woman´s clothing section placard jumping in the air to show off her jeans on the wall near the changing booths. A woman who had been filming the whole scene from behind a rack of khakis cheers, her phone in her hand, as the crimson rivers from dear Dalton's blown open skull wet the carpet in a crimson wave that pools right near her shoes. DJ races towards his father and throws his arms around him, tackling him like a linebacker. I place the gun on the counter as though I'm returning an empty glass I've just drained, placing the pony right next to it as a guard while the crowd swarms me – you could say we've just won the game on the final play in a comeback victory, and I'm about to get the treatment of the quarterback who ¨killed it.¨

FOUR

To describe the speed at which virality happens in this country – with its eyes always peeled to televisions, phones, jumbotrons, bathroom televisions, TikToks, computers, computers they take to the bathroom with them – I shall allow THE WISE OWL to give a poetically abridged version of events following my *heroic, miraculous* actions. NOTE: The research department will be pleased to find that killing someone in broad daylight for a clearly justifiable reason had an even greater impact on my recognition than originally projected in testing.

THE WISE OWL:

Never have I seen something so strange,
As a Doorstore parking lot victory parade:
They came in their trucks, in their carts, with their families
And fried cows over blacktop at avoiding calamity.
The news networks flocked with their cameras and quotes,
With people tapping the DAFT ONE's hand at the hope
He'd given them by taking the life of the teen
Whose neon hair and sad face shone on their screens.
"These incidents really could happen every day."
Exactly what you'd expect Master Jones to say
Having dodged the bullet of mental illness manifest
From an idea on the internet to a hole in a kid's chest.
We got free drinks, free cigars, pledges from the locals,
Their eyes shining like the blood on the tiles, now hopeful

That their theory of good people with guns has been proven
And, despite our vast training, we were stunned by the movement.
The camera footage posted by millions, worldwide,
With nearly every commentator taking our man's side.
There was no choice, no time except to do the right thing;
DJ said his ears from the gunshot still ring.
They didn't ask him much, brushed, pushed him aside
To get THE DAFT ONE's reaction and his azure, glinting eyes:
"I did what any true patriot would've done
If I saw evil in motion and had my hand on a gun."
Brave warrior, true American, they hailed him as one
Who holds the ocean's sparkle and the heat of the sun
Yet stays calm under pressure — and a hell of a shot
"If you're looking for role models, he's the best one we've got."
Such is what the local representative said
As he stared at the footage bored into their heads
They made memes of DJ crouched behind the display case
*Called him a pussy, a f****t, some sort of disgrace*
For being locked between his father's life and cold, quick death
Thus, in our shine, DJ seems depressed.
The state rep told us we could stay with their family,
Included in their orbit by the celebratory insanity:
While driving, cars honked, people cheered, they all waved
For the actions of the scrawny kid and the life that he saved
And they asked, "What's the creature that looks like a horse?"
And THE DAFT ONE answered, "That's my pony, of course!
He's been my good luck charm since the days of peewee features,
When my dead parents would hold him aloft in the bleachers."
At the news of our parents not being around,
We slid straight into the hearts of this idyllic little town.
They asked where we were from, where we lived, our address

Lifting us from the oblivion as the unwanted guest.
Even the jean jacket man, with his eyes wet, voice feeble,
Said he'd thank God for the both of us when under the steeple.
We thanked him in turn, took the fifty dollars he gave,
And as he left, he gave the smallest little wave
Of his grisly, grimy palm, some preternatural calm
As we got back in the hummer and the day went on.
During dinner, there were phonecalls from across the nation
From every representative, journalist, and wealthy news station
Trying to speak with the boy whose hand held steady,
About the importance of living free while always being ready.
We told them the key to our machinelike success
Was the pony by our side and the owl on our chest!
The pony for reminding us of our true potential,
And the owl for reminding us everything's eventual:
Life is short, THE DAFT ONE says, Hallmarks memorized
And from the energy of his voice, these people were hypnotized
They asked where to buy the donger ponies made of stone
To decorate their entrance halls, bedrooms, their mobile homes
"If you ever run for office, you would set new records,"
Said the state rep, wearing a tanktop of Def Leppard.
His wife had hugged him, kissed him, cried on his shoulder,
The three of them united now that the moment was over.
We found their cuisine to be predictably bland,
And something else we couldn't even try to understand:
Around the house hung firearms, a plethora of types,
Even on their tables next to where they sleep at night.
THE DAFT ONE asked, "Sir, why were you not armed?"
The state rep: because I could never do that type of harm.
Killing someone changes you, 'doting wife' Charlene said,
With the smell of strong cleaners surrounding her head.

They asked THE DAFT ONE multiple times,
If there were a tear in his heart, a tear in his eyes.
Yet the one thing that would've been universally despised,
Is acting like an action hero and then trying to be kind.
He answered, "I'm a bit shaken, but honestly relieved,
These are the kinds of resolutions we all love to see."
The father seems like he'd make love to us if we were of age,
Between harsh gulps of poultry, his teeth his own rage
At nearly being shot, and worse, his own son
With all his prior training nearly killed by a gun.
He compared the risks to driving a car on the road
One of those scary parables kids are always told:
Watch out for the swervers, the alcoholic pilots —
I half expected the pony to shout BE FUCKING QUIET.
To them, he explained, the car and gun are the same,
Especially when it's the tool being charged for the blame.
The afternoon's events were as inevitable as storms,
Someone should've done something, should've been warned,
But its not the fault of the owners, as he always says,
For dealing with someone with such a misguided head.
And so they thank Jesus loudly, proudly, clenching us tight
Thanking us for that day and for seeing another night
As a family united, by the good, bad, through it all
Feeling like a baby bird blessing the ground after a fall.
Thus, into the spotlight we were thrust, our small hands bloodied
Like royal robes or red carpets, the sequence unstudied.
And so time continues, at the speed of bullets in this town,
Before the stains are even cleaned or a body's in the ground.
From DJ, we're sorry, but this whole family we'll borrow
Especially when we go back to school with him tomorrow.

FIVE

Going to the same school as DJ was as if white Jesus Christ himself sat among the pews, except with none of the pressure and with my first miracle already completed. Well, maybe it wasn't quite as revered as that, but at least I wasn't one of the few kids at the place that had never experienced a shooting before. People took pictures with me, asked to pray with me, the cheerleaders all looked at me with a strange hunger in their eyes they usually reserve for people with abs and pads. Not wanting to appear like an involuntary celibate – these strange, darkened men who sneak around in chatrooms filled with rage and hungry for weapons – I allowed them to hold the donger pony, service vest included so as to be permitted to enter the school. DJ stood awkwardly by, probably evaluating us the same way a director of a pornography video looks at his models. One of them, a girl named Stacy and a senior, bonded with me by saying she hadn't had a gun on her during the two shootings she'd already survived, but thankfully, with teachers being armed now, we could all feel protected by the English teacher who called me the best thing to happen in her life since the Ides of March. Seriously. And this was a woman who was obviously lonesome, her skin pale from eons spent behind her own curtains and inside her own thoughts, who roared like a velociraptor unironically while having a hip holstered fucking *glock*. That way, if any of the kids were to go postal, as she told me, she would be able to do exactly as I have done, about how

I inspired her the same way the knife in Caesar's back inspired Brutus.

I know, Owl: I've committed literary metaphor suicide with the witchy woman's glock, the same woman who calls *King Arthur* the wart while reciting shit poetry from the middle ages, am I right?

THE WISE OWL:

Correct you are, my daft one, my savior, my king,
You are the distance around the center of these things;
However, your metaphors misfire like the gun
Strapped to the side of that godless, gray nun!

Indeed. Thankfully, we pivoted from the time of kingdoms, fiefdoms, epics, and heroes to what was mandated be taught in the English classes at this almost-charter school: this is one of the ones, according to DJ, where you have just as much a chance of sitting beside legitimate royalty as sitting next to a representative or congressman's daughter. At least, at this school, DJ was somewhere in the middle of the peer tier, this strange, perfume and cologne choked wasteland where every emotion available on the human spectrum hangs in the shadows of firearms. Thankfully, though, with Mrs. Becker packing absolute heat and the lungs of a dinosaur destroyed by exploding crystal meth, demonstrating her obvious mental stability was more easily achieved when analyzing the CORPORATE POETRY mandated for consumption by these little chartered brains sailing through uncertain times.

OH. And it's worth mentioning this species is undergoing a battle with a disease, the likes of which they spread to new continents in their cargo and their unconscious discoveries, ones with apathetic wrath, mechanical efficiency, and heavy crosses. If a single germ or a tectonic twist from their earthly mother can kill them, then they are to the rest of us as they must have been to each other before they understood the physics of losing wars.

I say this because these little fuckers aren't wearing masks. I'm the only one, me and the teacher, whose face appears like a deteriorating egg pumper as shown in the species' sexual education videos due to the way her mask splits her straight down the center of the skull. Sorry, my brain's frazzled by the fact I, the owl, or the pony could breathe on one of these fuckers and cause their chest xrays to change colors. And now DJ is told to stand up at the front of the class and read the corporate ode he's chosen to recite – from a list of sponsors for the school, including the gun manufacturers – which he must've crafted after a hardcore masturbation binge and joining his mother in huffing Drano 'til their eyes spun.

Ode to PIPELINES (Gaben Love Me Better)
Oh, if there's one thing that taught me to survive the apocalypse,
It was how Dead Air and Death Toll taught me to never quit.
There's No Mercy to be found here, we are without a Parish,
We're wandering in the frigid air asking if we still care
As we're zombies by any other culture's word.
Don't you think it's all just a little bit absurd?

"What the fuck are you reading, DJ?" The teacher with the glock asks, crossing her arms over each other like she's wrapping herself in plastic. "I told you to write about the *company*, not the game!"

"I'm getting there, Mrs. Becker!" DJ says, his voice alight with emotion over serenading the game where people get murdered by the government after they became infected. Remember, this is the kid who saw a bullet almost nail his father through the heart a couple days ago, and now he's singing about one of his blessed, connected escapes in a way that resonates with these other people.

I don't know if I like people, The Pony says, hopping up and down, its neon pink support vest labeled SERVICE ANIMAL (Cock Pony).

You and the fucking rest of them, I say back to him. Then, as DJ is about to start rambling about steam *fogging up his glasses and bringing him to tears*, there's a knock on the door. Before anyone can respond, the door's wrenched open with a jerk and three more humans, dressed in their classiest, richest suits, wander inside the room like they're celebrities walking out on stage for a talk show. They smell vaguely of alcohol. One of them is DJ Daddy, and the other one is one of the guys who works for the Southern Legend Himself, Senator Jim Baetz. He's not the one they named the Bates motel after, but he's known to like motel rooms with women various steps away from being married to him. *Allegedly.*

THE WISE OWL:

Is it true that these men prefer leaders who choose,
To have sex with girl children by illegal avenues?

"Of course, you stupid bird." I tell him. "They've been doing that shit since the invention of the human asshole. You really think it would stop today, but a lot of people who claimed to swear to God were the ones introducing hell on earth."

And what a hell on earth this has become. They've brought *another* fucking camera crew with them, this time for what I think is the fucking school news channel. They're trying to cast us as a celebrity in the same way they pump their bovines with drugs and then suckle their infected, bloated milk. I am angrier than I thought I would be at this consistent exposure, but I remember the training provided by the committee and am able to accurately shelve my emotions. This is another advantage of inhabiting a body that's white, and I'm smiling at them like we aren't sitting in the room of a little sociopath ready to give that cheerleader her *third* experience with a shooting. Stranger things have happened. Like what DJ Daddy says as he stands in front of the room and the applause has stopped echoing off the Barnes and Noble posters for *One Hundred Years of Solitude*, *1984*, and *We Need to Talk About Kevin*:

He first apologizes for his dipshit son's comments about an American corporation, saying he needs to remind him that corporations are people too and that you can hurt their feelings. Then, he says that it's a real honor to be sitting in the same room as a man who not only has received the blessing of Jesus Christ, but who was able to act in the way God intended when he pulled the trigger, blah blah blah. I feel myself being venerated, with their glassy, bright eyes crawling all over my skin and along the back of my neck. *Peculiar* sensations, these humans experience, like the ability to stare at this recognition and feel as though our plan for all this is working *too* well. Obviously, I don't believe this – I couldn't be happier that the donger pony has made its way to the front page of the *New York Times* as the newest white, hairless dick to grace the cover – is a terrible thing, at all, but being in a room of little drones reciting their loves for Apple and Tesla and Amazon with heart-pouring sonnets makes me feel as though there's no communicating with some of these *people*, although we're damn sure going to try. And that's how we got invited to be the featured guest at the school board meeting happening that evening, and got ourselves to stand right in the center of the place where the lines of the country have been drawn the clearest.

Country Satan feeds me yams, The Pony says, the absurdity cracking through its complexion.

I am going to feed you too, child. We are going to feed you all the yams you want whenever you want them. We will be having our Thanksgiving with them when we know the time is right.

SIX

The huge, iron cross hanging over the center of the library, under which sit the seven members of the Dickson County High School board, is large enough to crush the three elderly community members sitting directly underneath it if it were to dislodge itself from the ceiling. *I didn't think this was a catholic school*, the donger pony says, his round hooves bouncing on the sterilized, piss and turnip colored carpet. This isn't a catholic school, Mister Donger Pongus; oh no. We are in the lands where near pedophiles sit on the highest courts and wish to inscribe the ten commandments into the walls of a neighboring state's capitol, and might even be one of the representatives we are due to meet in our course with DJ. Basically, they're a secular, private school that just has *religious influences*. They're what they call themselves: Cafeteria Christians, or people who figured out that reading is widely overrated, especially in school. None of these kids read in the fucking cafeteria, they're too busy watching the table of the kids in the corner who wear the hoodies and praying to god they don't wear trenchcoats when it snows.

THE WISE OWL:
Oh Daft One, my dongus, I don't mean to trifle
But why does the school board have sniper rifles?
The president this year is a man who has made his life's work an extension of selling oranges. This being the sunshine state, he's one of the men who comes from a family who make their

living squeezing fruit into cups with a thing called pulp, that sounds like a warm clump of vomit being drunk down your throat. Some of these people *like* this shit, Owl. DJ isn't one of them, thankfully; instead, he's sitting with us in the front row, as close as he's ever gotten to being recognized in this school by the people in charge, while his dad has taken position as nearest to the dais as possible. If that cross fell, it'd be those members right beneath him, guns and vests and all, crushed by the artwork right in formation with Daddy DJ and the most *presidential suit* Charlene could muster after snorting all those drain cleaners this morning.

"How old is that one lady?" DJ whispers to me. She's at the point of blissful, acceptant decay that humans do when her entire existence seems tethered to smells of freshly harvested vegetables, or the Ticonderoga pencil clenched between her fragile fingers as its eraser conjures smells of schools constituting a single room. She thinks the internet is something you use to fish. And yet even she has her own hip-holstered revolver, one of the ones her family must have passed down like their trauma. If she were to fire that palm-musket, her arm would probably snap in half. However, even this aspiring gargoyle of compassion could do nothing against the waves of conflict rippling through the school like the way Dalton's blood rippled across the tiles when we *accidentally* stepped in it. As a matter of fact, five members of this counsel, all of whom are white as come and over the age of 50, some of whom who have been educators and some of whom probably think teaching kids is overrated if they don't have divine belief, well, despite these predispositions, they're actually *Democrats*.

"It's amazing half these fuckers haven't burst into flames," Daddy DJ whispers to us.

"The secretary's cunt probably tastes like rotten cheese." DJ says, loud enough for it to be heard in both directions.

His father reels his palm up to strike him, but then he remembers he's wearing a watch worth about a quarter of his kid's tuition here, so instead he leans close enough to spit on him and says, much like a snake showing its fangs, "Listen here, you little shit for brains: I understand that we've *all*," when he says all, he grabs the air in front of him like he's gripping a crystal ball. "Been through some events that would make a lot of people shit themselves." He nods at his son first, a thin mask of sweat across his glazed, reddening forehead. His blotches are the same shapes as the potholes on this state's atrocious roads. Then, he nods at me and bows, as though I've somehow reflected a little bit of the Christ they placed inside that cross above us. "But DJ, your friend needs to know that we're in a *warzone* out here."

A shrill banging fills the room as the dude who looks like he just wandered out of a convention for balding hunters gables us in like this is Judge Judas. One of the two student school board reps, dressed like a teenage version of a GQ commercial, but *nerdy* instead of *flirty*, actually has a copy of *Robert's Rules of Order* right next to his pretty blue personal folder and the sense he'd watch his future wife getting fucked and actually enjoy it. Anyway, these barely-past-animals are falling quiet like we've suddenly just engaged the same switch they do in the Capitol, at least not when its being broken into and filled with people dressed like the man sitting with the President's tag, plastic with white lettering, directly next to his gable. And directly next to him sits his uzi, which he keeps fully loaded and sitting next to him like it's simply a really fancy, lead bobblehead or LEGO model.

"Alrighty then," he says, glancing around the room with

a cross between a smile and a grimace on his bearded, Duck Dynastic maw. "We can't keep a hero waiting long!"

When these creatures look at you, their eyes create a pressure along their skin. It's very light, but when people say its crawling, I think its rather pushing, a movement along the Z axis versus the X or Y. And they're gravitating to not only me, but to the Owl perched on my shoulder, the donger pony underneath my chair wearing its faithful neon purple service vest, and to the man whose life I saved in something so miraculous, it must have been touched by god, whether he be Christ or simple physics. Despite my years of training and the various forms of torture I endured to do this job this way, I feel the temperature in my skin increase like I'm a kid learning to drive who has accidentally floored it. DJ Daddy, though, nods at me with genuine sincerity mixed with the fact they've brought along the cameras. The President thanks everyone for attending, once again, before mentioning the fact we need to say the pledge of allegiance. So we all rise, exactly like we would if commanded to stand from the pews, and I have to grab the donger pony so hard my knuckles go white trying not to laugh at watching the way the second school board representative is mouthing the words and looking around like he's a drunk puppy in a playpen. The nerd has his eyes closed, finely manicured nails pressed over his dress shirt's breast pocket, but the kid next to him, who is dressed well enough but a little round around the edges like the strange, marshmallow creation on the tin cylinders for oven-baked croissants, and looks like he enjoys those, as well, must be *on* something. I don't believe its weed, I don't believe its alcohol, and he might legitimately be at the point where he's so high on either a tab or liquid spray that he can hear the donger pony speak.

"What the fuck?" The kid whispers, his pupils fully dilated

in both the natural light and the fluorescents, the sounds they make ringing in his ears as though a bee has nested next to his earlobe. "Is that sculpture *talking*?"

"KILL THEM ALL, DAMON!" The Donger Pony says, warping into a hellish red color and bouncing around in front of the kid's unseeing eyes while black smoke pours from its unseeable anus.

No reaction.

"Good try, Mr. Ponus," I tell him, the anthem nearly over. "I think he's on just enough to see colors, not nearly the level needed to understand our arithmetic."

Everyone sits back down. DJ taps me on the shoulder. I look at him. He points a thumb over his shoulder while the President begins droning about some procedural bullshit and the sanctity of keeping everything in line while his one school board rep nods every few seconds and the other is contemplating if there's such a thing as time. Deciding the hour is ripe to say *fuck it*, I pivot around in my seat and cast my eyes back through rows of faces who smile when I light upon them as though I've placed a drop of holy water right atop their foreheads. At the back, there's a group of people who are wearing masks similar to the signs we saw spread out on that absurd beach on which the horse and I washed ashore, where seagulls intermingled with the Owl and told him some very interesting things about the people whom they shit upon. The kinds of things you could tell with the signs clutched in their hands, one of them wearing a shirt implying there would be a resurrection of the President whose head got blown apart in order to endorse one of their former leaders. They really, really like this former leader, to the extent there are pictures of him tattooed on their bodies with reds and whites and blues and blacks, filled in. These people are so strange. They love their pain and wrapped it right up with pleasure from the very second they decided to try and care about each other. Absurd, absurd beings, and the air these parents breathe make me happy there's a protective cloth over my face for the sole reason they can't see me smiling at them as they simmer. Then, in a burst of static, the big man with the quickest, coolest gun, like something out of *Batman*, taps the ball of his microphone. The feedback makes the Damon kid flinch like he's jabbed him in the soft part of his skull.

The president, Jay G. Poorhouse, says, "We will now open the floor up to public comments." There's a bit of a murmur, and then a woman with a face that makes her look as though her bones themselves are sagging, wearing a cowboy hat and with hair wirelike enough to confuse an eee-leck-trition saunters up to the microphone three feet from DJ Daddy's shoulder, in the center aisle. She says a thank you ringing with a hollow insincerity on the same level of the echo reverberating in our ears, the ones that make THE WISE OWL flash back to his own days before knowledge, before he spoke in rhymes, when he was adrift on the wings of sorrow and felt himself to be some kind of bird flying through the clouds above the fallout in the way everything was going for him. There's something ominous about the sound of a machine. That's something I think we and these *people* can truly agree on. Once she adjusts the mic correctly and Damon's worked his way back from the tunnel, she thanks the president, clearly, and points over to us.

"I think it is amazing that we are in the presence of *two* true champion patriots," She says, nodding the big brim of her hat over her sparkling, horse-wide eyes so similar in feature they make the donger pony shuffle. There are woops and hollers, claps and a couple stomps. The very reverberation of those things off the walls and high ceiling make it seem as though someone's pouring gold over DJ Daddy's face, falling into relaxation and basking in the glow from the smiling teeth in front of and behind him. It would be romantic if DJ didn't look like he needs to vomit. She continues, having successfully used us to snare their attention like a celebrity ad during the super bowl. "I just wish I could see both their faces!"

There's a strange, human cocktail of laughter and gasps in their reactions. The Pony turns away from the woman, all romantic energy discharged, and I stroke his dicklike snout as the woman basks in the sound of palm skin on palm skin for the second time in three minutes. DJ Daddy is shaking his head no, and whispers something to the woman. The President gables us in order again, decorum hanging thin like the threads tethering the cross to the ceiling.

"Miss. Kerstankowitz," The President says. "You need to respect the rules of the Dickson County School District."

"Duel me, Jayson," She says, kicking one of her hips to the side and placing a stirrup boot inches from the high ass school board rep's terrified, enchanted face. "I'd like to see you lick the rust off my stars."

"Is she inciting violence?" Another parent asks, this one looking like a librarian with tattoos in his modest t-shirt and fogging glasses, over a mask that says *I don't know how to read* with a picture of an elephant.

"I'll incite my boot right up your lily liberal ass!" Kerstankowitz says, dropping into a combat stance with her feet spread apart and growling like a big kitten on *Tiger King*.

"Ms. Kerstankowitz," The President repeats, not even bothering to raise the wooden hammer. "Cut the bullshit, please. If you could state your reason for appearing in front of us this evening past wanting to give me a brain hemorrhage, could you get on with it?"

"Thank you for asking politely," She says, planting her spurs in front of the mic with a friendly, ringing jingle. "Now can you not call him *racist?*" She flings at open hand at us again.

"Who called him racist?" Asks another board member, this man the one who most resembles a schoolteacher with his whitened silver hair and the lines from decades of disappointment streaked along his cheeks and forehead.

"All of you!" Kerstankowitz responds, in the tone of a woman who has said the sky is upwards. "Liberals would use Critical Race Theory and say he's racist just because he's white!"

"Objection!" Screams a woman with a voice leathered by raising multiple children. "Cathy Kerstankowitz, your daughter is a bitch and so are you!"

"Oh, *really*, Margaret?" Cathy says, turning around and whipping her revolver out of her holster, spinning it by the trigger. "Your daughter's boyfriend must like saying hi to his uncle whenever he comes over to your house."

"You cunty little gator *fucker*," Margaret replies, beating her tangerine, plastic surgery inflated tits like a gorilla whacking her chest before war. "We're trying to engage in civil discourse and you're here just making shit up!"

"This bitch voted for Moe Wyden," Cathy says, explaining it to us as though we're an aside in Shakespeare.

"Hey, Cathy, I'm talking to *you!*" Margaret says. By law, she's required to carry a weapon in the state of Florida, so she has to control herself from reaching into her purse and pulling out the pink pistol to have a barrel measuring contest with Cathy.

Cathy shrugs. She says into the mic, nonchalantly, the board sitting there like teachers watching the kids in class, "Any parent dumb enough to make their kid wear a mask is an example of how education's failed us in America."

"We're *all* wearing masks." Damon says, nodding furiously, sweat dripping down his brow and staining the concaves of his suited elbows. He's tapping his leg so fast he clips the desk and lifts it up off the floor a couple inches. "We're wearing masks *every single day.*"

"Damon's right," Kerstankowitz says, her party behind her with their flags and props cheering as they've been told to. "And we don't need no extras."

I'll allow THE WISE OWL to summarize the next series of events, because life as we knew it was about to be upended in the same way Damon's concept of logic currently flip flopped inside his hot, opened skull like an IHOP pancake stack frying in front of hungry eyes. He's lived and died a thousand times in the space of our most recent excursion, and so, like a poet ducked in the trenches of the First World War, THE WISE OWL reports back to our people from the bowels of a country as unfamiliar as us to peace was to the boys who wrote about the gas – those types of things.

THE WISE OWL:
Amidst the current of a land so rich, yet so strange,
The stars in the skies must have sought to arrange
Due to the commotion caused by the surprise attendance
Of a man for which these people have particular reverence:
He's a man with a complexion fit for magazine covers,
Who is the youngest of six boys, two sisters, three brothers,
An example of family in the finely-refined flesh,
With the American flag pinned just left of his chest.
Behind him followed people who spoke for others, here
To greet THE DAFT ONE and DJ like we were their seers.

Amidst the applause, the standing ovation they gave
While Damon looked on a completely different page
The Senator walked up the same center aisle
And greeted us five with a movie-star's smile.
He smelled like cigarettes and toothpaste when he bent on in
And told us we had prevented an unspeakable sin
As though we held out our hands and caught the bullet in flight
While DJ Daddy's eyes opened in animal fright.
Here, we stood, a bridge between the two polar sides:
The one who fights for health, the other one for rights.
We felt as though among jungles of perilous creatures,
With terrible souls and unmistakable features.
What are these breasts? Does their milk taste plastic?
And the hair? Does it not hurt being tied by elastic?
What about the mothers with bumps and yellowed teeth,
The ones who cheer like someone's leather seat?
Worst of all, the citizens standing at the town tribunal
Have ignored or even attended so many recent funerals
But it's the position of these people to keep moving after death
Believing only when one's buried do they have the right to rest.
The Senator shakes DJ's hand, offers a consoling word
In the tone of someone who knows what they're doing's being
    heard
Not only by the kid's father, but by those across the globe
Who have come to know the pony as a symbol of hope.
Then, when he gets to the Daft One, he drops to a knee
And says I am so lucky to have finally come before thee
We wonder how it felt walking across water
In the peculiar ways these people now bond with each other
A moment after violence seemed nestled in every barb
These women threw at their opposite, ugly, pumping hearts.

He invites us to visit his office and discuss the state of things
And has Damon imagining kissing his rings.
For a soft kiss from men whose hearts and dicks are hardened
At the thought of dying for country, those dearly departed,
It makes him picture lords in robes made of resplendent threads
And the masked doctors who wandered with noses of dread
Packed with flowers to prevent scents of flesh blackened, rot
People's organs bursting, what once was becoming not.
A final time do the Daft One's eyes catch the lens,
With everyone in the school offering to be our friend
We are humbled in the light, the pony neighing once again
Knowing this year will not be forgotten.

SEVEN

It became apparent to us, following the conclusion of the board meeting wherein the country's divisions were once again successfully distracted by the shiny light of current public figures and the sun reflecting off the spinning death shuriken known as the news cycle and the internet, that we needed to take DJ deeper into the web. There was absolutely no way in which to process the screaming velocity of existence in this nation without properly utilizing the channels by which we came to be inhabiting DJ's mind, including going home with him and his dad and being allowed to sleep in the guest bedroom with the pony and the owl. They even offered to get us a bird cage and some shitty *New York Times* lining, but the Owl said he'd rather be shoved up the ass of a Harley Davidson than shit directly onto Moe Wyden's face. The creature has a strange sense of dignity more befitting his anthropomorphic kind, the sort of thing that would get him battered, fried, and bitten into teenie tiny rhymy chunks by the kinds of blobs with waves upon rolls upon avalanches of fatty fat. Fucking Wall-E, a movie meant for children, where there are people who just masturbate with their springy dingles and pleasure caverns while riding around in chairs that do more thinking than 103 of them combined. The only thing DJ's house is missing is an automated blow up doll, the kind that would have any sane woman divorcing her spouse instantaneously upon the discovery of the android in a closet or some such. The thing is, as I've told the pony multiple times, his hooves placed firmly upon a glasstop nightstand next to the bed under a lampshade older than DJ by twenty years, DJ's Daddy should be begging he suddenly gets a *hankering for robot pussy*, in their words, because the women he's been fucking, if his wife knew about them, would have her snorting so much Clorox she burns her nasal cavities worse than Sherman ripping through Atlanta.

THE WISE OWL:

Oh Daft One, I must ask, in your best estimation,
Why is Sir DJ so earthly obsessed with masturbation?

Well, Mr. Owl, what an amazing question for you to ask. If there were to be the end of the world, it would look a little something like this…

Can you smell the smells of what's cooking, good looking? Let yourself fade into that glow, let the amnesia seep into your mind, take my hand, we are merging with the spirit of the DONGER PONE …

Aliens crash down in a 1950s UFO spaceship into the middle of a nuke-fucked field way out in Arizona. Or Manhattan, there's no difference. Anyway, they come walking out of their spaceship, looking all green and alienlike, with the webbed feetsies and the dick-shaped heads and the desire to shove a number of foreign (heh) objects directly into the anuses of every paranoid motherfucker on the face of the planet since nineteen-Area-Fifty-One, right? But no, when they land, they're looking around at the red sand and at how their crotches are being pulled skyward by the gravity of bonerdom on the planet, blood and plumbing and all that, feeling the hot ass wind with its specs of red earth flapping against their gelatinous, pulsing bodies, they look at each other and are like, Wow, they finally did it, they finally killed each other in a way that will defy inhabitability for millenia! The United States of Chernobyl. The Laughy Taffee

Empire brought down to its knees, all of human achievement vapor-
ized in the space between existence and the void. That fast. That's
how it happened, they suppose, and how every single edifice, appli-
ance, person, monument, mausoleum and record of any achievement
was turned into smoking, self-made fallout.

Except for this motherfucking computer tower between them.

"Thank goodness," The one alien says, bending down, his 'rec-
tion scraping the top of the computer tower. "We have a record of
humanity to add to our archives."

"Excellent," The other alien says, inserting his USB tip directly
into the computer's port. "Let's see what kinds of things this DJ kid
was into, shall we? I'm sure it'll show us the absolute best of humanity
with some of these video titles …"

"DJ."

Dead silence, aside from the pony's mute neighing.

"Dylan fucking James."

Yep. THE WISE OWL is about to shit out some bars.

I tap him on the back of the forehead with the donger pone.

"Huh?" He says, sitting up straight. We're in a room that's
completely black, the kind of black you remember after drinking
too much alcohol. The Donger Pone's hoof patters echo around
the empty chamber. The Owl spins his head 360 degrees three
times and flaps his little green wings. Then, we start moving, as
though pulled through some series of internet ethers as if bound
to whatever's coming to us by some inextricable force of human
logic; it feels as though we're moving towards a lighted tunnel,
down which we can hear what might be a hundred people shouting …

EIGHT

In a click, we're transported into a classical forum with columns painted red, white, and blue, their shadows trailing cross a fake Athenian stage where anyone can wander up from the audience and blab shit into the microphone. Except, instead of any kind of decorum, over a hundred grotesque, bullet-munching, flag-waving, firework-popping, Jesus-selling, home-working, procrasturbating, distracted, soulless fucking ghouls are all yapping their mouths, hands, and asses off shitposting in direct view of one of the most prestigious, journalistic institutions to ever grace these humans' miraculously limited minds. A 60 year old man wearing a red cap and with jeans stained by gasoline, dirt, and his own sweat, urine, and unidentified crusts diarrheically erupts on a picture of Trancy McCowski, the Democratic speaker of the house who herself looks like a surprised cryptkeeper at this point. The man's anus makes a squeaking noise and the man rolls his eyes back in his head, allowing drool to carene over his chapped, tobacco-burnt lips and down his dribbling chin while releasing a sound of relief and smell akin to ripping open a dead horse's abdomen on a 90 degree afternoon. Next to him, a white kid who can't be any older than 14 flexes his infant biceps next to a gun that's three times as long as the donger pony and can kill people with a simple flick of his finger. The kid screams n****r over and over and over again while letting an entire belt of ammunition rip straight up into the moon, the shell cases bouncing behind him and scattering on the dirt floor already stained with blood, gas, vomit, shit, and what are either bone shards or cocaine islands in the muck. Then, a woman whose eyes are crazier than a rabid tiger's, wider, too, shining with unreal moonlight, laughs in the way all Karens laugh when summoning the manager while bending down, picking up the spent shells and raining bullets, wiping them on her knitted, cozy cardigan, and then chomping the metal between her immortal teeth screaming NOM NOM NOM and reaching for the pony's soiled, terrified form before I beat her back with an American flagpole worse than *they* did on their 'Washington Tour.'

"DJ, WHAT THE FUCK!" I scream at him. He's quivering like a bitch, in his father's words, in the center of the dais while the symphony of carnage pounds in his eardrums.

"I need my dad!" He screams, trying to pull himself up using the owl and planting his palms in the dirt, dust, and dental shards.

"Your dad's too busy eating raw meat out of a hooker's asshole, son," I yell at him again. The Karen's grabbed hold of the American flag wrapped around the blunt end of the pole with which I'm trying to tame her and is now accusing me of being a paid actor. I really don't want to have to blow my cover using violence, so I command the owl telepathically to kill her with a poem. He obliges, his wings already ruffled from DJ's attempt at leverage, and sings,

THE WISE OWL:

Seller of candles scented like faraway places,
Who goes absolutely berserk in public comment spaces,
Please take your bloodshot eyes off of Facebook,
The Democrats have no more children to cook!

"FUCKING LIAR!" She howls at the owl through her

broken, violent mouth, just enough for me to finally wrench the pole away. Then, a white woman who has tattooed the words BLACK LIVES MATTER across her forehead in bold comic sans, already primally yowling in a way she never did in the five natural births she's bragging about on her shirt:

NO MEN

NO MEDS

FIVE BOYS

Kicks the bullet-muncher right in the no-fun-zone with a precision only possible by a person who *knows*. This turns into a wild volley of scratches, kicks, grabs, a headbutt, two tit torchers and them yelling shit that has DJ's eardrums ready to pop on their own accord:

YOU LIBTARDS LOVE THE CHINESE SO MUCH YOU'D GET CORONA JUST TO KOWTOW

YEAH, WELL YOU'RE A RACIST, SEXIST, MISOGYNISTIC HOMEBOUND WOMAN WHO SPENDS MORE TIME ON FACEBOOK EACH MORNING THAN YOUR KIDS WILL SPEND VISITING YOUR GRAVE, BITCH

MOE WYDEN (current chief executive officer of the United States in DJ's Dreamland) HAS BEEN DEAD FOR AT LEAST 15 YEARS AND COULD PLANT CHIPS IN YOUR KIDS ASSES, YOU'D STILL FUCKING VOTE FOR HIM AND LET HIM SMELL THEM, TOO!

YOU'RE THE KIND OF WHITE WOMAN WHO WOULD CRY IF ARRESTED AFTER SHOOTING A BLACK GUY IN THE STREET!

HOW DARE YOU ACCUSE ME OF CRYING AFTER KILLING A –

Before she can curse or choke on the bullet casings halfway down her throat, the white woman, who looks as what another white man with a beer belly and a sick, animal grin shouts is a *professor who wants to teach our kids to hate each other*, knocks Confederate Cathy's dentures right back to 1860 with the right hook she throws. The mob, of all ages and many skin colors, dives upon them and clutch their stomachs with their broken nails and lacerated palms while their faces laugh so hard, their tears squirt out in unnatural blues and contort their faces into the same shapes as the ancient masks which used to hang over amphitheaters like this one. Through the crowd, a group of white men with skin paler than DJ's and the paper in his daddy's home-office printer, their teeth large as iPhone 13s and their dicks harder than trying to find accountability for slavery wander through, their arms completely rubber and flopping at their sides as if rippling in hurricane winds. The three of them dance in strange, off-beat circles around the women, who have stopped screaming and are now rabidly biting each other as they twist in the soiled dirt. Across the mayhem, his legs still kicking out to his sides like *Pennywise* from those King movies if he took Stephen's cocaine, the Human Troll chuckles in a voice hijacked from a trailer dweller stereotype:

I ain't seen two bitches wrestle in the dirt like this since Hillary and Kamala argued last! #owned #1776again #Freedom #Trumpcards #QalwaysKnew #letsgoryland #homeofthebrave

This incenses the packed *LEFT* side of the crowd, decidedly more various in their skin colors while resonating in ferocity stoked by the heat from the words and their fire, and they start shouting things into the void of noise amidst the women, who are now trying to kill each other by DDOSing each other's brains and ripping off each other's faces to see who they really are, how many kids they have, where their kids go to school, where each other's husband went to school, whether or not they'd fuck the other one's husband when the other one's kids went to school, whether or not they'd be able to send disturbing messages to their mailboxes, whether or not they'd go and record each other's houses for 'safety purposes', you know, take things into the *real world* – and the other troll on the opposite side is ready to emulate the voice of the woman who identifies herself online as *antiQwhist*, with the Q meaning Qanon, the *whi* meaning white, and the whole political portmanteau being an awful fucking thing to have on a headstone. The troll says,

BITCHES???? HOW DARE YOU INSULT BOTH WOMEN AND ANIMALS ALIKE WITH SUCH A MISOGYNISTIC, DOGGIST DECLARATION? THIS HAS TRIGGERED MY POST TRAUMATIC STRESS DISORDER AND NOW I AM GOING TO REQUIRE AT LEAST THREE HOURS OF THERAPY TO SMOOTH OUT YOUR DISRESPECT. THERE IS NO SAFE SPACE FOR WOMEN IN AMERICA AND THE ONLY THING WE CAN DO IS TO CASTRATE ALL MALES AND FRY THEIR APPENDAGES IN A MASSIVE, BOILING POT TO THEN CONSUME AND BECOME PREGNANT!

#blacklivesmatter#LGBTQIA+ #BLM #lovetriumphsoverhate #fucktherighties #timesupnow #latestagecapitalismisgenocide

"These mimics are terrifyingly skilled," I whisper to the Donger Pony, whose hooves softly clop on the disgusting dais. DJ's managed to rise to his feet, the shock of being engaged by the internet trolls filling him with the confidence of his online persona.

"Oh my god," DJ says, shaking his head. "That last troll is a *chaos bot*."

"A what?" I ask him.

"Stand back," He says, pushing his hand on my chest and making me nearly stumble over the zoned pone. "He's about to turn dreamland into memeland!"

The troll stands completely still, clutching his hands at his sides like Arthur's fists. His face inflates to the size of a really big drone and his eyes glow red like he's just witnessed the creation of the universe. He says, in a voice older and more higher pitched than God's own, "KEKW. LOOOOOOOOOOOOL TOTALLY A FUNCTIONING DEMOCRACY WE GOT GOING ON HERE, KEEEEEEEEP UP THE GOOD WORK LMAOOO" The troll takes its own buttocks, removes them from his body, and starts clapping his own asscheeks together like two entirely fleshy, tremulous pom-poms whose claps echo more than the ones in "Industry Baby." "IMAGINE," The troll says, placing his cheeks squarely back around his puckered asshole again. "BEING ABLE TO PAY FOR RENT, PAY FOR HEALTHCARE, AND PAY FOR PILLS IN THE SAME BILLING CYCLE, AND THEN PUT A CRYING JORDAN FACE ON ME, LOAD ME IN A HOWITZER, AND SEND ME SCREAMING TOWARDS THE SUN."

"This place is not meant for us," I whisper, the words curling into the madness of the mouth-frothing throng dancing around the violence like their ancestors did flames. I stroke the pony's actual head, and THE WISE OWL flaps his wings before staring at the current discourse like eyes waking up to Nagasaki.

"This place is meant for *nobody*," DJ says, his hands shoved in his pockets now. "That's why I love it so much."

"We need to *give* them something," The Donger Pony suggests.

"You already gave all you needed to give, friend," I tell him, patting his hollow, cylindrical flank.

"No, no," The Pony says, backing up a bit through the sticky ground around it. "You don't need to give *me* to *them*," It says, silently. "You need to give *them* to *me*."

I pick up my equestrian friend and raise him before me, up towards the frowning moon and his dead, endless, cratered eyes and allow the glow to reflect across his skin like Simba being held up by a hairless, dumb, white monkey. Then, in the center of the melee, where people are gnawing at each other like chipmunks on crystal meth at a Christmas tree farm, making pleasure noises mixed with pain sounds and a general sense of numbing, dumbing incoherence, the pony appears above them in a form nearly holographic before solidifying above them like Jesus pissing down a miracle.

"What is *that*?" A white man asks, his gums bleeding and his tongue sore, soiled.

"I've seen it before," The dude next to him says, a Black man who has been eating popcorn this whole time just staring at the oblivion and seeing not much new. "It's the horse thing the kid who shot the guy had."

"*Damn*," the first guy says. "Looks like you could … *do stuff* with it?"

"Like what?" The Black guy asks, wiping his buttery fingers on his jeans.

"I don't know," the first guy says, his voice suddenly becoming uber-polite. "Looks like something someone would use to bomb a school."

The Black guy raises his eyebrows, piece of popcorn nearly to his mouth, and remembers a story he read somewhere about white people in Oklahoma. I can tell, we researched the same thing trying to be prepared to enter this ridiculous shitplace, and now they've got the pony above them calming them down as though they're all crows who have witnessed a shiny object.

"I AM THE WHITE HORSE WHICH HAS COME

HERE TO SAVE YOU!" The Donger Pony says, in a booming voice derivative of the divine one they hear while praying (some of them). "RIDING THROUGH A DISTANT LAND, WHERE BODIES STACK AND PEOPLE BURN!"

Everyone claps. Everyone. They put their tattered, twisted hands together and clap for the donger pony and for me. A version of my face projects next to the Donger Pone, standing with my arm around DJ and his dad, at the center of the picture with the jawline still premature but enough to evoke the status of a number one overall draft pick ready to sling my American heroics all around them. Then, the Donger Pone takes the lead from DJ Daddy and turns itself into an American flag colors. People whip their wallets out and start tossing quarters, dimes, nickels, and credit and debit cards at the pony, who inflates in size to the point where their thumbs lift it up and nearly out of the amphitheater and towards the moon, who, with a blink of his endlessly gazing eyes, pushes the pony back down until the entire trojan horse falls like an equestrian meteorite and slams down onto the lot of them. One of the humans runs screaming, his broken leg dragging behind him, "FUCK ME, IT'S THE MODERATORS, PLEASE HELP IM BEING CENSORED! #cancelculture" Thankfully, DJ and I are saved from the imminent heat death of the universe and by people tearing the donger pony in half just to use it however they wanted by a click that has us twirling up into a place that's seemingly sky blue, as if we rocketed into a song lyric about the nature of all the things, but instead of being cold enough to freeze us to death and blessedly, finally popping our brains like kid's balloons in the bullets of that woman's demented mouth, well, the ground and walls and space around us feels feathery, and its moving in my fingertips ...

NINE

THE WISE OWL is stuck like a dollar bill colored gopher in the middle of a neon blue sea, a feathered carpet of brainless, soulless birds who are looking at us as though we've just been dropped out of the moon's black, cratered eyes.

THE WISE OWL:
Our asses in feathers, we've landed among
Avian carpets, this teal, silent throng.
Behave as though each is a blue, rustled bomb,
Thrust up toward the sky like a cumulus bong!

"Holy hell," DJ says, with the little birds already starting to perch on his shoulders, atop his head, on either side of his crotch. Their tiny feet dig into the surface of his Levi's jeans.

The Pony gallops its way over to us as though skipping through water. On his way, he accidentally taps one of the little birds too hard. It rumbles, opens its beak, and then *screams* in the voice of Alex Jones: *YOU'LL TURN THE FRICKING FROGS GAY.*

"Oh my lord almighty god," DJ says, his ears echoing. The writhing mass of twittering, hopping, twitching birds gets triggered again at DJ's elbow slamming into one of them, which says in the voice of a young, white, gay man, *DAYLIGHT SAVINGS TIME IS THE EQUIVALENT OF A HATE CRIME.*

At this, some of the other little birds around that one start flapping and skipping and climbing their way straight towards that one's anus. They begin pushing it up the wall of birds in what is a demented cavern with a blinding white light at the top of it, with each tweeter either pushing up or down or sharing in a ladder system of crazed, howling, chirping, singing, blathering blue *birds*. And it just spins around and around and around; the Donger Pony tweet with the American flag birthed from the bacchanal message board has caught some kind of virality, and the little birds are pushing the three of us up and around as though we're the stupidest toilet bowl ever assembled and the flapping, feathery walls are the chlorine duster. The Owl pitches his beak open again and says something we read in some of the ancient tomes that shaped this civilization, ones about slouching beasts and the like:

THE WISE OWL:
Like history shared at the simplest click,
By hands, hearts, and hatreds giving no shits,
History spins like a helix-bound spire,
We are inside the colon of the world entire.
We spin round and round, each like and share
Bathing us in a feeling of which we're well aware:
It's great basking in the eyes of people who adore
Anything we do, touch, and say in their world anymore!

"Planting a bullet through the back of that kid's Doorstore vest is the best thing I ever could've done, huh?" I ask DJ, who is as familiar with the cyclical shittiness of this site and the internet at large as we are.

"Might've been," DJ says, nodding at a rippling wave coming towards us. "But now we're about to meet the *sirens*."

Three harpy looking winged bitches, the kind that make potions in myths and are professors in Harry Potter, come surging to us counterclockwise in the clusterfuck of bitrate birdsongs.

One of them is as though Big Bird from Sesame street is pregnant for the third time, but the overweight, well-hydrated-piss colored avian is wearing a McDicks vest and clown shoes and one of those backwards caps on her feathered head, as though she's about to serve me in every way she means. I poke her, the curiosity animating my figure in an illogical way. DJ looks like I've just sniped him across the map with a pistol, and I wink back at him, thinking *at least one of the two of us knows when to best pull the trigger.* This, I suppose, is his punishment of sorts, but the woman-bird crosses her wingtips across her breast and starts rapping in a language only possible in the aborted afterbirth of this system they've got called *capitalism* and the inherent, personal need for them to make everything into people, too, the same way this site turns them into birds. She raps,

Well what up fellow kids, how do you do?
My name's McDicks and I want to know you.
The Internet is where we find all the memes,
Fast food is where kids go to eat their dreams!

The Owl goes flying right at it and slams into its forehead, knocking it loose and sending it free-falling down the chasm of irrelevance at which everything here starts. I don't blame him for ending the attempt at Corporate Friendliness early, especially one that *cringe*, but to troll me back, DJ hits the second bird, which is an anthropomorphic ostrich with a pipe hanging out of its beak with the BURRITO EMPEROR logo buzzed into its meaty, scrumptious flank.

"Guess that guy had to go fix an ice-cream machine," He says, winking an avian eye at us. A bunch of the little birdies around us laugh. *They are such a simple species!* The Pony exclaims, having found equilibrium in the rhythm of the whirling tweets. The last bird is an Eagle wearing aviator sunglasses

(HEEEEH) with an AR-15 strapped across its chest. In a voice ruined by chain-smoking cigarettes and sucking on the same exhaust sending black clouds across New Smyrna beach, the Eagle says, "THESE GUYS LOOK LIKE THEY VOTE FOR MOE FUCKIN WYDEN! WHAT A STUPID LITTLE FA**Y ASS SCULPTURE YOU GOT THERE TOO!" He points one of his grimy, stinky talons right at the Pony. This causes the Pony to enter DEFENSE PROTOCOLS. It hums a seismic, invisible vibration and channels its anger from its violation earlier by the pornstars and their silky ilk into a void where matter can be created and also destroyed, where yes is also no and everything becomes the moon. Observe for yourself what he does as he dives at the man's throat like a rabid, plastic bobcat shaped like a penis and skewers the man's Adam's apple with a blow so bold, it reverberates through the pone's bone frame and has the eagle choking worse than if it had inhaled the very food it was trying to vomit into the mouths of its children. The little tweety birds all laugh as the Eagle coughs its brains out, and the Pony publicly declares, in the same godly voice as in the Grecian amphitheater but toned down to 244 characters, "THE DONGER PONE CONDEMNS ANY WORDS OF HATRED COMING FROM PEOPLE WHO RESIDE IN THEIR MOTHER'S BASEMENTS, ESPECIALLY THOSE WHO CAN'T READ THE POLITICAL AFFILIATIONS OF THE PEOPLE ASSOCIATED." This gets a *ton* of little tweety birds to surround the eagle and start pecking at him, breaking right through his sunglasses and ripping his corneas out with their beaks, the tweety birds themselves diving into its thrashing throat as the Eagle starts blindfiring bullets with the AR-15 into the proverbial cloud, calling them so many hateful things and trying to shred them as they spiral downward fast enough the birds they're falling through on the walls catch fire. They go tumbling down the teal tunnel until they're down there with the people inscribing essays as to why someone else on the internet is wrong, the people who use chalk to keep track of their internet argument wins, the people who love to jerk off after they *own people* as much as white Americans today, like this representative we're on course to meet, when they envision Calvin Candie as a life goal, salivating just due to the power.

Whelp, they're all the way down there with them in the time it took for someone to open their mouths and say words in such a low character count, and before we can even catch our breath, the Owl ready to serenade us again, we find ourselves face to face with a tweety bird colored in the same American flag camouflage fatigues that the pony wore during our ascension to this higher form of discourse. The only thing missing on this one's feathered exterior is the Seal of the President of the United States, or it could be about to open up its platinum-plated mouth and tell us something that could change the course of the country in a single instant. It could even be a poll that will be used to determine policy in the form of democracy where all but the numbers have faded away.

Instead, this one opens its mouth and speaks to us in the Digital Voice of mister Baetz himself, the Senator having already seen our glorious killing in the war of public opinion with the totally legal, good guy endorsed firearm and trails a wake of followers so long, they could be just replicas of his soul following behind him:

"Gentlemen, I absolutely love patriots exactly like you!" The voice says, the little bird's beady eyes channeling the full power of its robot brain's empathy enablers. "I thank God that I am able to invite such amazing heroes to my office here in Washington this upcoming week!"

The bird tilts its head, looking straight into the Donger Pony's invisible eyes.

"What exactly is *this* thing?" It asks us. DJ and I share a glance across the carpet of birds permeating the distance between us. DJ smiles, and this time, following this shared adventure, part of me believes its genuine. Oh how I'll love to make him a lord when it comes time to establish our kingdom beyond these demented shores; he's truly one of the Good Ones.

—FIRST INTERMISSION—

Due to the speed at which these mutated apes love to live their lives – planes, trains, automobiles, walking down the street with their headphones deep in their ears and tight around their necks – I find it appropriate for THE WISE OWL to remind our travelers, at this point, of some important context. It's not *every* day, as they say, that a national hero in the making, his trusty steed, his sage advisor, and his new, best friend get invited to the office of a Senator at this famed place called the United States Capitol, which really looks like one of their strange, squishy, milk-bulging infant nurturers when viewed from a distance (to say nothing of the gargantuan-length, white-bricked, planet-sexing monument across the horizon). However, as we, collectively, have been well aware in our preparations for our arrival, even the Internet and its divine absurdity takes place in the shackles of this human word called *context*. In my understanding, these are the things that happen around a thing, such as the sentences around this one. Simple concept, I'm aware, but the paradox with these people (especially the semen-skinned ones) is that they would take a part of this sentence and vomit it up like a stupid, quipped, manipulated hairball exiting the throat of a domesticated feline. The irony, of course, is that they chuck these things on Twitter, and then the birds eat *them* alive. Anyway, without further ado, I present to you A SUMMARY OF THE SHIT WE'RE WALKING INTO, as presented by the honorable WISE OWL with nothing but his guitar, his voice, and the assistance of some friends who like telling stories using just their tongues ....

THE WISE OWL:

The disease spread from the shorelines, shimmering, complacent,
Laughter and life passed, directly adjacent:
Partiers – drinking, smoking, dancing, raving, raged
And in the land of plenty, death took a brand new name.
It came from a bat, from the Chinese, they claimed,
The kung-flu turned into something they blamed,
To keep working and turning, spending and earning
The laughter never louder than when the bodies were burning.
They said, this is all in our own heads, the brainless, the dead
Centered around the right to keep living instead
Of locking down, shutting up, cancelling graduations
With minds never designed for strict contemplation.
If it's God will, then let it be so much as it is,
"I don't give a fuck if it kills someone's kids!"
There's no shot at them stopping to see what they did,
Because to do so would mean they'd have to admit
The fires and factories and makeshift facilities,
Nurses numbed down to their core sensibilities.
Nails broken, eyes sunken, the relentless disease
A vengeful sort of deity no person could appease!
And the election they ran was decided by the mail,
Oh what a terribly dumb process that entailed!
They counted the ballots of team life and team death,

When the day turned to night, their kind got depressed.
He said, counting only works when the numbers are real,
The nuclear football right next to how he might feel.
On the day they came to Washington to tailgate with guns,
They marched, screamed, demanded, had utter tons of fun
Clashing with barricades, shouting the lofty names
Of politicians they claimed should feel totally ashamed
For forgetting math's principle: the numbers can change
Depending on the person by whom they're arranged.
They waved navy blue flags with names rippling high
And unleashed on the world the hell hidden behind
Their friendly, polite smiles, the voice's pointed tone
Which ends as soon as they put down the telephone.
These are the people who'd shoot us to shards
If we tried to march on their towns or children's schoolyards.
They moved in a throng, tracking dirt, grub, and grime
Recording, enjoying, feeling this was their time.
Ever since they first put hands on the clock,
There's never been moments to rest or to stop
So onward they went, through each metal fence
The lonely guards own bodies now held up to prevent
Something terrible, historic, amidst the euphoria
Of knocking someone down and them not getting back up.
Chills! That's the feeling they say crosses their skin
At the images of the Shaman celebrating his win
From the podium of a person normally as far away from him
As the universe between what they said and what they really did.
They broke and they shattered, they cheered and they howled
For once they were inside, all had to come out.
Jesus was being denied his right to selection,
And their candidate secured their children's protection.

The army showed up like a coroner to a scene,
The people split to both sides with a chasm between
Brothers, uncles, friends, neighbors, fathers, daughters, sons,
No longer able to say they've been United as One.
They erected tall walls, stationed troops outside the dome,
Then, after hardly even pausing, everybody went home.
This is what disturbs THE DAFT ONE and our entire race
There was no sense of shame, no sense of disgrace
For when something unholy enters what's supposed to be sacred
*   space,*
Is there anything sacred to this perfect, proud race?
So in the land of the free and the home of the brave,
Where everyone's a sentence ripped from a torn page,
We ascend through history so thick one might choke,
If they hadn't already lived their entire lives in smoke,
For to be blind is to be free, and to be stuck is a disease,
It's time to see what from us Senator Baetz really needs …

Poor little thing's been taking PCP to feel better recently, all the history combined with this country's gravity weighing down his 85% brain under his avian skull. Luckily, the rest of the animals in Senator Baetz's office, according to his campaign website and electoral advertisements, are dead. Along with the thick smell of cigars permeating the space outside his thick office door, I do believe we're about to meet what some might call another *American hero*!

PART II: THE DONGER PONY GOES TO WASHINGTON

TEN

To here we have traveled: the eternally venerated District of Columbia, less than a single blip in the hour of true time. Time to these people either thickens or thins in a way, if they were smart, they'd study and turn into some kind of commonly acknowledged variable. Thankfully, traveling at the speed of the Internet has allowed us to perfectly represent ourselves in the city of dreams. As a matter of fact, there was a bonus included in the offer by the wonderful, patriotic "thought" leader set to receive us at the Capitol today, Senator Jim Baetz: we would get to spend three exclusive nights, DJ daddy and DJ and I, at the Watergate Hotel, with the money coming out of Mister Baetz's *personal* re-election campaign fund. When asked, lightly, about the implications of this legal jump roping, as its called, DJ Daddy simply said, on the flight that we had to take up there on Southwest Airlines which was also financed by the DAFT ONE goes to Washington fund, that we, and I quote, "Shouldn't hate the player, you should hate the game."

With the Donger Pony strapped in my lap, wearing its American flag camouflage vest, plus the WISE OWL safely in his stuffed form underneath my arm, I was able to shuffle them both around in my lap atop my DJ-loaned Levi's jeans while squinting my eyes at this man.

"You've never heard that one before?" He asks me, having selected the aisle seat, allowing me to sit right against the window and for DJ to cramp his legs in the seat in front of him. The people in front of us are a family of three who are apparently traveling up to DC for some kind of Guinea Pig Convention – they have shirts that say it, around their very pronounced stomachs – and they've decided that now's the right time to stop wearing their masks. They wore them while sitting in line and shoving fast food down their gullets, slurping and sucking and licking and loving every single twist of their tongues, the chomping and the chewing and the disgusting motherfucking chapped lips thing that these people do, like holy SHIT, well, these people are now once again exposing their superior genetics to the rest of the airplane when all anyone asked them to perceptibly do is to squeeze their lard-asses into the too-small seats, order the entire A to Z airplane menu, and shut the fuck up. And do you know *why* this is the thought that pops into my tired, ragged brain after being thrust into this insane bullshit faster than a trailer park in a tornado where the tornado can't pick the trailer up off the ground? Because these people are saying they don't care about anyone else on this plane. And they're not just saying it to me.

No, really, yeah, they're having a three on one argument with a flight attendant who is tan-skinned, muscles bursting out of his arms, rolled up at the sleeves, who is also Black and bald and basically trying to tame a screaming, rabid walrus with how this woman is "bitching him the actual fuck out," in DJ's modern terminology.

"You can't ask me to compromise my own ability to breathe!"

"Ma'm, I promise you, it's *not* the mask's fault."

"Don't you talk to my wife that way!" The man says, sticking his asshole-smelling armpit hairs directly over the crack in the seat in front of DJ. I can almost see the green tendrils violating the air the same way the dude's truck clouded our lungs on that beach. "I will not have my constitutional rights impeded on this flight!" The guy's saying, his sunglasses covering eyes that I'm sure are red with both rage and half-day meth withdrawal. His hairline's already so thin he could be approaching the age where its acceptable for him to die to run the economy. He's going on now about how, as an American, he will not be bullied by this (somehow) fascist *and* communist regime run by Moe Wyden and the Demonrats, which sounds like a psychedelic rock band who makes bestial torture porn. Trust me, it exists, just ask DJ's dad, who is caught between trying to feign concern for the potential altercation going on in front of us and not cracking up in laughter in being selected for *another* potential violent internet meme. Too bad they don't allow guns on airplanes, I feel like someone should open a company called Bullet Airlines and make that happen. Instead, we're forced to sit here and watch as the flight attendant nods with the complexion of Mother Theresa at these hocking, honking hogs raging about being placed back in their cages. Their *intellectual* cages, of course, the son says, having finally spoken up to affirm that he's the type of guy who's a shoe-in for AutoAdmit. He says that Southwest Airlines has been secretly supporting the Communist Chinese in their attempts to induce chemicals into the atmosphere, and in return they've provided them with human-robot staff who can kick the utter shit out of any number of military personnel. Oh and also the Democrats. Blessedly, once again, DJ Daddy is not the voice of reason – he's a member of the right political party who might have a chance at un-fucking the next example of how rights are delivered with clenched fists and broken jaws.

"Hey, hey," DJ Daddy says, appearing over the side of the father's shoulder like he's a big, hairy, sexually deviant angel in a suit too nice for his jawline. "Now's not the time for arguing, people." To show solidarity, he's taken off his *own* mask and is now clutching it as though it's a handkerchief in a medieval drama. The three big piggies underneath him all turn and approvingly nod their heads, saying *hell yeah!* And *you look familiar?* Then you've got people realizing that there's a celebrity on their hands, the congressman whose son is not only wearing a mask, but who, in the words of the snorting mother of the bunch, was "not man enough to defend his father when he was the one holding the gun. That's how far our kids have fallen."

"What, from killing themselves working in factories at the age of 5?" The flight attendant says, his cheeriness replaced with a knifing, faux-polite tone.

"No, from killing themselves at the age of 16 for having to work until midnight in order to even support their own existences in Wisconsin," DJ says, into the crack between the seats.

"DJ!" Daddy DJ says, threatening to backhand him. "Don't you start spouting that liberal *bullshit* while we're on this flight!"

"Plane would get there three hours faster without this row on board," DJ says. The flight attendant bites his own knuckles trying not to collapse laughing. Meanwhile, Baldy McBaldman's also unstrapped his seatbelt and is standing two inches away from DJ Daddy's perplexed, furrowed eyebrows, placed his glasses on his forehead, and is now peering down at DJ with a violence in his eyes to rival the previous duels between disease deniers and the people who staff these planes.

"You're a scared little bitch boy," The man says, hissing at DJ in a wave of spit. "You should be lucky for your friend sitting next to you."

"Sir," A different flight attendant says, a Black woman who is done with this shit in her mid-30s with multicolored curls. Her nails are long and sharp and pointed at the man's chubby, bouncing chinrack like knives about to skewer an albino balloon animal. "I'm going to have to ask you to sit down."

"Seatbelts signs are fucking tyranny!" The man yells, punching his fist directly into the air and clanging into the bottom of the overhead compartment. "If I want to get fucked around by turbulence, I can do as I damn well please!"

"Explain to me how there's turbulence when the earth is flat!" Someone else screams from up somewhere in the plane.

"Yeah!" A man shouts, three rows behind us, with a mask that says LET'S GO RYLAND on it in big, bold, white text over a crimson red cloth. "Let's see where they keep the *chemicals!*"

"Ah shit," the male flight attendant says, as the woman and her son have both unbuckled their seatbelts as well. He looks across the aisles to his coworker, who immediately talks into a handheld radio she's procured and says *this is a code 103 217, code 103 217.* The idiot who slammed his knuckles into the plastic is now reaching into his overhead compartment while the woman who radioed the code in and her mid-40s, similarly talon-handed, papyrus-skinned coworker are attempting to close the compartment while standing behind him. DJ Daddy has sank back into his seat with his hands rubbing his temples, making sighing noises. The man in front of him is now saying "You can ask this State Representative sitting right behind me, I *don't* have to wear a mask on this plane!"

"The Governor has said mandates aren't necessary, nor do they need to be followed." The kid in the center says. If he were a normal ape, I think they would've drowned him in a river shortly after birth. He pushes his glasses up the bridge of his acne-riddled, snotty-clogged nose through his victory grease, the little air-thingies above the seat absolutely helpless in the face of peak male argumentative form. "If you touch me or my mother or my father, we'll be forced to sue you."

Oh sweet fucking *Jesus*. He's said the S word. Everyone on the plane has simultaneously unplugged their headphones, folded their newspapers and books and magazines (as if people actually *read* anymore), and craned their necks around to participate in the most American ritual of all time: suing someone for something you can create after it's supposed to have happened! Like a reason to feel violated for being asked to wear a facemask, or for the flimsy flight attendant behind the man to nick him or his precious, laminated constitutional copy with her claws. Instead, the flight attendant who radioed in comes out from a place near the cockpit three sections up the plane, and whatever the hell she has on the end of that leash has these chubby bunnies running back to their seats faster than they stack the drive through at the local IHOP. Upon further inspection, what the flight attendants seem to have domesticated, for their own protection, is an alligator, painted white and yellow and blue and with a model of a plane strapped to the crown of its skull. Apparently, and this is all shit we learned *after* what's about to happen, of course, in their interpreting of allowing decisions for public health to be made by the businesses, who are, of course, people in and of themselves so you can't restrict *their* rights, either, especially if they make money, which Southwest does despite situations like the one in which we find ourselves, well, these companies can choose how to enforce their own policies. In this case, following the violent, rapid rise of cases involving complete fucking troglodytes and their offspring with the people who spend their entire lives traveling to destinations they wouldn't even dream about, they brought Abby the Alligator from her comfortable cockpit playpen, and she's now smiling with her serrated jaws – alternating white and blue and yellow, naturally – right at the big chunk of the Free Thinker's back calf. It would be like biting into a plastic grocery store bag filled with pure, hot fat. For the sake of the own animal's heart and the man who is now whimpering like a little bitch, in his own words, himself at the sight of those friendly jowls, I do hope they're listening when they say the employees really are looking out *for their own best interests*.

Meanwhile, inches from the reptile's smiling eyes, DJ Daddy looks down at DJ with a sideways glance, stroking his five o'clock shadow with his palm. DJ reaches into the seatback pocket, takes out his packet of peanuts, and starts feeding them to the hungry corporate mascot who has suddenly brought a sense of calm which will prevent any emergency stopping for the care of people who couldn't be fucked if the people on this plane all slammed into the ground, so long as they died on ventilators and in hospitals and alone as they've been doing. Such is why, with even my own celebrity status being juked by the orderly procedures of the flight attendants, I can only pet the Donger Pony, squeeze the owl (who is now damp and squishy with all sorts of perspiration), and ponder the shapes of the clouds in this pretty planet's atmosphere and how they could all look like Ponies if we tilt our heads the right way.

ELEVEN

The dude's styled his hair to look like a young John C. Calhoun, according to our records department, with the hair shorter and almost straight black over a ridiculous, Hollywood face, with the jawline and the twinkling, masterpiece eyes just *beaming* to welcome us to Washington. The fact he and his posse and an entire camera crew greeted us right as we exited airport security, with the front part cordoned off and the cameras clicking like we were about to meet Princess Diana, suddenly made me feel as if the Donger Pony were actually increasing physically due to monetary value. The hexapodildonic horse is starting to recover from its terrible treatment at the hand of DJ's favorite pornstars back in the day, but Senator Baetz's jawline and his regal mane are making the pony worried we've accidentally wandered into a political pornographic parody; this is especially true, he silently whinnies to me, due to the women who are following in the Senator's wake: they're rabid, rose red capped BAETZ BABES with screams that echo down the asshole of the Southwest terminal. Thankfully, the circle's closed behind us, after following, of course, the local police down the connecting bridge to go unfuck the standoff between the guinea pig people and the corporate reptile. As he approaches DJ Daddy, DJ, and our ABSURD TRINITY, I can almost feel the Jordan Belfort radiating from his smile as he grips my hand firmly and squeezes like it's a Florida orange on juicing day.

"I finally get to meet the rock star!" He says, having apparently forgotten his red-carpet reception at the board meeting. To be fair, he was coming from a campaign event in the district and was so furiously high on what I concluded to be methamphetamines that it seemed like he was about to gnaw right through his own fucking gumline by the time he was done talking that night. We ignore this amazing stupidity to notice not only the perspiration on Mr. Baetz's palms, but the fact he's gotta be at least twice as high as he was that night right now, only half a football field away from the cops who are about to break their hips trying to unscrew that Gator's teeth from that poor kid's left kneecap.

"John Mejora," I finally manage, the handshake ending with my joints smarting. *Such inferior designs as these start to hurt with age, humans.* "It's an honor to meet you, sir."

"No, no, the honor's all mine," he says, with some weird twang in his voice that makes it sound like vaccinations are a cuss word in his household. "I get to host a few Florida heroes in a town filled with villains." He says, making DJ grin and DJ Daddy legitimately laugh despite the commotion behind them. Apparently, the alligator is now threatening to sue for emotional distress, according to what the Pony's saying, having intercepted their signals by using his equestrian ears to listen through walls (which he's not supposed to do according to the treaty, I'm aware, but look at how deep we're in this now: we're *empathizing with the Wall-E people.*)

"Swamp creatures?" DJ Daddy says, shaking the man's hand and staring him in the eyes like he wants him to grab him in the men's bathroom like these Republicans love to do, but only if they're divided by sex!

"Are you *sure* you want to work here?" The Senator asks,

clapping DJ Daddy on the shoulder like he's a kicker who just made an easy field goal. "So nice to see you again, Carl. You look like you've been healing well."

"Oh," DJ Daddy says, like he's just been rejected asking someone to Prom. "Yeah, I mean, it's been a little difficult, but thankfully my son's been here to help me out."

"Your son – he *and* his friend – are national treasures, sir," Baetz says, bowing to us like we're his ancient, wartime generals. "Your son for having the wherewithal to keep his gun with him at all times, and his friend for not being afraid to be the Good Guy we don't see enough!"

He pivots back to DJ, a thought popping into his mind. "Say, son," he says. "Are you on the High School Shooting team?"

"No," DJ says, keeping his voice politely lifted. "And my father's name is *Paul*."

Baetz whirls back to DJ Daddy, his eyes widened, the look of panic as the bugs have started to come out with their shadow-crawling sounds. He keeps it together, though, and then places his right hand directly on DJ Daddy's left shoulder, wrinkling his suit and squeezing like he's about to join him in prayer. "Paul, Paul, *Paul*," He says, placing his wrist into his forehead and pressing hard enough he leaves a red mark. He then grabs him with the other hand and looks like he's apologizing for just not being ready right now to love someone the way they need to be. "I'm sorry, friend; it's been a long, hard day fighting for Florida's rights in Washington." He releases him and steps back to adjust his tie. Bashfully, DJ Daddy says, as respectfully as a grown man wearing a GOP bowtie can, "Sir, I know you knew me when you shook my hand."

"That's what counts!" Baetz says, shooting him a finger gun with absolutely no sense of irony what-so-fucking-ever. He knocks a fist into DJ's shoulder too, as though they're in the locker room, before finally moving past us and addressing the clusterfuck occurring on the bridge. The cops are in the process of truly testing fate and gravity by walking the family across the bridge (with the parents both red faced as hellfire from whatever shouting match must have occurred). Meanwhile, the kid is being rolled out by police on a wheelchair, his leg wrapped in gauze that's already almost bled through. THE WISE OWL is trailing behind the wheelchair and stumbling as if drunk, while Abby the Alligator is being carried on a satin pillowcase by a team of flight attendants walking straight in line, as if this is some procession where the parents are going to jail for whatever they did to the gator, the gator is going to be crowned the new queen of DC, and the kid's going to the hospital only to leave with a medical bill rivaling the first year of his tuition at whatever dipfuck school they send young contrarians to these days with his leg forever scarred. THE WISE OWL, with the cameras, DJ and his father, and everyone here follow Senator Baetz to the mouth of the tunnel, through the peculiar smell of fish and the floor squeaking strangely underneath some of these women's stilettos and flat tops ... THE WISE OWL takes the time to issue a warning to me and the brilliant, bold-colored Pone next to me on the airport tiles.

THE WISE OWL:
This crossing of paths has made me suspect,
That senators are those who get most respect.
They are a hundred who represent the entire land,
But how this one won elections, I don't understand!

"Let's see how he deals with his constituents," I say, the crowd parting as the three of us make our way up to DJ and DJ Daddy's side right next to Senator Baetz, who has folded his hands in front of his crimson suit, blaring in the sunlit afternoon, and is staring down the head flight attendant from Southwest who sicked the gator on the guy along with the parents, whose Guinea Pig Festival rodentia are now covered with specs of blood and snot and what might be shit, I don't think I can smell it from here. The cameras are right behind us like vultures at the sight of carrion in the middle of the starving desert, and now the Donger Pony is front and center to what might turn out to be a crucial piece of this nation's history! And Paul is legitimately, fully erect at being this close to the warm touch of power. Abby the Alligator, meanwhile, opens her jawline in a smile and you can legitimately *see* bits of flesh stuck to the underside of her teeth like what pork fat caught between the molars must feel like to these stupid people. Oh, and Senator Baetz has the whitest teeth I've ever seen, an amount of bleach on the bone like washing skeletons for the catacombs in Paris, but when he's this inquisitive, as he's been in some of his internet *ownage* compilations where he pwns the libtards, you can only see him scowling at you the same way Papa Calhoun must've stared down Jackson with that noose in his hand.

"What's the situation here, fellas?" Senator Baetz asks, echoing like a plantation owner's voice across an expectant, working field. "Seems as though there's been a bit of conflict in the air."

"Good afternoon, Senator Baetz," The head flight attendant says, Abby's leash still wrapped around her hand. "We are currently attending to a criminal procedure."

"Why exactly is she speaking for the police?" The Senator asks the two men on either side of the parents, the same color as the cops at the Capitol.

"With respect, Senator," The one policeman, an exmilitary dude in his early 40s, says to Calhoun. "We've already concluded our investigation: these here three people emotionally damaged this here reptile." His voice has more banjo than the Senator's three times over. The alligator, meanwhile, looks as though it's debating if it could hop off that purple satin pillow and go for the other leg before someone grabs her leash.

"Well, what was the disagreement about?"

"It was about our freedoms, senator!" The mother says, her voice quivering with white anger at being caught. "They told us we couldn't refuse to wear masks on the plane!"

"Does the company have a mandate?" Senator Baetz asks.

"Yes," The flight attendant says, shrugging her shoulders. "We have all the permits for the gator usage, too."

"I see," Baetz says, looking between the cops and the flight attendants as though trying to piece them together. "And so are you telling me someone's *rights* were infringed upon?"

"No," The flight attendant says. "They have no right to put other people in danger with their reckless behavior."

"Reckless behavior?" The Senator asks, raising his voice and nodding faster while taking three paces towards the woman. "Excuse me, Ms., I don't even know your name, but I can tell you right now I'm not liking the sound of these excuses." He gestures wildly towards the kid stranded in the wheelchair, reaching behind him and swatting. "Usually I don't mind seeing a little blood spilled argumentatively, but this here family's been on their way to the Guinea Pig Convention!"

The flight attendant blinks. The cops sigh, shuffling their feet behind the parents, who are now radiating vindication through their up-tilted multi-chins, the perspiration soaking through the front of their shirts, and the fact *their* nipples are now as hard as the group of women who are swooning like the Senator's had his cologne lining each one of their collarbones before this happened. And *these* women are definitely on the same shit he's on, because they've been snorting every few second like a herd of hogs trying to both clear their nostrils and intimidate the people holding the handcuffed human swine into believing they're some other type of pig, too; at least as they're standing between their chosen man and whatever he's looking for, how quickly those things seem to turn. Anyway, after a series of glances back and forth, plus the cops telling the cameras to back up a few feet, the flight attendant arches her eyebrows solely due to the strength of three years dealing with constant, insane customer bullshit, and asks our dear Soap Opera star Senator, "What is the guinea pig convention?"

The crowd of people behind the Senator all gasp as though the Donger Pony's suddenly invaded their personal spaces. The Senator himself smiles, nods his head, and points a very waggy finger right at the flight attendant in way that will be called *extremely racist* after this whole shebang is over. He attempts to soothe the shouted curses from the women behind us, while DJ is trying not to laugh like a hyena, his cheeks puffed out and his pursed lips making noises of nearly failed suppression, and I think the spot on DJ Daddy's pants means that he either got caught by one of the spit lobs being hocked by these women in the flight attendant's general direction, or he's already had his manhood absorbed by Senator Calhoun's Shakespearean drama at the woman not knowing about his fucking domesticated rodent gathering. And now he's got them enraptured because he's about to explain it.

"The National Guinea Pig Convention," Senator almost-Calhoun says, winking at one of the women and causing her legs to legitimately convulse across the tile like she's dancing the electrocution. "Is a fundamental expression of people's rights as personified by their beloved rodents."

"It's both a celebration *and* a competition," DJ Daddy says, nodding his head right at her as well.

"Exactly, Saul," The Senator says, causing DJ to cackle into his elbow. "You see, the guinea pig to me represents freedom in the sense that people can use any mascot to encompass what freedom means, so long as they share the same kind of spirit." He flexes his hand in front of his face as though it's been numb from pointing so long. "I believe that freedom and Democracy can make people from entirely different backgrounds able to join together and celebrate that which brings us closer in a time of great strife."

The kid, who has been in the wheelchair the entire time, stamps his remaining foot on the ground in an angry, squinted-eye morphine haze and shouts, "When am I going to get my leg back?"

"When the alligator shits it out!" The flight attendant shouts back. This causes a ruckus that in turn causes the entire rolling staircase to rattle on its haunches. Senator Baetz, however, curses at his supporters and steps right in front of the crippled kid to stare down at him like a venerated statue at the people trying to tear it to concrete chunks.

"What's your name, son?" The Senator asks the kid.

"Reginald Baxter Typhus the Third," the kid says, the Senator's address triggering the internet troll part of him and having him imagine this is all just taking place on the forums. "Respectfully, senator, I feel the opposition has no argument."

"What, you think this is debate club?" The Senator asks, rolling his eyes into the back of his head. "Reggie, I want to know what you said to make the alligator bite you." Ms. Abby gives an approving hiss through her serrated lips.

"*Excuse* me?" The Karen says, stomping her flat-bottomed foot on the ground. "Senator, we didn't do anything wrong!"

"I didn't say you did," Baetz says. "But I am following tradition of needing to hear both sides of every story before I close my case."

"Wow," one of the cops says, tilting his brimmed cap approvingly. "A real American thinker!"

Undaunted, the internet debater extraordinaire says, "I said the alligator was working as an agent for the Communist Chinese Democratic Party of America."

"Son," The Senator says. "They're *lizards*." He places his hands on his hips. "I have great respect for independent thinkers, but I believe the Democrats are worse than lizards."

"How's *that*?" The flight attendant asks.

"Lizards are cold blooded," The Senator says, pointing at Abby on the satin pillow. "But the Democrats *slither*."

The group of women behind him make a terribly coordinated series of hissing noises like they're all trying out to be part of Medusa's hair. Then, the Senator snaps his fingers and calls for *Georgie!*, who turns out to be his personal assistant, a Black dude in his mid-20s in a perfect Kashmir suit. Georgie runs through the crowd carrying a cage that appears to be filled with small, bloody roses, until you realize they're actually a series of guinea pigs who have been painted to resemble the Senator's campaign colors. This causes everyone to become focused on the guinea pigs, with the Senator smiling for the camera and snapping pictures next to everyone's faces with that radiant, white bone wall smile being only reinforced by the grinning skin around him. And we got to pose with both the alligator and the family and the alligator with the guinea pigs until the alligator tried to eat one of the guinea pigs, at which point the senator told Georgie to come hither again, pulls a shotgun out of a gun sheath, and shot the alligator dead right there on the metal, blowing its brains through the bottom towards the burning tarmac.

"God *dammit*!" The Senator shouts, flexing his arms together in front of his chest and popping his top button under his collar so it clatters to the ground amidst the dead silence. His voice echoes down the crossbridge along with the ear-ringing noise of the shotgun blast and the cheers from his crowd. "That scaly motherfucker ate one of my dear guinea pigs!"

As it was clear that this situation was about to become a fiasco that involved bullets and lawyers and things, DJ and DJ Daddy and the Donger Pony, plus the Owl whose eyes were spinning around and around and around the *entire* time, Georgie and his team whisked us away to one of those limos that you see politicians driving around in with bulletproof, tinted glass. The fresh smell of shotgun powder still clogging my nose, I waited until we were well away from the snapping camera lenses to whisper into DJ's ear and ask, "Is this man popular in his position here?"

"Hell yeah," DJ says, as we squeeze into the backseat of the semi-limousine. "He's been unopposed in the primaries the last three elections."

Suddenly, the air-conditioned, leatherback interior no longer felt only like the waiting room to see a doctor maddened by age and prescribing anything you say you need, but also as though we were about to be whisked away on a siren-escorted journey to a place as close to sacred as you can be in this world, where bullets and broken glass are just part of the procedure these days. Oh, the wonders of how these people use their time …

TWELVE

We float through the high-security fences into the United States Capitol like Jesus Christ himself coming to Jerusalem. Only here, the difference is that we're no miracle worker ready to command the attention of everyone who holds crosses in their hair and made of gold and silver across their collarbones – we're something greater. We're *witnesses* to history, and to what's now making Senator Baetz rub his paws together right atop his desk in his private, Senatorial office. When we watched three senators living in an extremely shitty, run-down motel afflicted with rust and foul scents, these are the places they would not sleep inside, except Jim Baetz has been extremely lucky in the fact he's got some high-ranking committee appointments that have to do with silly things like justice and has a pinch of seniority, what, being on his third term as a senator after making the switch from private fiscal investing. But now his nose is twitching worse than watching the stock market with Martin Scorsese, and he actually already has a small vial of coke stationed next to the framed picture of John C. Calhoun staring up at him, as though he's less of a reflection and more of a reincarnation. He rips the lid off the vial, spills the cocaine on the desk, and proceeds to rip the coke straight off as its been mixed with bits of ash and wood shavings; his nostrils must be *leather*. He doesn't even flinch as he blinks his eyes and slaps the underside of the table with his kneecap three times until he stops kicking. Then, he looks at all of us: me in the center, DJ Daddy to my left, and DJ to my right, with the pony placed perfectly perpendicular to the Senator's desk on my lap and the owl cocking his head to four o'clock at the idea of cocaine's rhythmic power.

Before the Owl can rap, however, the senator, wide, bugged eyes over shadowed crescents in his skin, looks straight at me and goes, "So who taught you how to shoot, John?"

"My father taught me how to load a rifle when I was three," I say, raising my eyebrows at DJ Daddy and feeling a cold wind from DJ on my opposite site. *Sorry, friend, I'm going to need you for a second.*

"Brilliant," The Senator says, leaning across the table and fist bumping me with a gator-blood splattered hand. He got most of it off, I suppose, but a few flakes remain on my middle finger's knuckle when I take my hand back. His phone started ringing awfully loudly, so he ripped it out of the wall and sent it clattering to the floor, where its resting on the spotless carpet of this glorified rectangular prism, the cord around it like a chalk outline on one of the District's many streets where men like Senator Baetz would never dare walk, unless his entire life gets ripped from him by the legal system in this alligator arbitration coming up. After taking the phone back from the floor and hastily plugging it back in its place on his desk, there's a huge, echoing pound on the closed office door and the voice of a woman shouting, "Jim!"

"Ah, fuck," The Senator says, shoving the cocaine vile back in the top drawer, straightening his tie, running a slick hand through his curls and snorting so loudly I could've sworn he's sucking up a nosebleed. "Hold on, Marlene!"

"Jim, I don't know what you think you're doing, but if you don't open this goddamn door right goddamn now, I'm going to resign. There's a pit of hungry wolves out there and the

Democrats are *raping* us worse than Bill Clinton in Alabama!"

"I'm sorry," The Senator says to us, nearly whispering through another barrage of pounds. "That's my press secretary. She's always trying to tell me what to say and think and feel, so I'm sure she's about to fully shit on my desk for the situation with the gator at the gate."

"We can leave if you want," DJ Daddy says, nodding at both of us to be sure, but the Senator pushes the motion away while shaking his head, sighing, eyes closed in frustration.

"Never, sir," He says. "These kids are American heroes, and you're an example of how to respond when people say you should be advocating for gun reform."

"I *am* an advocate for gun reform," DJ Daddy says, openly, happily. "I want everyone to be able to participate in bullet sports with full endorsement deals."

"*Wow*," The Senator says, whistling, the banging decreasing in both velocity and volume. "I was asking your son earlier if he was on the shooting team. If his friend here would join, he'd –"

The door swings open so fiercely the wood's arc nearly catches the pony. In walks a woman whose hair reminds me of coiled copper wire, jutting down to her shoulders. Her lipstick's scarlet worse than the woman who wore the letter back in the ancient tales, the one nobody in this room can even remember, and she's wearing a scowl with the intensity of someone who has been caught amidst an argument with a lover. I can assure you, from our external investigations of Master Baetz's marital status, DJ Daddy is not only metaphorically offering to lick the man's puckered, bleached asshole (the same one that's been spread across I'm not sure how many forums anonymously), he's going to do just that after this most recent transgression ends this work-place relationship forever. Marlene's about as tall as DJ Daddy, maybe about a head shorter, yet I feel like in her condition she could vault over the desk and stab the man clean through the throat with the sharp part of her high heels.

"You've gone and lost your actual fucking mind, Jim," she says, tossing a bundle of articles together from CNN and Fox and MSNBC, all with headlines screaming about the incident:

BADASS SENATOR MAKES LIBERAL CROC GO EXTINCT

"IF YOU KILL ONE OF US GUINEA PIGS, HE'LL SEND YOU BACK TO HELL!" Shouts woman in aftermath of reptilian emotional damage case

KILLARY'S NEVER COME CLOSE TO THIS SENATOR'S RHETORICAL EFFECTIVENESS

"Brilliant," The Senator says, his cocaine-fueled eyes shifting over every page. "I'm so glad to see our supporters have latched onto our most recent campaign message so emphatically."

"I'm going to bite your cock off and then push it down your throat," She says, phone in hand, silencing another call looking to speak to either of our heroic shooters here. "Great, this one I have to take, it's from the White House again."

"I told them earlier PETA broke three of my family's grave-stones," The Senator says, reaching back into the desk drawer, withdrawing the cocaine, and eyeing how much left is in there before flexing his nostrils. "You want any, Marlene?"

"After this call," she says, walking back towards the hallway and closing the office door behind her as she leaves. Before she completes the arc, though, she turns around and says, "Oh, Senator?"

"Yes?" The Senator asks, already having cut the cocaine into thin lines across the table with his congressional identification card.

"The f****t flag across the hallway's back up there again."

"*Liberals*," The Senator says, a naughty, glinting look in his eyes at the *non-pc language* of his campaign associate. "Guess its time to fly the snake flag again. Wish I would've shot the woman, cops would've high fived me walking out of there." He blows a goodbye kiss to Marlene, who's out the door and blabbing, and after it closes he rips the cocaine off the table in one fell swoop of all the lines, together. The man could've been a starving anteater the way he vacuumed up that powder. According to our research, we're not sure if Kennedy actually did meth, but if there's one thing that suddenly makes a whole lot of sense, its how Senator Baetz is able to speak so motherfucking fast in all his internet propaganda. He's like if Ben Shapiro decided it would be a good idea to start experimenting with ways to make his wife's pussy actually wet. This is a liberal joke I heard that when I told it to THE DONGER PONUS, it retreated inside its individual shell to tend to the horseys in the donger stable, and now it's on my lips again as I observe the small donger pony model the man's already got decorating his desk. We'll be able to hear if he pushes his hard thing into the woman's pleasure cave on the very desk he just ripped the lines off of and where he rolls his cancer sticks on his own like they did in the olden days. I am sure there are some members of the oversight committee who will enjoy the soundtrack, but before we can get anywhere near there, we're caught in another loop of Senator Baetz's inexplicable, *honest* charisma, the one that had that group of good, Christian women standing behind him with those signs and with their ovaries kicked into overdrive from the sight of such a God-fearing man working magic on a situation. And that's where the dude pivots now, because he turns around to his mantelpiece and selects one of his earthly idols straight from the place where it had been chillin' in the violent, downcast gaze of John Calhoun himself.

The Senator places the guinea pig sculpture on the table, engraved with a name that says

PRESIDENT PIGGASUS

(Along with the little rodent's irrelevantly numbered birth and death dates. I guess it's better than snorting his ashes.)

The rodent effigy looks like its made of smelted gravel, and the eyes being as fucked up as they are, askew and bulging with no irises, makes the thing look closer to a frog you'd find vomiting out a constant stream of water in any semi-rural fountain. However, the guy strokes the top of its terribly textured head and gets a look in his eyes like he's staring into the mist lingering over Arlington.

"This was my first guinea pig," He says, touching the thing's nose with the tip of his finger. "He was a trooper. Died of rectal cancer when I was in the third grade."

"How unfortunate," I say. DJ offers a nod of sympathy, as his father parses his lips and laments his defeated penis. Cocaine might be able to solve a lot of his problems, come to think about it. Now, the Senator's grabbed the gravel guinea pig effigy and is hopping it straight across the desk to where it can converse with the donger pony sculpture, the pasture of his thoughts nearly childish in display.

"I empathized with that little auburn, glowing furball more than any kid when I was school-going age," The Senator says. "And I feel as though we're the same today with the kind of people on their way to the Guinea Pig Convention."

On the place's site, where you can donate to the campaign of the man in the leather chair stroking the rodent R.I.P. figurine like it brings him physical, actual pleasure, there's an entire sub-site devoted to the Guinea Pig Convention and the fact everyone who goes there is a Guinea Pig who's been Awakened. The little rodents are their personifications in the same way the Senator's now waxing nostalgically about the fact the rodent was able to be dressed in patterned clothing purchasable on a website that makes such things. I wonder if this man has ever attempted to buy a child on the black market, because this entire situation is making me feel as though we've accidentally entered a time-warp induced by an ′overdose′ of marijuana. However, this is not the case, seeing as the point of the Senator's whole rambling tale about the rodent is the fact we've been made into Guinea Pigs (light emphasis on the *we*) by the American government; ergo, and yes, he actually *says* ergo, we need to bond together in a herd. He has over 103 Guinea Pigs now, he says, but the whole point of the operation is to engage with the community whom he loves so much, who are the closest to seeing him both in this office and the way he behaves on the forums.

"Do you want to visit them with me?" He asks. "Have you had enough of Washington?"

"We haven't burnt or broken anything yet," I tell him, with a wink. "I'd shit in the rotunda but I went before we got here."

"I *like* you," he says to me, pointing with the ferocity of a sports owner at their number one draft pick. "I'll show you why I brought you here."

With a click of a button on the rusty, Dell tower, he turns on his senate PC, brushes the dust off the hot, whirring fans, and invites us all to join him this time on a guided exploration of top-tier American politics …

THIRTEEN

We explode back into the D.C. streets like we're surfing in a lucid dream, except instead of trying to unfuck the subconscious mind of a man who can represent the country while his mouth works at warp speed, its as though the Garden of Earthly Delights, a crowning, holy achievement by a human far away from this tortured, broken place, has been manifested in concurrence with the content on Senator Jim Baetz's campaign site. However, instead of us being immediately fused with the torrents of the internet as though allowed to cascade into our conscious minds like dams breached by invisible holes, we are now traveling along with DJ Daddy and the Senator, who is fully inhabiting his persona as a posterboard face by appearing nearly comically animated, as though he's from Disney's "Hercules," but instead of cleaning bullshit out of a stable for countless hours, he's tossing it down the throats of the throng of "campaign contributors, local patriots, and Americans invested in their country's future from across the universe."

These people are the Patriotic Tourists who await us outside of the rotunda's moat-protected walls with their patented Tourist Weapons, trademarked with the SenBaetz logo, emblazoned on everything from the gun barrels to the bullet casings to the actual CannonZ they're rolling around with, ready to fire them into statues like Abraham Lincoln's head (outside of a theater production and parasitically consumed by this current age). They're the definition of peaceful tourists: people howling at the top of their lungs in a way you'd expect from a wild force of nature, who are chanting FUCK MOE WYDEN and LET'S GO RYLAND at the same time. There's an entire bus of them where the driver is employed by the same agency responsible for training the school-teachers in firearm protection, so he's offering a deal to any visiting teachers from the Florida region that if they want to have their staff's license to be good people with guns renewed, all they need to do is break three different windows, snap the legs off of eight different chairs, and – the easiest part, according to the bro-chure clutched in their hands – if they manage to injure a police officer, they'll get a discount of three free legal defense funds for their friends once they get referred to the Peace, Respect, Freedom, and Justice tourism board. Apparently, they're starting similar services in Portland, but these people here have mostly gotta be from either Florida or the neighboring states.

The Militia of Friendly Smiles, who have those dead-eyed, line-faces looking like emojis who have known the taste of death, are jokingly eating candy canes and pretending they're smoking joints, save for the ultra religious ones who are carrying tote bags inscribed with *HOLD THE LINE PATRIOTS, GOD WINS* that contain plushies of the Shaman who took a face-painted shit on the lectern of the house speaker, back before Trancy McCowksi was almost nearly as decrepit as old Moe Wyden himself. Any celebration of the woman's basic functionality in this country's legislative body, to say nothing of its executive branch's post-expi-ration President manning the helm, gets championed as though her opponents haven't made it legally possible for women like the velociraptor English people to pop a cap in their students' asses mistaking DJ for people like those two kids in Colorado. Thankfully, all of the teenagers in this crowd (on a class trip, apparently!) are Responsibly Armed, meaning their AR-15s have *themselves* promised to be kind today and not be held responsible for any stupid incidents like the one committed by our dear Senator earlier this morning.

However, in response to this, I can smell smoking alligator on some of these portable grills these people have stacked in front of us, and there's even three stuffed gators who have been completely skewed on stakes in the crowd that are being slammed down on the pavement and making grotesque, percussion sounds of metal scraping cement. These people have had their tours expertly arranged in order to coincide with the GPC this weekend, and naturally a couple of the pigs who have been openly pissing and shitting and licking and humping on the capitol stairs are all wearing service vests but also wigs that make them look like men from the 17th century. Dragging them across the ground when they're misbehaving or starting to whine is the closest these people will ever get to sashaying in their mortal lives, meaning that the Senator has to thank them gratefully for their continued support following the brutal death of his guinea pig who he held directly in front of the alligator's mouth as he told the alligator he was going to demonstrate the bonds of inter-species trust. The adoring crowd shows their affection by howling like they've become wolves, which itself triggers the people who are currently chiseling the base of the Washington monument in order to better reflect the jagged divisions of American history to begin howling as well against the clink of hammers – that's right, by the way, in this part of the tour you're able to pay pretty much $15 to smack the shit out of a monument and demonstrate the strength of your patriotism, leaving an indelible mark on the massive stone cock visible from the high heavens above which blessed this cumstained land the same way being born in a place so grounded in freedom molds every single life that wields those branded red, white, and wave colored hammers.

The hammering, however, is giving the owl obvious issues, so we ask the Senator to take us to the reflecting pool where the people pretending they're ducks and chucking themselves into the sacred, sunlit waters while dressed like 18th century pilgrims gleefully chuckle at their pathetic attempts to splash into Thanksgiving while the trees are lit on fire by visitors, who are obviously just trying to clear space for more businesses in the district; their desecration of the arbory accompanied by screaming NO MORE CHILD PORN LOVING DEMOCRATS HUGGING THESE THINGS! is obviously just a man expressing his god-given right to scream his lungs out with the same ferocity as the fire pissing out of his gascan holding hand. All around the reflecting pool, the democratically demented, the representations of every memer on the internet manifest in a way that will be granted either clemency or absurdly short prison sentences, have expanded across the national mall, tossing the scents of burning skin and piles of shit being set ablaze into our lungs and make the owl almost choke on his own tongue. The pony, meanwhile, has cordoned off its invisible nose, and as we're floating through the sacred air filled with disgusting smoke with the Senator as though his coattails are a magic carpet ride, people start thrusting when they see the pony no matter what they're doing, uplifting us and causing people to click their tongues like a pack of dogs who have peanut butter stuck to their mouth tops. There's so fucking *many* of them interacting with us as the sacred arbors burn, including a white woman who is so orange she looks like a hooker Oompa Loompa whose bare nipples are serving as the eyes in a smileyface bent and twisted to look like the Senator's, his Howdy Doody facial features draping down a pink carpet of a tongue leading straight to her vagina, which is stained through her yoga pants with her holy bush burning for the man's dick in a way the donger pony dildo will be able to satisfy – given to all those who request it at the end of their tour. This woman's simply breaking park benches by leaping into the air and slamming them with her brand new sneakers, embroidered with the Qanon Q taking the same arc as the Nike checkmark, saying *Just Q It* next to them in colors merging stars and stripes and pizza slices into demented, specialized art that squeaks across basketball quarts of people she calls *n****rs*. Then, a few feet down the path from her, there's a group of what are probably football players or jocks who are having total sex with a woman who's painted her body to look like lady liberty, with their cocks penetrating every single orifice of her. This, of course, is a piece of performance art sponsored by the campaign, because its demonstrating how justice is meant to serve every man who is white, rich, straight, and would be the type of guy to high five his bros next to him while fully desecrating a gift given to the country by other people, and having it called love by those who are marketing it. Such a performance is going to get each and every one of them a discount to future tours preserving and creating the history of the United States, and then the woman suddenly stands up and births a child whose umbilical cord curves into a massive Q and the child itself opens up its filthy, placenta juice saturated lungs and screams I WAS ALMOST AN ABORTION, I WAS ALMOST AN ABORTION! in an animal sound that makes the pony nearly die of fear. The men then proceed to all fight for ownership of the child before realizing it's a fusion of them all, so then they take the child and proclaim it to be THE HOTTEST INFO DROP OF 2021 and allow it to match the burning canopies in intensity with what it shouts next:

THE BOY AND THE HORSE AND THE OWL WERE SENT BY GOD. THEY KEEP POPPING UP IN SUCH AWESOME PLACES AND WITH THE BEST PEOPLE WE'VE GOT. IF SENATOR JIM BAETZ LIKES 'EM ENOUGH AND WOULD DEFEND THEM THE WAY HE DID IN FRONT OF THAT ALLIGATOR, THEN WE KNOW THEY'VE MET Q AND WE'RE JUST WAITING FOR THE PONY TO TURN ITSELF IN A COUPLE DIFFERENT DIRECTIONS

We fly away from the hellish insanity, up through the curling smoke, and head towards the tip of the Washington Monument. From there, we're able to see each stroke of the tourist's hammers from underneath us as they pound into what's left of the legendary erection. Then, as soon as we get up there, we're able to accelerate our way down to where the campaign's set up a stage and a podium and the people in the crowd are firing happy shots up into the air and making sure their boots stomp as hard as possible into the swampy ground, leaving holes where their heels have been. Senator Baetz steps up to the microphone and says to them, "Tourists, thank you for coming to help fix Washington DC!"

They all scream and cheer and clap their hands together, more shots being fired up into the sky with the previous ones landing as though shat out by fighter planes.

"Your benevolent destruction and spectacular use of household items to inflict massive property damage and bodily harm is something that makes our divine creator proud, and I as well."

YAAAAAAAAAAAAAAAYYYYY they all say, banging their hammers and tongs and fireworks and dildos and dynamite and pipe bombs and hash pipes and flag poles and baseball bats and pieces of metal, wooden, and brass fences together, including branches from the trees with burn marks all over them in an unholy percussion befitting a parade of death itself. On that topic, the Senator gestures for the Donger Pony. I bequeath it unto him while kneeling down as though he's knighting me, and the crowd starts chanting BLESS THE PONE, BLESS THE PONE as Senator Baetz holds the pony up so the crowd can hold theirs up as well. It's possible on his social media sites to use the donger pony as a reaction icon, so his supporters such as these are able to plan all they want about their auspicious visitations and share photos of the destruction captioned with MOST BEAUTIFUL PLACE ON EARTH!!! and other slogans so hilarious the pony can't believe the things he finds on all these people's Facebook pages. And here they are, holding little ponies of their own in their meth and ash and shit and vomit and cum and blood and dirt and holy-water covered hands, holding something they knew jack shit about before I put a bullet through a kid's brain and the Senator started speaking our name in situations just like these. And the man continues, booming into the microphone from his stupendous platform resistant to the flood of turbid, shit-filled water sloshing up from the reflecting pool, along with the bodies of the people trying to be ducks that the ducks have now started eating, "We need to aspire to take out liberal arguments, rhetorically speaking, as fast as the kid was able to teach that kid's brains a new way to say goodbye that day!"

"YAAAAAY!" They all chant, in their digitized baritones and altos, their keyboards clacking and their cheeks clapping. "WE LIKE TO SEE BLOOD AND LOVE TO PAY FOR IT!"

"And you know what?" He says, placing a hand on his chin. "I've been thinking about something I need to ask the swamp creatures here in D.C."

At this, the crowd starts making snarling and retching and vomiting and shitting and bursting, exploding sounds, their faces contorting as though warped by the very devil who first planted sin in the hearts of fallen men and lifted their faces up to be beautified by sculptures in rose filled gardens and cast across the very internet with the clouds in the burning sky taking the shape of his own smiling visage. These people are so bloodthirsty I witness what must be a 70 year old woman with a spiked collar around her neck and her baggy tits inside a bra that says BAETZ 2021 on either cup, with the campaign's teal threads hanging loose across her spotted, wrinkled shoulders, snap straight through her denchers and pierce her own gums while trying to gnaw on a bobblehead shaped like Baetz's democratic enemy while shaking her head back and forth like a dog that's got a steak in its wild, ripping jaws. Another man who is beating his head repeatedly into a shield with the Senator's face on it screams THE LIBERALS INVEST IN 5G, CHINA RUNS OUR UNIVERSITIES while his shitty tattoos ripple down his biceps and his jeans sag down his asscrack already glinting with glossy sweat underneath the purifying atmosphere. And then there's a kid dressed like that little shit who shot the protestors in the comments section saying I AM GOING TO BE A TOUR GUIDE FOR THE FLEX YOUR FIREARMS EXHIBITION WHERE WE GO AROUND RECYCLING LITTER AND INSPIRING SAFETY IN THE COMMUNITY WITH THE BULLET CACHES ON OUR CHESTS. I AM DOING THIS VOLUNTEER WORK FOR MY COLLEGE APPLICATION AND AM THE CAPTAIN OF MY HIGH SCHOOL'S RIFLE SQUAD. REPORTING FOR DUTY, SENATOR, IF I SEE ANY UNRULY PROTESTORS GOING TOWARDS A SHOPPING MALL I'LL LIGHT THEM UP AND GIVE MY

LIFE TO SAVE OUR TARGET!

"A mass shooting. In Target," I say to DJ. "Where did God go so wrong?"

"When he lied to us about free will," DJ Daddy says, left hand gripping right wrist in front of his own dick. "That's how we ended up with communism."

"THIS HORSE," The Senator says, calming down the ravenous crowd still delighting in the afterglow of violently dismembering a liberal user who left a feedback post and flossing their teeth with her bones. "Belongs to a person who I know *you* know is a tremendous American patriot."

They all cheer again, turned to happiness and with tears of joy in their eyes as fast as it took them to skin that poor woman alive and post responses about how she should've had an alligator who hadn't had such a history of being disciplined beforehand, he never would've found himself having to be a slave for corporate America if he'd made better choices in life. The instant switch from rage to adulation has THE WISE OWL almost ready to vomit a verse, but before he does so, I sneak behind the Senator and catch a glimpse of the crowd's warm wave of praise while nicking the vial of cocaine from the senator's trans-dimensional suit pocket. I tap a bit of it into my hand and allow the owl to bend over so I can forcefully palm feed it to his suctioning anus. In about three minutes, he's going to pop off in front of that mic in a way that will make every Speedy Dickhaul radio show fanboy want to start listening to people whose skin looks darker than the mayonnaise they bathe in every morning. The Senator's talking about me as someone to emulate, with one of the less bloodthirsty, smiling tourists wearing a shirt with a picture of Moe Wyden's potential tombstone on it with a snake engraved as the epitaph shouting her comment that if I were a few years older, she'd want to see me shoot her and this makes me force myself to send her a heart sign with my hands. I now feel as though the fact I'm wearing fake skin on this fucking internet rally tour through the valley of the DC damned is making me heavier with manufactured guilt (based on the emotional equations we studied to become one with these people) than the lizard people wearing skin and playing scrabble with the codewords to call off the nukes when they get tired of the "bat eating kung fluey c****s." That's something else she posted in this comment section, but of course, in the favor of free speech, the utter paradoxical destruction of Washington by foot tourism in the aftermath of sanity here allows her to say whatever the living fuck she wants so long as she keeps chucking coins, cash, and cryptocurrency straight into Senator Baetz's wide-ass bank account. I can feel the owl radiating heat next to me, nearly vibrating with his increased temperature, so I interrupt the rambling Senator himself in the center of his speech praising us as the best thing to bless this land since Jesus gave Egyptians guns to put the scalding owl up to the hot mic and to allow him to blast these inbred nerds into the next level of existence, seeing if he can be the sort of scribe appropriate to use his voice the same way Nero's bow scraped across that existence, helicopters blazing over us carrying banners saying WELCOME TO THE FRIENDLY SKIES! Surrounded by smiling faces until a tree branch ablaze catches the very silken corner and causes them to drop the banner into the stagnant pool of shit below, reflecting absolutely nothing.

FOURTEEN

After the shitshow at the 'Reflecting' Pool ended (there's no reflection here let's be serious), the Senator directed his armed tourists to the next, most important destination of their gun-bearing, sightseeing lives: The National Guinea Pig Convention is prepared to start in force at the historic and affordable Watergate Hotel, the place where Richard Nixon learned to hear through walls and a place that's gone full-scale Doorstore when it comes to selling merchandise. Senator Baetz's presence at the event as the keynote speaker, coupling with the domestic rodentia tragedy that just occurred at the airport terminal, gives the place a mix of momentary reverence yielding quickly to unadulterated, batshit insanity. Even DJ Daddy's appearance on those fated, lice-infested sandshores of New Smyrna doesn't even come close to the sort of shit they've got set up here, initiated by the doors being protected by three massive guinea pig furballs about the size of wrecking spheres flanking the door as the armed security. These titanic motherfuckers inside those terribly suffocating, burning suits of fur and glue and scarily sharp, sterling white chompers are carrying custom-made shotguns with pictures of guinea pigs open mouthed, razor sharp maws like the gunsmith's equivalent of warpaint. Their guns could blow a hole in an elephant so wide you could fly a drone through it, cleanly. And finally, the Senator approaches as the head of our pack, with DJ Daddy having bought a guinea pig at a corner shop that he's now carrying around in a case better meant for a dog than something with claws and teeth that can rip through plastic lattice fairly easily, DJ himself wearing a just-purchased shirt with a picture of the dead Guinea Pig on it, captioned with the words EXTINCT THOSE ALLIGATORS IN THE 2022 ELECTIONS with a picture of a target over the face of an alligator-donkey hybrid.

The Donger Pony sniffs the golden, gigantic guinea furby and clops its hooves on the power-washed sidewalk concrete. I agree with him: these people have sex in these things, with *gunplay* easily being one of our favorite examples of humans fetishizing their guns and bullets and their ammunition, especially when they need to aim and shoot and run in either direction according to their Boston Gospel. But here, I'm unsurprised to find a squad of fur-wearing cheerleaders, probably from a local high school and potentially check-keepers of people with signatures in our immediate vicinity, are waiting for us with pom poms that are meant to look like celery and with carrots held in-between their glossed, sticked lips making eyes at the Senator like he's the Owner of the Team and has just made an offer for instantaneous career advancement with the option for later expansion. As luck would have it, the Pony says, trying to keep its delighted, silent whinnies between THE UNHOLY TRINITY, one of the Pig Cheerleaders happens to be one of the women whom DJ Daddy has contacted at one point or another. He gives her a slight wave that DJ must mistake for general friendliness, and she smiles back up at him with a wink that would make any decent human being want to bolt from this Guinea Pig furball carpet leading through the Watergate's main doors faster than a ball-point pen across one of DJ Daddy's pages, the ones his woman berates him about before finding the thing closest to bleach that she can exhume up her nostrils until her brain stops pounding her for marrying a prostitute-fucking politician who can't even keep his boner down in the presence of a Senator and a squad of "prospects."

Thankfully, the cameras are focused on THE DAFT ONE plus Senator Baetz himself, who immediately relieves the pressure on DJ Daddy by shaking hands with a man dressed in a guinea pig mask, black priest robes, and fake toenails that are bouncing atop the concrete as though they were talons of a little guy scurrying his way towards his full freedom. The man whets his lips looking down at my 14 year old, blonde, blue-eyed host like he's about to make me smoke some incense and weigh me on some ballsy scales. Instead, though, he informs the Senator that the owner-guinea pig church service to commemorate the blessed opening of the event is about to commence in the big stage conference room they've set up here, so we're immediately ushered past people carrying cages of all shapes, colors, and sizes with fashionista rodents peeking out of every cage and crevice towards the place where we'll be able to pray with the man in the Guinea Pig mask as he preaches to us on stage. We're all encouraged to buy as many deep fried carrots as possible, which we'll stick an unholy amount of salt and ketchup and mustard and mayo on top of and suckle at the metallic nipples of the water bottles they've mounted to the walls, big Rubbermaid cylinders holding gallons upon gallons of tap water every human needs to drink like a guinea pig in order to both bond with the other participants at the conference, and, more importantly, personify their beloved animals the same as they're personifying them in their choices of dress. This, as Pastor Piggaso reminds us, his breath reeking of gin and a jawbreaker-sized wad of gum stuck to the left side of his mouth, is the most important thing: we must have man and beast and God united if we are to properly stop being guinea pigs of the federal government, meaning we need to advocate for each other the same way Christ has blessed not only Senator Baetz, but the entirety of the Republican party through the blessed, incalculable arithmetic of fate, fortune, money, country, and pride. The man says this under the dead, rubber eyes of the guinea pig mask on his face, a cocker spaniel colored plastic atrocity that looks like it, too, has witnessed death so many times it no longer stings. Thankfully, the person wearing it is ready to connect us all with god, so we're blessedly led to the best seats in the auditorium while the master of ceremonies, the honorable PIGGASO, stands beneath a $400,000 tapestry that's been custom made to have the same three guinea pigs from outside with their miniature automatics strapped to their backs cartoonishly, Alvin and the Chipmunksishly stand over the fucking donger pony, who itself has been transformed into more of a donger guinea as though some fucking unholy ritualistic photoshopping has been done to combine our symbols the same way we're now in spitting range for the Piggago pastor. Either way, there's a raucous wave of applause for him and us and the DAFT ONE, especially, with a couple whip-crack curses at DJ too in the form of people gut-shouting PUSSY and BITCH and COWARD (much to the chagrin or the LOL of the people seated around them) when his face pops up on one of the mega-screens they've got mounted next to the makesehift crosses they've hammered into the walls.

"Everyone," Pastor Piggaso says. "Please remove your Bibles from their seatbacks and your guns and firearms from their holsters."

"Amen," everyone says, getting their guns in one hand and ready to fire in agreement with whatever the pastor says.

"Are you prepared to bless this service's opening and the sanctity of this event, in the name of Jesus Christ the Lord your

GOD?"

"AMEN!" Everyone screams. A couple random gunshots go firing into the ceiling, which has been smartly bulletproofed by the same blankets they advise to be thrown over middle schoolers to protect them from AR bullets the same way their jackets cover rain. Then, the pastor places his plastic face super close to the mic, enough to cause a bit of feedback through the truck-sized speakers, and makes a noise I've never heard made by any other human outside of that cursed fucking chamber before, after, or since that moment.

He goes, E E E E E Y Y Y Y N Y N Y N N N N N Y N Y N Y N Y N H H H H H H. That's the closest I can get to it. It's as if a creaky door had feelings and was pumped in disapproval through the lungs of a rodent small enough to crawl up a grown man's colon in a classic single by Eminem, or something. He does this, and to the best of their ability through their COVID-vulnerable lungs, the maskless, white, Guinea Pig ear and claw and fur wearing fucks all repeat the noise back to him. EEEYYYYNYNYNYNYNYHYHHH!H!!!!!

The Pastor leans back into the mic and goes, "E E E E N E N Y N Y N N N Y Y Y H H H E E E N N N N N N Y Y Y Y Y H H H H!" Repeating it twice and with his own eyes bugging underneath the mask and behind his glasses to the point where its clear he didn't mistake the cocaine on the table for sugar when he snorted it, or whatever the fuck bathroom they locked themselves in to cook meth using the hot part of the coffee maker in the presidential suites. Either way, the crowd echoes it back to him with a bit more ferality, some people jumping up and down, others placing their hands directly in front of the seatback in front of them and scratching at the fabric, the rarest of them all placing their chompers, already fucked by chewing tobacco and chainsmoking cigs and whatever gets stuck inside the crackpipe, all over that fabric and trying to nibble at it like it's a piece of crimson celery. The priest is winding up at the podium like his lungs are the equivalent to a pitcher's arm before striking out the final batter in the bottom of the ninth, and I share a concerned glance with DJ as the woman next to him, herself not the lightest person to ever grace this sacred, sticky floor, has successfully chewed through the seat in front of her and is now making pleasurable noises of consumption alongside slurps and chomps. The PIGGASO raises his masked face towards the rafters already riddled with bullet holes and goes,

E E E E N N N N N E N E N Y N Y N N N Y Y Y H H H E E E N N N N N Y Y Y Y Y H H H H H!

This causes a mysterious phenomenon to entrap the theatre in a spiritual wave equivalent to soul reverberation: I believe the proper term in English for this is bloodlust. However, right as the call of the wild awakened in our experimentally-ready bodies, poked with vaccines and fed chemicals they wouldn't give to actual barn-raised hogs slopping in their mud and shit, the stage goes completely dark and the spotlights shut off, causing an angry reaction as though we've all just been denied collective orgasm. This causes a couple of muzzle flashes to erupt in the darkness in the direction of the stage, but thankfully anyone who died in this setting would be considered a martyr for the guinea pig cause, having been shot to death in religious exultation while resisting the control of the government through divine, limitless freedom.

However, before we can get swiss-cheesed by the people who have trained their rodents how to dance, the stage lights up again while little shadowed forms are making their way around to where the podium used to be. Father Piggasus is standing in the back, his robes discarded to reveal the fact he's actually grown fur on every part of his body except his crotch, which is covered by a GOGO BAETZ 2022 campaign thong. His legs have been shaven entirely bare to better match his toes, which have been banded together to be three big toes on each foot with impossibly sharp nails that might be able to cut a bullet in half mid-flight. Then, the guinea pigs underneath him begin dancing in the way they were meant to dance: dressed as cowboys and cowgirls and cows and cheerleaders and miniature football players and like Ronald Reagan and Dick Cheney and Donald Rumsfeld and Tricky Dick Nixon himself, these little guinea pigs align themselves to the rhythm of a fast paced, discotheque, godly-worship song that interspaces the EYYYYNNHNHNHNHH on repeat with things like IN GOD WE TRUST interpolating. It's at this near climax, wherein people begin fully climbing over their seats on all fours and leaving their own guinea pigs to chill inside their cages, that Senator Baetz taps me on my thin shirted shoulder and asks me if I'm ready to go for the bigtime. From above, large chunks of what look like carrots but are actually flavored chocolates with the campaign slogan NOBODY BEATS BAETZ in colorful text on them are now flowing down from the ceiling; it's amazing none of the bullets from the earlier celebration didn't pierce one of the special holders keeping them all up there. After quick consultation with the donger pony, and before the cheerleading gopher girls who are now on stage become the next to worship whatever Pastor Piggasus is packing underneath that aggressive expansion of his contribution to our campaign, I take the owl and make my way to the podium, ready to address this gnashing, gnawing crowd in their own language and with the ultimate goal of feeling what the Priest himself felt when they all echoed back in unison the words Senator Baetz told him to say in the spirit of God and guns and country: it makes you feel like you're flying like we were inside the tower, and it makes you feel like you can do it so long as you follow their affection the way a smoke line trails a tungsten shell.

FIFTEEN

Depending on who you ask – the Oversight Committee's Official Report both notwithstanding and nonexistent – versions of what happens next inside the conference center differ entirely. That's the strange thing about these creatures and their inability to remember: even when they do remember something, there's no way any of them could possibly agree anywhere near unanimously as to why it happened, how it happened, even when or if it happened. Therefore, rather than simply present THE DAFT ONE's version of events, I am going to describe it from my and THE DONGER PONY'S and THE WISE OWL'S best efforts in terms of our collective vantage point while acknowledging some things we'll never know. First: whether the Baetz 2022 campaign staff 'instigated' the 'incident' that occurred right after we took the podium in the middle of maelstrom. Second: how to properly clean guinea pig blood from priest robes without ruining the fabric. And third, most importantly: who in the ever-loving hell decided it would be a good idea to call the Watergate staff and have them enter Battle Mode to try and contain what would be termed a riot if any of these people were a Demonrat?

Let me be clear – their favorite phrase after vomiting some uncommunicative glop of thick, senseless English words – we did not intend to be whisked under the lights of incredibly hot superstardom in this political party through the orgy of pleasure, violence, and back-breaking absurdity. We didn't intend to engage with the primitive species of this planet only to have them exalt us to the highest levels of their social echelons solely by being young and white and blonde hair and blue eyed. If anything, the sheer absurdity of what occurred and what's happening now, what with the school board campaign and all, well, it makes THE WISE OWL confused in a way everything these people do has made him confused, and THE DONGER PONUS having his face plastered on every webpage and billboard, on TikTok and Instagram makes him afraid one of these people is going to snap him in half or do to him what those 'discourse lovers' did to him and with him and on him and around him. And that's just the point, isn't it: looking into the crowd of crouching, gnawing, dead-eyed faces, their gnashing and chewing and air-shitting amplified by the glaring heat from the spotlights above, we didn't feel like we were any sort of god or like we'd been chosen by the force that spun this little blue ball fast enough through the cosmos to inspire people to discover math. No, standing in that microphone static, with invisible cords attached to the throat and hips and right through those same eye sockets to coil around their feeble brains – humans have smaller brains than we do, it's been entirely scientifically confirmed – I felt as though I'd be just as 'happy,' if that's the word they'd use for this, to either make them dance in grand formations like a batch of hippos taught ballet as I would be feeding them straight into the protestors who have lined the sidewalks outside the Watergate and seeing which one of the inferior species gets to sit at the table for our Thanksgiving.

To make a long story short, we chose to mix the two.

Anyway, THE DAFT ONE digresses. Here's what the audio logs and camera footage and webcams from the desk show at the moment one of the rally-goers phoned in for backup:

DMDMDMDMDMDMDM

The man sitting in the back office at the Watergate Hotel – the one where they keep both the shrine to Tricky Dickery and the keys to open the hidden reservoirs underneath the foundation – is watching Tucker Carlson when his cellphone rings. He puts his chips down on the rickety table in front of him, flashing the two peace signs at the picture of Nixon (the same one tattooed on that walking corpse's back, THE WISE OWL reminds me) before picking up his pager and pressing his greasy, stubbled chin right into the receiver with an ear kept open and his eyes kept on the television's predictable, pedestrian interview with the mother of the kid we shot in the back of the head. Apparently, delving into a potential mass-shooter's internet history and watching this poor, greyed woman try and rationalize her son's death and our celebrity concurrently was just enough to numb his brain and glaze his eyes. This changes, however, when he hears who's on the other end of the phone, as well as what appears to be a mix deadlier than the emotions inside the dead kid's mom's brain, only sonic instead of emotional. Moans. A couple stray gunshots. Screaming like guinea pigs in the background while the echoes of angry biting and someone howling BAES FOR BAETZ, BAES FOR BAETZ over and over aren't what make him so concerned, enough to lean forward in his chair on his destroyed-by-40 kneecaps and grasp for the cross around his neck. No, at first he hears nothing out of the ordinary from the fellow Watergate employee who is cowering in the back row of the theatre watching the bacchanal: there was a sense of religious fervor so enrapturing a spotlight exploded, raining glass down upon the podium.

"Sounds like a typical revival to me," The Guard says.

Then, the terrified employee told him of the people fucking each other in their guinea pig costumes, unholy sounds emanating along with smells of shit and sweat and spit thrown into the collective conscious with about the same amount of empathy as toxic chemicals dumped in a river.

The Guard shrugs his shoulders, listening to the dead kid's mom talk about how she could have done better by her offspring in a way that didn't involve the "dammed internet."

"They've got all their forms signed," he says, glancing up at the Nixon stencil on the wall. "I've seen tons of Dicks at Watergate."

Then, the next thing is the thing that makes him sit up straight in his chair and knock his television dinner off his lap onto the floor, where the macaroni and cheese stains and stickies his shiny black hotel cop shoes: it's not the gasoline they poured over each other, it's not the one of them who amputated the engorged arm of a woman in her 50's and tried to cook it over a Black and Decker grill Piggaso gave them, it's not the homemade fireworks being tossed off the stage, it's not the GOD GIVEN GUNS chant we lead where men flexed their forearms until their little blue veins popped and the bullet-holes in the ceiling, properly proofed prior to this spectacle, are enough to have turned the entire canopy a darker shade of black in their rising, and its certainly not the fact the guinea pigs themselves have infiltrated their owner's mobile devices and are streaming the carnage to every social media site in a three-planet radius while we, at the microphone, simply watched them all unfurl with the eyes of DJ and DJ Daddy and the proud, sonless Senator behind us … no, shit got fucky when two of the Guinea Piggers, one of them an inflated blow up doll version of Honey Boo Boo's mom and the other a man who looks like he sells insurance during the week and gets his ass waxed on weekends, while in the throes of licking each other's belly buttons cleaner than high school whistles, decided it would be a great idea, in their passion, to knock over a sculpture unproperly moored to the floor. One second, it was a bust of a Grecian who invented a thing they all loved but whom none of them could name except the hotel owners; the next, it was in pieces on the carpet, sinking into the already soaked floors like a priceless artifact dripping into a sunless, sunken chasm where no light has ever shone.

This, in the words of the Guard, triggered the PROPERTY DEFENCE SQUAD to man their battle stations, knowing that they had the chance to make the ultimate sacrifice: to give their lives and to enter the Watergate equivalent of Sodom and Gomorra to protect the most American thing they ever could – the things they all leave behind in this twisted, godless planet. And, by the way they stormed into the auditorium, with their military-grade assault rifles and shouldered bazookas and GOP-colored lightsabers plus an actual fucking tank parked in the hallway (I thought the pony was talking until I noticed the ground shaking), they were ready to shishkabob those two disgusting lovers with a flick of a trigger faster than someone could sue them for property damage.

It's into the glassy eyes of that same guard, dressed in the captain's uniform of the PROPERTY DEFENCE SQUAD with matching medieval shield, the hotel's logo emblazoned across the steel like a family crest, with his concierge's vest shinier than a tunic in the rising sun, that I stare and witness the most passion I'd seen from any of these people, much more than when they themselves spoke about their fellow humans. All for the dusty, shattered shards now inhabiting at least three orifices between them of the people sitting right there on the floor.

Remember your training, the committee told me. All they really want is to be ordered.

DMDMDMDMDMDMDM

"Senator Baetz!" The Guard screams, in a tone trying to sound mighty but only sounding mighty far away from the zombie-like murmur of the trance-broken pig convention-goers now milling about like cows after their evening graze. "What in the name of telecoms is going on here?"

"Listen, gentlemen," Senator Baetz says, his palms stained with the blood of Christ, his penis only having halfway lost its hardness in the open mouth of his trousers, his fabulous hair tussled and slightly sticking together due to a substance that smells way better than its parts. "Everything's been paid for and I thought everyone was of age!"

"There's a first for everything," the Guard says, snapping his fingers at a home service employee wielding a blue and white battleaxe almost as tall as she is. "Karsonya, please secure the featured speaker."

"Woah, woah," Baetz says, trying to block her path down the mutilated center aisle. This causes the other guards to get testy and shoulder their weapons deadly enough to blow us all to fucking hell if we weren't already halfway there. "Okay, he isn't of age."

"That's not the problem, Senator," The Guard says, casting a wistful eye toward the fallen statue on the floor. "The problem is … you killed property."

The Senator freezes. We can see the tip of his ass hair protruding out the top of his khakis; he's solid as a glacier before the Industrial Revolution right now. "He's forgotten the golden rule," The Pony says, tapping on the glossy floor amidst the humming, crawling mass of flannel-vested guinea pigs crawling all over his form. "He's going to seem so callous, so removed!"

The white plastic cock horse is correct, of course: what kind of Senator worth his bath salt, from the great state of Florida, would care so little about the very thing by which his ownership proves his worth on the planet he inhabits?

"You mean the concierge with the battleaxe?" The Pony asks, nearly toppling a guinea pig dressed like Ted Nugent.

"Silly pony," I tell him, shaking my head, my eyes never leaving the Senator's scene. "Just because we're in a theatre doesn't mean its 1865."

THE WISE OWL's head spins a full rotation so fast he's punch drunk, which is good, because I would wish nothing more at the moment than to down an entire bottle of liquor for how they're lining around the fallen statue like the dust was left behind by its soul ascending through the punctured rafters. Even Piggaso, his robes returned to him, has found a cross from underneath one of the seats strewn with unholy grime to go and bless the statue, a whole $2000 investment that can never be returned to this earthly form. The only sounds that break the silence of the PDS holding each other's hands and weapons while murmuring in prayer are of the people who lost their limbs and who are currently in a drug-fueled daze, but just as the PDS squad are honoring their fallen soldier, we get our shit back in order, things falling from a boiling pitch back down to normal with the temperature of the room.

"Nice job, kid," DJ Daddy tells me, clapping me on the shoulder. "You did it better than we ever could."

We'll pay our respects to the fallen statue, surely, and hear stories about the great men and the great items that have been lost, knowing every toaster taken from Target in a riot deserves its own obituary. And then, as it seems to be the constant state of things in this insane country, we're interrupted by one of the door-sized Guinea Pig men with the huge-ass machine guns, who snuck his way past the tank in the hallway and who dropped three honorary dollar bills straight down on the small pile in front of the statue. He's got news for us from the Watergate frontier: the protestors have found the stream.

Confidently, I turn to DJ Daddy, stare into his mortal soul, and tell him, "Daddy ..." I pat DJ on his slumped back hard enough to make him stand straight. "It's time to open up the floodgates."

Yes, finally: after our internet exploring, our natural patriotism, it was finally time to redeem myself for the property destruction by owning the goddamn libs. And I get an entire team of guinea pigs to do it!

DMDMDMDMDMDMDM

"These people will wave flags for anything," Senator Baetz says, as we're slouched across the front of the tank parked in the foyer about to face the roaring, raging crowd outside the Watergate Complex doors. There's a line of security thicker than bullshit standing in front of the woke mob gathered right in front of the glass, clutching protest signs against Senator Baetz and the rest of the Guinea Pig Convention which has been sandwiched now in-between the demented church service (ft. absolute Hades unleashed on earth) and the intervention of the fucking property security forces, all running around like Lyle Acquittenhome himself and the fat SUV driven by his fatter, dumber mother across all lines of logic and directly into the doom-spiral in which the DAFT ONES find ourselves. The Owl is prepared to go down singing, since he's got his bulletproof vest custom fitted across his feathers and has been ready to whip up a storming lyric ever since he was positioned on the podium and parroting death sounds during the vicious, interrupted orgy.

The Pony, meanwhile, is receiving the maximum security possible: we've strapped three campaign-associated children directly across its front, ass, and flanks, and they've sworn oaths that their guinea pigs will be taken care of by their parents so long as their parents don't sell them to people like us for our diabolical, political uses. Ooops. Well, the pony's uses range from the perverse to the profane to the sacred, and we've got these kids ready to die in the service of protecting the physical body of a literal internet meme. Thankfully, each one of the kids is wearing one of the bulletproof, school mandated vests the kids have to wear after they've celebrated during gunplay at recess: if the kids go to the kinds of schools that DJ goes to, which are financed by the kinds of people depicted burning in effigy on numerous pieces of plastic and cardboard atop the writhing crowd, well, those kids start shooting airsoft and paintball guns at recess and play man-hunting games as their personal version of relaxation. To be an all-star in the militia games, which DJ says he's down to be after not pulling the trigger last time and getting verbally fucked about it by losers, that shit requires people are able to transfer their ability to hit a blatantly racist, fuckload of an opponent in a game like Counter-Strike into the actual version of the people who pull the triggers on pieces of metal. What a mindfuck, as they call it, when you think of what a bullet is: it's a piece of metal shaped like a chode that can crack a skull into a red and white Rorschach which sparkles brightest when mixed with the open water of a calm, crystal ocean before it fades to the bottom of everything. It's an object that can bequeath a future onto a young man who proves he could defend the very country from which they come and where they seem to want to stay despite the madness mere inches from our kneecaps. And the most hilarious portion of the entire thing is that, as he adjusts his tie and smooths his chin, his team having sprayed, brushed, and dried his hair, this man has absolutely no issue engaging with these people. We're going to just walk right the fuck out there and hear the Senator try to appease these howling, cursing, weeping, goons ready to be OWNED! in an internet video. We are frolicking amidst the grips of libtards, please pray the pony finds safe passage through the sheen of screams outside these opened doors …

And that's just it: Gaetz wasn't kidding. As THE WISE OWL says it best, he caught the rhythm of it all, and he knows exactly where to place the efforts made by Jim Baetz to straddle the line between the Guinea Pig cultists and the armed protesters outside, since there's something both fucking hilarious and tragic about the way he called for them to be quiet and had a dildo hit him right underneath his chin. It must've smacked right off his Adam's apple, which caused someone to leap into the crowd and for the melee outside the gates to probably look to someone like the Fall of Troy from up above before the security was able to get the protestor who chucked the cock at the Senator's throat the fuck out of the District, as he screamed towards the Senator, "YOUR HAIR MAKES YOU LOOK LIKE MORE OF A FAGGOT THAN ME, BITCH, AND I BOUGHT A BOOTLEG RUPAUL ORNAMENT!"

The Senator catches the insult with a wry smile as the crowd laughs at him with the ferocity of a horse trapped in the corner of a glue factory realizing what must be done to save its life. Then, he opens his palms and arms to them, and says, "Can't we all just come together for the guinea pigs?"

"You said vaccines cause autism and that retards shouldn't vote!"

"I did not claim those things," He says back calmly to whoever shouted that amidst the throng of Blacks and whites and browns and every color we've never seen in DJ's native habitat, at least not in the places where his family lives. "I said that vaccines are filled with demon semen and that the Democrats love jerking off to it!"

"HA HA AHA A HA HA HA HA," The line of mouthy, shitty, intellectually deficient fucks who were just defiling each other's corpses chuckles behind us like someone's fed them information about John Kennedy coming back to life and they're hearing everything they've known about the Zapruder film be confirmed. Then, right before our eyes, the faces behind us start warping, their fat and skin and multiplicity of chins being curved as though someone's melted them down into a tube and is squeezing them atop cinnamon buns. The broken jaw of one of the poor fuckers aligns itself again and then, exactly like everyone else's around him, elongates into a penis of its own with his chin as the tip and the double donger dicking down at an exactly 103 degree angle to make his entire face a Q. If you look through the lines of all of them, they've all warped so far in perfect alignment I can see all the way down the tank's barrel that's positioned right in the lobby, just waiting for the command to claim the tank commander got scared by the writhing mass of protestors and had to fire the primitive, yet highly effective ballistic straight into the crowd because he was scared for his family's safety; he's not a military man, after all, he's just one of the many Americans who have begun driving publicly available war machines (sold by John Deere and Chevrolet and Mitsubishi) that compete in the Militia Games section on racing. Perhaps that's what we can do: we can make DJ a Trojan Horse which right now, if adjusted to historical size, would rival the one that went straight through the gates of Troy, since the morphing of these people's faces and the contortions of their bodies down to strangely thin wisps that wave eerily in sync with one another happens in three seconds, as though pushed by the same malicious wind in their thoughts and forms and actions. How I wish that tank commander would pull the fucking trigger, the shit would fly right through their heads and blow us all to smithereens.

Instead, the Senator manages a smile at his constituents regardless of their facial shapes, hearing the Baetz Babes fulfill their namesake in earnest worse then DJ on a Tuesday evening. Proudly, one of them places an entire barrel of burning masks right next to the senator and allows the Senator to ask the crowd if they have any sacrifices they'd like to offer before the real intellectuals arrive. The sound carries through the rippling wind of the flags these protestors are flying, the ones he was talking shit about: they've got pictures of Moe Wyden on them with his face reanimated into a smile, sniffing the heads of children in a way that's meant to be the opposite of wanting to cook them in a pot instead of strap them to a pony. They've also managed to somehow encircle their own faces with mystic masks that say WE BELIEVE DALTON SHOULD LIVE and other magically whack things about DJ his dad and we. They've got pictures of burning towns and cities up there which were radiated by the sun, and they've even got pictures of the moon staring down at us with unholy disapproval at the travesty we're about to unleash before their eyes. There's a tension in the air that could electrocute an angel on its way back up to heaven at the moment, and wouldn't you know the moment everything snapped is when someone shouted at DJ "Kid's such a little bitch he wouldn't even protect his father!"

At this, DJ Daddy draws his own gun out of its holster on his side and stares down the mid-20s looking kid with the ferocity of Alexander Hamilton when he stood across from Burr and before that made so many white, liberal tears it could've rehydrated Moe Wyden's decaying, atrocious skin. We've barely had time to put our own masks over our faces, expanding it to a full face-coverer with its bull horns and scarlet mixed with white painting over a gray, wooden, circular base the color of an erupting storm cloud. Now, we're about to witness a father fight for the honor of his son against a man who's made a sign that says LEGALIZE METHAMPHETAMINES!!! with a cartoon picture of the senator smiling like Howdie Doodie dropped some x. However, before these two super patriots can turn each other into swiss cheese in the miraculously ordered destruction of this country's natural law solely to not have to measure each man's hard thing with the sort of shit they buy at Lowes, Senator Baetz reaches out an arm and stops DJ Daddy from going towards him.

"Now, now, Charles," The Senator says, having regained his own decorum over this situation. The army of Q-shaped monstrosities behind him are ready to make this afternoon feel like a sunny day in 1776, since these are the people who are protecting the people who spirit cook their own children. The Senator shakes off a couple shouted insults and continues, saying, "Sorry, I called you Charles, I meant Saul."

"My name is Paul!" DJ Daddy says, throwing his hands down at his sides like a desperate housewife finally snapping at her asshole of a husband.

"I thought it was Karl!"

"You already called me Carl!" DJ Daddy screams, the crowd laughing at us from both in front and behind, their circular faces making them appear like fucking human moons.

"I'm saying it with a K this time!" Senator Baetz yells back.

"WHAT THE FUCK DO YOU MEAN?" DJ Daddy screams, and its at this point that the same person who must've thrown the plastic dick throws a tape from the audience right at DJ Daddy's feet and says, "You raised a fucking pussy son and you're fucking women as young as him!"

There's a fucking brutal, crucial fight between the Q-heads and the protestors and the security who were woefully unprepared to face the creatures with just these fences. I don't even think the tank commander needs to invent the fear this time, because some of the legal bazookas that the protestors are carrying are now being aimed in its direction with their holders screaming for the motherfucker to let his go first so they can send it right back at him. Eventually, though, the tape bounces around until THE WISE OWL, acting on instinct and ready to scorch this twisted species back to when it still ate its own feces, grabs the tape in his mouth, flies high into the sky, and then finds himself in the crosshairs of the entire fucking crowd in front of us and the one behind. In our shared mind, we know this is the point we've trained for, the one where the vitriol is ready to explode in a bunch of twisted memes that would shatter DJ's life to fucking pieces. So now we have to try and be the fulcrum in this situation, and if we manage to reach out and take this trust that's right in front of us, we may be able to successfully engineer this planet and our presence on it to harvesting the cash crop that's legal in this capitol. First, though, the owl has issues with bullets to deal with, yet I have a feeling he's going godmode. Next to me, DJ is sweating so hard, and just to try and imitate one of these fucking empaths, I reach over and clap him on the shoulder three times. "It's okay man," I tell him. "Lord God Owl has fucking got this."

"I'm going to fucking win the militia games," DJ says, steel in his eyes like he's playing a high ranked match. "It's time to be a superstar."

"We're about to see a supernova," I tell him, THE WISE OWL ready for its time of unadulterated poneration, the dongality that powers the priceless cycle of absurdity known as this planet's fucking existence. "And you know the best part of it all?" I ask him

"What?" DJ answers, as the crowds still hold their weapons on our avian companion.

"I can't see it anymore."

"Can't see what?"

"The place where your world stops and where the internet begins."

If I could have a flag, here's what I would wave with it: a picture of THE DONGER PONGUS covered with 50 fucking stars, with its rounded hooves bearing the stripes of white and red like he's the demented steed of Target. He'd be standing right next to a picture of the planet earth, and next to it would be the moon that stares with endless, judging eyes, asking what the fuck he's seeing and exactly what the fuck he's looking for. And THE WISE OWL would be right on there too, much looking like the way he does right now, in a form befitting that of a bardic legend, Virgil's fuckboy rocket prophet who speaks only in rhymes and verses: glowing more golden than Ra itself, holding in both its talons and its mouth the chance to change the fucking universe.

SIXTEEN

THE WISE OWL:

Oh humans of red caps and billowing flags,
And people who love calling others fags,
Your quick lust for blood and gluttony of needs,
Stand only behind your insatiable greed!
And the insane amount of food on which you feed,
Comes second to the way you spread your own seeds!
Down cheeks, on chins, tops of mouths, sides of throats,
The same mechanism by which some males will fuck goats,
Turns out to be the pride on which the rest of you choke,
When you can't even repeat what the other hath spoke!

"Holy mother of baby Jesus CHRIST!" One of the Q-heads screams, wrapping his bone-white fingers around the three-inch-thick circular skinpiller next to the engorged dingdonger at the end of the Q. "That bird is SPEAKING to me!"

"Speaking words of wisdom, let it beeeeee," Sings Senator Baetz, with the liberal protesters just as shocked at the scorching, scalding bird as we are at the fact they can hear him. DJ and I share a glance, but before we can try to make any of it make sense, THE WISE OWL continues his diatribe over the enlightened, twisted crowd.

THE WISE OWL:

Our wisdom embraces our instant, earned fame,
When most all of you don't even know the boy's name!

You mock one for protecting Daddy elected man,
How you criticize our actions I'll never understand.
Would you trust your life in the hands of a stranger,
Who when they come 'round makes you feel as in danger?
Would you blame the Good Guys for holding the very gun
They used to counteract the actions of the unfortunate ones?
We find ourselves alive in the age of instant memery,
You've gotten yourselves totally blind to the scenery,
Climbing trees and fucking them as you burn the planet whole,
My, your own fucking species is out of control!
I don't want to hear it's the fault of the polar opposite,
So please, Q-man on the tank, please hop down off of it.
I can smell the holy scent of marijuana burning in the air,
And I want us all to have some so that we no longer care
However, we all know to smoke it is to inhale an unholy vegetable,
Which you can put on top of Big Macs at your McDicks of the Devil!

"The Owl's speaking the truth!" A person with a normal head shouts to the crowd. "My main man back in Baltimore's the Cannabis Manager at McDicks!"

"Really?" A woman whose head was an engorged, enraged, pulsing Q of thin skin and silvery veins is now slowly congealing again into the face of a woman who has nearly burnt her entire skin the color of a Florida orange itself. Imagine frying an orange and then squeezing it so hard the entire thing threatens to pop like a plump blood vessel. THE WISE OWL successfully deflates the curlycue Karen back down to rational lengths, and the bird continues alternately ripping them new assholes and saying everything's a blessing in his bars.

THE WISE OWL:

Now, to those who have charged a son who was protecting his
father,

For being frozen in his own place about to witness a slaughter,
I want to bring up a point to those who own their huge weapons,
Why do you keep them from their ammunition, why have them
   separate?

"He's right!" A man whose face now resembles more of a watermelon shot with a high-powered revolver at close range with specs of shrapnel as sesame seeds. "A friend of mine has an AR-15 in his three year old daughter's bedroom and keeps the belts of ammunition ready right next to he and his wife's sleeping heads. How is she going to lock, load, and hit the road when she's like driving in a car without headlights?"

As always, some people are just fucking albino monkeys better meant for erasure, these parts of this inferior, barbaric species. These limb-bald apes have the gall to insult those with the darker skin for being born with a certain amount of chemicals in it, while these fuckers whose largest organ successfully doesn't protect them from the sun cannot hold a candle, literally, to the realm of the Wide Eyed Moon. Although I can tell the attention of our Commander is upon us for breaking the rules and having the Owl get so shiningly pissed, I can only smile nervously and note the disgusting, freezing afterbirth of DJ grasping my hand when the Owl started mystically challenging the people making him want to go HAM in the Militia Games. The Owl, however, is now holding the tape in his mouth and is ready to almost bite it in half with his beak. This causes the formerly conversational adversaries to train their weapons on each other again, and with the tape gleaming from his smiling jowls, THE WISE OWL prepares a freestyle rap that transports time, space, and context into a dimension powered by the Internet, delivered across the world through a series of tubes at the speed of clicking something …

SEVENTEEN

THE WISE OWL:

Right there, at the intersection of history and the present,
I had an entire species on my shoulders, a Dream to represent:
How, in a land split along lines unerasable,
Could I make the Donger Pongus seem wholly interchangeable?
The cameras had shown up, ready for blood to be displayed
Across the tank, the Q's, the protestors, ready for the depraved
To crack open a beer, spark a cigar or a cig,
Light ones muttering under their breaths about the "barbaric
   n*g."
They'd grabbed the guy who tossed the tape, who wore a pallid
   mask
And as they tried to get his name and information, someone
   asked
Who exactly are you working for? Another asked, What's your
   game?
The bearded man shrugged his hoodie'd shoulders and said, "it's
   his fame!"
He said the tape shows DJ Daddy engaging in crass deeds,
Having exchanged money for sexual favors, his own walking
   seed
Gleaming red next to THE DAFT ONE on the other side of

the barricade,
It's amazing from such a stiff dick such a vibrant life could be
made!
Senator Baetz tries to bargain, lift his voice, steer the crowd,
But every time he speaks voices in the back shout:
Traitor! Dickhead! Cocksucker! – he's trying to BRIBE
All because this dirty white man from Florida lied
I heard his wife huffs bleach, the Anonymous man concurs
"If you think that tape is bad, just wait 'til you see hers!"
It was at this point that DJ Daddy, his knees set to buckling
Attempted to accept he'd been secretly recorded fucking:
"I have not been a perfect father, husband, or representative,
But sir, if you don't show that tape, I'll give you an incentive!"
"I don't want your money, and I don't want your help, neither;
You're an example of how to get places by being a bottom feeder!"
"Bottom feeder?" Senator Baetz raises his bushy eyes,
As though the evidence clenched in my beak can be easily denied.
"Sir, you're the one hiding behind that stupid mask,
And if you want to talk extra favors, all you need to do is ask!"
"I have a right to privacy," The man says, struggling in the grip
Of two burly, bullish security men with an abundance of clips
The kind that would rend the man's flesh worse than a traffic
stop
And we've only got a few minutes to tone this down before we
get the cops.
Just as THE DAFT ONE thought it, someone shouts, "Oh here
we go!"
The sound of a thousand sirens came shooting down the road!
Wheels scream across pavement, at three different pitches,
After their feral howling blues and reds, my ears need stitches!
The highest belongs to the cruisers with enough plated steel,

They're armor's harder than the skin of a man who cannot feel,
DJ Daddy might've seen his face reflected off the chrome,
The flashing reds and whites and blues of them bringing it home,
Here was his mayor smoking meth in the hotel moment,
And now, even on his suited knees, he couldn't now own it
For the second, tenor siren belongs to the hovercrafts
Who are painted Metro PD colors and leave clouds of floating
    black
Drifting up to the spotless sky like throwing ink into a fishbowl
They're like floating, metal elephants, and could vaporize whole
The entire city block directly around the complex,
Carrying weapons their budgets must've bought directly off the
    internet:
They've got ion cannons mounted right under their wings,
And enough queued explosives to make every DC thing
Look like American Chernobyl, their energy burning undersides
Staffed by testicle-shaped turrets with moustache cops inside!
And worst of all, the lowest noise cast a shadow like a cloud
    itself,
Making us think we'd suddenly gone to a new circle of hell:
The Police Mothership above turned out not to be a storm,
But its own low, echoing note reverberating like a war.
Washington, Lincoln, Jefferson and MLK
If they could see through stone eyes would remember today
As the time they saw the reason for Democratic election,
To give intergalactic weapons to those responsible for the
    protection
Of the citizenry in the shadow of the warship never built to lose
And that's when THE DAFT ONE said to DJ, "they've got fuck-
    ing NUKES!"
What he says is true, of course; our race has fully built the donger

horse

To withstand the weight of atoms breaking, but maybe not the divorce

Impending on DJ and his father's lives like the eclipsed, burning horizon

In the shock of the show of force, DJ asked, "Who's the one deciding?"

At the mention of a sacred word in this species scarred history,

From the mix of cops dressed like robot soldiers, a voice came from between

The Batmobile cruisers, the cop tanks, the black-white plated four doors,

Like another savior sent in white male skin to reunite the discord

Except this one emerged in a cloud of blue steam and the sound of asses

Braying in the eerie chill of the stunned, silent masses

Every camera makes a person age at the speed of viewing eyes,

So they roll out the azure carpet, and to nobody's surprise,

He emerges from the limousine like a toy from its store casing,

The words APPLAUSE flashing on the hovercrafts, embracing

The union of force and choice, and as the crowd starts to boo

Moe Wyden stands like a puppet on strings, and says, "I need to talk to you!"

He sounds like Microsoft SAM took a handful of ecstasy,

But before I molt from the star striking me, he's standing next to me!

He reaches up a hand with beeping circuits clearly wired

Through his skin, bones, veins, and muscles, the engineers tired

This is the third appearance he's made today, his oil needs changing,

And if he starts using the True Tears, his skin will need

re-arranging.

In his Presidential voice, through the rough exhaust, he pleads,

"Mister Bird, will you please leave these degenerates to me?"

The Q-heads have warped back into their lettered forms,

In a low voice, THE DAFT ONE says to DJ, "We've been warned."

I'm protected by PETA, here: if I were to be harmed by these guns,

PETA would show up with meat cleavers and guillotine everyone,

So as I've got the android executive reaching up an open palm,

I decide to take advantage of this unnatural, un-American calm.

"Gathered citizens of the planet where the water can be lit,

I implore you to look around and ask why we give two shits,

About the life of a married man who holds no true power in his life,

Do you really need to see him deep throat raw meat to sleep at night?"

"That's not a decent question," says the clearly undead president.

"If you show us all that video, you're setting a real bad precedent!"

"BALDERDASH!" A Q-head screams. "Children boiling in water

Is just practice for when we all get systematically slaughtered!"

For all their gear, gadgets, and war machines, those broken, violent dreams

All the cops with their Super Suits can do is point their guns and scream

For a sense of order to be imposed, a sense of respect for the law,

But the man smiling behind that icon's mask has no respect at all

For whether DJ Daddy, in his slumped, numb, defeated form

Becomes the most recent, lonely man to get famous thanks to porn-

*Momentarily, I consider allowing the tape into his wrinkled
    hand to fall*

*Yet through the unease rippling around us and those starting to
    call*

For the return of president Kennedy at the speed of flying metal,

*In a way, looking at the animated corpse, I think everything's
    eventual.*

*Thus, I send a prayer to the sky straight to the moon's watching,
    wide eyes,*

And swallow the tape whole solely to see if it will play inside!

*They all watch me do it with their lips, hands, and jaws hung
    open,*

*As though my cinematic mouth means some greater force has
    spoken,*

*Then's when I felt the ion cannons trained on me from straight
    above,*

And realized that no matter the amount of care or love,

There was something they needed to see now in my very stomach,

*Which is exactly when one of the Q-people, with a shotgun
    shuck, says*

"FUCK IT!" An eighteen year old armed with a rifle painted
in the blue, green, and white colors of his professional sports
team shouts, the Eagle decals glinting with malice on the side.
"TIME FOR SOME TAR AND FEATHERS!"

The resulting melee begins with one of the fisherpeople in
the crowd, one of the classical gatherings, managing to snag
THE WISE OWL with the sharp end of a fishing hook modeled after the shape of a Q, with the sharp part landing right
in the owl's breast with a shunk and the resulting pull being
worse than the man trying to detach his rod from a snarling

gator. THE WISE OWL engages DEFENSIVE MANEUVERS while the Watergate Defense Force, the local cops, the presidential escorts, the Q-people, and the protestors all engage in the classic American tradition of Civil Discourse, meaning they're clawing and biting and beating and slapping and spanking and shitting and cursing and clubbing and drubbing and owning and drowning and D E S T R O Y I N G each other worse than a pwnage compilation on the YouTube algorithm. Robot Moe Wyden immediately engaged the Anonymous video-owner in a Mixed Martial Arts dance straight atop the pavement, honoring the traditions of the American duel using his augmented joints over fully decayed tendons and muscles to crack the man's mask with a knee right into his temple like the smack of a palm atop a tombstone. The Owl, meanwhile, successfully pops a rocket out of its feathered asshole and drags the whale-sized fisherman, vest and all, directly up into the range of one of the gun turrets from a hovercraft, which plugs him full of lead while he's still in midair and causes his blood and guts and fat to go raining over the writhing, twisting, screaming crowd like confetti dropping on the new national champions. Donger Ponies painted red and white and blue, along with guinea pigs who have arrived as reinforcements against the tyrannical government in its terminal, traffic-blocking form, are being pushed along the top of the crowd as though they're plastic and furry floats, and we barely have time to grab DJ and his father before THE WISE OWL, having used his rocket powers too hastily, shits the tape directly out of his ass at Senator Baetz's face, who, himself engaged with a protestor telling him to MAKE CALHOUN DEAD AGAIN, ducks the flash drive, where it whistles through three curlycued heads and flies right down the barrel of the same Watergate Hotel tank, rips through the protected steel, and impales the tank driver who's had his hands hovering over the fire button ever since he saw the protestors were Black expecting deliverance to arrive through a human who was still alive instead of the half-lizard-half-robot chief executive executing his political enemies with a series of Bruce Lee kicks. In his inspired defense of American property value, and in his aggressive position, he left himself as vulnerable as a peacock spreading its colorful feathers in front of a starving, growling wolf who only sees meatsacks like him as iron deposits, so the irony of him getting his skull ran through by a wisdom-propelled reel is enough to make his own deadened corpse fall right against the armor's self-destruct button, causing a huge picture of Nixon resigning in front of that memetastic helicopter to display itself in ASCII text with the slogan, "LOOKS LIKE THIS DICK'S TURNED HIS LAST TRICK!" cheerily displayed next to a countdown timer.

5

4

(10)3

2

"What the fuck are we about to witness?" DJ asks me, or the void, or the crowd frozen mid-fight.

"PeOpLe." I say, as the world goes blank, and we fall back into the Internet, where every second's counted and millions of people have their eyes peeled, waiting for something just like this:

EIGHTEEN

MEATING MISS AMERICA!
(2021, Florida, Undisclosed Location)

DISCLAIMER: The following events depicted in this video were consensually undertaken following US Legal Code, State of Florida, 420.69 dated July 4th, 1969, as pursuant to all legal modifications, protections, and restrictions as outlined in the law. This tape was recorded for PRIVATE USE ONLY, and any dissemination, retransmission, or reportage of events detailed within shall be prosecuted to the furthest extent of applicable United States Law – and the Main Man involved is a UNITED STATES STATE REPRESENTATIVE, meaning the LAW will WORK for HIM!

The darkness fades. It's DJ's parents' bedroom, with a master bed in the center covered with saffron, velvet sheets that must've taken hours for his wife to iron, let alone un-stain. It looks like it smells like scented, exotic candles, one of which burns near the windowsill, lightly reflecting off the metal grates right behind the modern venetian blinds hiding the inside of the room from the quiet, suburban street. In the low lights, we get an opening shot of DJ Daddy, sitting at his computer, a Miami Dolphins Budweiser can barely drank and lukewarm sitting next to his keyboard. On his screen, there's a doomscroller's banquet on his

40 inch, lightly stained LCD monitor: pictures of Dalton's emo-scene hair splayed across CNN, MSNBC, Fox News; pictures of us, we have a cameo!, giving the poker-face to the camera as we're blasted across OANN and the other, smaller news stations; and then there's a picture of DJ himself, buried near the bottom, which DJ Daddy's glassy, bloodshot eyes roll right on past. Above his desk, which is spotlessly bleached, of course, there's a picture of the state of Florida, with the ripest, proudest, juiciest oranges you could ever imagine slipping between your puckered lips. An Eagle stands at attention with his feathers making deuces across his forehead in a peace-sign formation, with a rugged under-beak and a pal-mal pressed between his razor jowls. Behind them, there's the picture of the orange guy himself on a motorcycle, silhouetted like Jesus in church during sunset on Sunday. Over the picture of DJ Daddy looking dejectedly, exhaustedly past his flatscreen, up at the flag, completely ignoring the picture of his family framed next to his desk, audio which sounds like it was recorded by a farmer whispering his darkest secrets to his potatoes says, "America. 2021. You are witnessing what men have been reduced to in this darkness."

The doorbell rings. DJ Daddy stops moving his mouse. Then, he reaches over to the picture of his family and grasps it in his hands. He holds it in front of his eyes, close enough to where his suddenly heavier breathing can smog the glass, and then places his right hand over his heart. The camera levels directly with his eyes, his receding hairline DJ's in 20 years with the same flick and flow black bangs across his sweaty, scrunched forehead. And then the man, of course, lowers his eyes in prayer, thinking about his patron saint of virtues, Mitt Romney, as hard as humanly possible while he addresses the big man from his state-congressional cum den:

God, I ask that you forgive the trespasses of the young man who tried to shoot me, the same way you forgive my son for being too pussy to pull the trig. I thank you that he will have plenty of opportunities to shoot more guns in his lifetime, and I hope, with time, his new friend and his entourage of suggestive animals are able to move here and shoot guns, too. I pray that you bless my gun and all my ammunition, and bless your name again for the land I am about to conquer in the name of my family, my faith, and the great state of Florida.

With this, he gives a crisp salute to the webcam, his eyes looking as impassioned and emblazoned as DJ's after finally finding the right video after three hours, and proceeds to stand up, allowing the camera to capture his hard thing at its firmest, pulsing point beneath his leader-of-the-free-world-type suit pants, themselves still spotless thanks to his wife's best efforts. Then, as he unbuttons the top button on his Brooks Brothers white collared shirt, he picks up his phone, which connects to the home intercom, and he says, "Is this my little dove coming home to Daddy Eagle?"

"Why yes, it is," a voice, as sultry as it can be from the front porch, floats back up through the static. DJ Daddy raises his eyebrows at the camera and cracks a knowing smile, banging his erection on the bottom of his desk as he races to spin around and nearly collapsing to the floor. He'll claim he edited this shit out when he talks to us later, but watching him bent over, the camera capturing his perfectly middle-aged-man ass right in the center of the frame, you could swear he was worshipping the bedpost before he gets back up, opens the bedroom door, checks in the closet that we can't quite see, and then proceeds down the stairwell, the room waiting in the auburn glow of the big chandelier, plus that candle still flicking in the window casting those shadows around that corner of the room …

DMDMDMDMDMDMDMDM

The next thing we see, a woman's opening the bedroom door who is most certainly not DJ's mom, mostly because she's the spitting image of America: in the candlelight and the bargain chandelier over the bed, her blonde hair's a mix of burning gold and simple brown. Her eyes, which scan the room with familiar, calm sweeps of her shining Pacific irises, are rounded and sharp, their corners slight curves like moondrop contours. DJ Daddy takes her fur-necked coat, opens the closet, and presumably hangs it inside while we get fuller view of Ms. America getting near the camera. She finds the huge thing and winks at it, her tight, round breasts flexing underneath her one-cup-America one-cup-Florida flag bikini. Her waist could've been plucked from any Victoria's Secret advertisement, except – and this will be hotly debated after the tape's conclusion – her stomach looks natural. Well, as natural as it could be for the kind of woman leading the troupe of three other masked, cloaked, silent figures into the room of a politician dressed half like she's from Spring break and half like she's from DJ's high school with the red, white, orange, and blue skirt she's wearing. She kicks her Nikes into the wall, twirls her frills, and looks up at DJ Daddy, her nose piercing a studded glimmer and her thin, pink lips already red where she's bit them like one of those internet ghouls that dongered the pone.

"Hi, Daddy Congressman," she says in a voice sweeter than eggnog in front of the family fireplace. She swirls a crimson nail right over the same spot where DJ Daddy pledged allegiance, his full-staffed flag respecting the colors and their small, frozen peaks three inches from his chest. "I'm so glad you elected me to serve you tonight."

The masked figures, standing near the bed with their hands folded, are like the three wise men if they worked for Brazzers: one of them's wearing an Eagle head with rubber, dead eyes bulging worse than avian Grave's disease. He's only a few inches taller than Miss America, and he's holding one of those thuribles you see altar kids swing in Catholic church. The other one's only about as high as Miss America's bulging ass, one of those which will be ranked in the top 1.03% of all asses worldwide after blowing in the porn industry – the metrics for ass-measuring, according to this species, involve roundness and clapability and curves inspiring the immense perfection of their nature, and if there's anyone qualified to evaluate said artistry, it's the guy wearing the cop uniform with the mask of a guinea pig staring straight into the nylon skirt holding what looks like a huge, black box in his gloved hands. Finally, the guy closest to the camera holding what must be a meat cooler, the plastic kind you find at tailgates, he's got a Publix tote bag in one hand and the other resting on the cooler's handle, and when he drops his robe to the floor, he reveals that he's dressed the same way a caveman would be, except the paint and dirt and tattoos on his lanky, rail-thin body are more befitting of a rock artist than his mask, which is a perfect replica of Thomas Jefferson including with the wig powder trailing over his shoulders down the white ropes of dry, curly hair befitting his wig. The Eagle-man, still in his priest robes, strikes the thurible-bong covered by the candle's lavender and the omnipresent smells of under-counter cleaners we know to inhabit every carpet, wall, and orifice in that house. While saluting the midget in the cop uniform with the guinea pig mask, Ms. America and DJ Daddy each rip a cloud they could exhale into the New Smyrna sky and plant right up there with the rest of the

136

honest, cotton puffs.

It is at this point that the tall guy and the midget take their parcels over to right in front of the webcam, right next to the one filming the bed, and the midget takes something out of the Publix bag along with a huge, serrated knife. Upon DJ Daddy wrapping his hands directly around the tangerine, Miss America – in her star spangled high socks and dollar-sign stretchy, silver choker around her neck – gets down on both knees on the bed in front of DJ Daddy and stares back up at him with her tongue playfully lolling right out of her mouth.

DJ Daddy turns around and asks the guy in the priest robes and bald eagle mask, "Hath thou procured the necessary legal documents?"

The Eagle nods. He reaches inside the Doorstore fanny-pack across his waist, and, from beside the stash of incense, removes a papyrus looking scroll tied together with a Christmas bow on top of it. Facing the wide-angled camera, DJ Daddy reads like he's giving a high school commencement speech: HERE IT IS PROCLAIMED THAT THE BEAUTIFUL YOUNG WOMAN PRONE ON MY SATIN SHEETS TURNED 18 YEARS OLD AT EXACTLY 4:20PM THIS AFTERNOON!

Here, here! The masked men say in unison. Bubbly and vivacious, Miss America's girl next door upturned eyes flutter in front of the camera as a little laugh escapes her tongue. Later, of course, they'll learn she actually does live around three doors down, which helps when responding to ads for movies about necessary cultural exploration as supervised by an upstanding member of the state of Florida's legislature. The midget guinea pig cop tosses a baseball sized tangerine right into DJ Daddy's outstretched palms. He raises it towards the chandelier, nods his head towards the cross right between the windows on the opposite side of the bed, and then plows the knife straight through the center, bisecting it and sending droplets falling down right onto Ms. A's face, collarbone, and breasts. He turns the orange towards the close-up camera he's using on his phone, and then places two huge fingers right into the gushy center. Ms. A comes closer to him and sucks on his index and middle finger in a motion so hypnotic, it makes him forget momentarily about the smarting, ring indent visible on his clenched fists. The freethinking midget cop tosses him a full orange, and Ms. America lies straight on her back, her lower stomach's rippling black ink tattoo of bullets with butterfly wings flying towards a target painted like the moon and stars becoming partially obscured by her hems. DJ Daddy proceeds to take a shuddering breath, turn on his iPhone's camera light, and gingerly, yet sternly, explore a realm of fruit, physics, and physiology unendorseable by anyone except the United States Government …

DMDMDMDMDMDMDM

"Jesus Christ!" Senator Baetz screams, trying to hide his own erection underneath the table around which he, Marlene, and the rest of us are watching the tape play on his computer. DJ Daddy's been sitting in the corner staring at the bust of John Calhoun the entire time, his neck and chest redder than 3 days underneath the scorching New Smyrna sun. The FBI representative tasked with watching the entire thing, a white career dude in his mid-40s with a round, stubbled chin and haunted eyes, makes a gesture around his plump neck like he's wrapping a noose. For the first time since the video began, DJ Daddy says to us, "No."

We turn to look at him, his face bulging as if one huge sore. "First, the juicing."

DMDMDMDMDMDMDMDM

Following the wormhole exploration via tangerine, a blender whirls on the bedside table, having been procured from the strange box carried by the tall guy dressed like Slenderman in presidential drag. The masked men, and DJ Daddy himself, down to his Celtic cross around his neck and white t-shirt above his khakis and multicolored socks, all share a glass of juice from the three oranges which successfully completed their excursions; the one that didn't had been removed by DJ Daddy's tongue and teeth, to the point where the cool juice mixed with a bit of ice must feel nice against his chapped lips. In the center of the room, between the bed and the computer, a huge, tarped object stands ready for usage. Ms. America, meanwhile, keeps the same mechanical smile and falsely-whitened teeth, having gone to the bathroom once to delight in the diverse smell of bleaches prior to THE BIG MEATING, which pops across the screen in excited Word Art that should've gone extinct during either Bush administration. With a head-nodding consensus on both the flavoring of the juice and the patriotism around them, the eagle-priest nods to the guinea pig cop, who reaches down once again into the freezer and, bending his short hips and lifting like going for a personal record at the gym, hefts the plastic-wrapped ball of raw meat directly onto the carpet next to the bed.

"Wow, Mr. Congressman!" The woman says, as though she found some helium leftover next to the family shitter. "That sure is a lot of meat you have for me!"

"This is the land of plenty, dear BLEEEEEP," DJ Daddy says, eying the raw meat like a vulture at a twitching carcass. "We are supposed to share the abundance!"

"Oh, mister congressman," she says, running one of her

star-spangled nails straight across the DJ-maker standing at full attention. "I want you to give me the biggest stimulus in HISTORY!"

At this, the Eagle reaches into it's own pocket and rips out a wad of hundred dollar bills. As though casting bread sitting in a park, the birdman throws the crumpled dollars straight onto the bed as Ms. America licks her tongue right across the zippered khakis. In a sign of thanks to god and heaven, DJ Daddy stares at the ceiling under which he's slept with his wife a thousand times and says, with the extasy of a climber summitting, "MEN, FIRE UP THE FUCKING GRILL!"

With the whip of a curtain being pulled back so fast the rope burns through the tumblers up above the stage, Tall Tommy Jefferson pulls the tarp off the thing in the center of the floor and reveals it to be a grill so chrome it could be a shooting star if it were catapulted 'cross the Everglades. The three masked men, to the envy of DJ Daddy and Miss America watching from the bed, get around it with their own hard things at the ready, rubbing their crotches across the jangling dials and the propane tank and the smooth, grimeless racks, the midget cop wedging himself between the top of the metal cover and the stainless metal with the Eagle man almost lighting the torch while cawing before DJ Daddy, barely containing his own lust for the incredible "machines," gets the situation back under control. By the time he's back on the bed, Ms. America's already planted her bare, gaping ass directly towards the camera, and when DJ Daddy bends down to take a full whiff of the hot air drifting out of the tunnel, he turns a sad, side eye to the picture on his desk. This is the way he's been reminded of his wife's perfume. "Perfection," he says, his wifebeater already sweatstained and his flabby, dad arms twitching with excitement as he reaches into the bag of raw meat. "Miss, are you ready to PARTY LIKE ITS 1776?"

"Super-size me, daddy!" she says, turning around and bashfully batting her eyelashes while DJ Daddy initiates the meat insertion. The three accompanying men have all started square-dancing around the grill, stopping only to marvel at the amount of meat DJ Daddy manages to fit inside the series of tubes before him. Then, after taking it out, while the masked men are still singing "Party in the U.S.A." like an adult Disney channel if it were tone deaf, the men place the raw meat on a silver platter they must've gotten from the holiday set downstairs. They sprinkle it with a bit of orange juice and, having pushed the perfumes and polishers aside on the shared armoire, Tall Tommy Jefferson, who now straps a chef's apron directly across his midsection, inspects it to make sure that nothing else has defiled the sacred meat before molding it with his bare hands into the patties to toss on the stove. They repeat this process until there's enough meat cooking on the grill to feed the entire room, and that's when, using the handheld camera, DJ Daddy finally gets his perfectly average hard thing out of its sheath, except instead of it being fully bare and fully there, it's covered in a condom so thick you can't even see it past the eyes of John Wayne staring up at him with a cigarette hanging out his mouth.

"JOHN WAYNE," He pants, ready as though God himself is waiting at the end of the tunnel right in front of him. "We're going bareback today!"

"Yee Haw!," Miss America says, her makeup-laden face mixed with sweat, and that's when DJ Daddy reaches right across from her and grabs the tall, cinnamon scented candle sitting right in front of the barred windows. As he proceeds to drip the candle wax right on the small of the woman's back, he reaches down to her curled toes and takes the high socks off as fast as he can, the burgers already being consumed by the three men in the foreground who have all the picnic food they could possibly need on this blessed evening. Then, DJ Daddy wraps her high socks around his neck and tries, while as invested in her rear as John Wayne to the frontier, to hang himself from the chandelier while plowing the almost-raw meat into her with a force so strong cracks form in the plastered roof and threaten to slice them both to pale, jagged patties in a maelstrom of broken glass and live copper wires. Right as he's approaching nirvana in a way no man or woman or child in that room or watching has truly witnessed, the three disciples have their double-stacked, barbecue drenched, red white and blue seeded burgers at the ready, and as DJ Daddy pushes against the woman's ass so hard she's almost screaming while gripping the bedsheets in holy tightness, they gather around him, holding their plates in one palm, saluting with the other hands, and chanting, in unison, "TIME TO PLANT, TIME TO PLANT, TIME TO PLANT!" Through their rhythmic recitations, DJ Daddy bellows as though he's just been ran through with a bayonet, and through the smoke you see him get just an inch taller on the bed when the camera cuts to a simple burger resting between two buns on a paper plate with the colors of a picnic flannel, and someone's hand – DJ Daddy's by the look of the pinkness under the fingernails – squeezes a tube of pure mayo directly onto the meat before slapping the bun on top of it and whisking off to Magic Kingdom.

In the same text as the constitution, pure white over the patterned background, it says, "THANK YOU FOR WATCHING, GOD BLESS AMERICA, AND ALWAYS MAKE SURE TO COOK YOUR BURGERS ALL THE WAY!"

DMDMDMDMDMDMDM

142

Around an office table, Senator Baetz, Marlene, and DJ Daddy's poor press secretary allow the black screen in front of them to fill their silence.

There's a three second pause.

"I mean," Marlene says, raising her stenciled eyebrows at Senator Baetz with the look on her face like she's just walked in on their son. "Who hasn't, am I right?"

NINETEEN

The flight back to Florida aboard the S.S. Cuntfucker (the rechristened name of Senator Baetz's private plane following DJ Daddy's ascension to the most famous celebrity sex-taper in the history of recorded fucking aside from Kim Kardashian) is a combination of an American mile high party and a motherfucking depressing funeral atmosphere. DJ Daddy's either been aboard the in-flight bathroom with the light off just sitting on the toilet drunk as hell or moping in his own private corner like he himself's the inventor of the nuclear family bomb. Meanwhile, we're still getting the hero treatment for attempting to bridge the gap between the Q people and the protestors – all of whom were so shell-shocked by DJ Daddy's sextape being viewed they went the fuck home instead of burning down the Watergate or shooting each other in self-defense – and now Senator Baetz wants to help me become the candidate for schoolboard. Now that I've become as much of a part of DJ's community, I suppose I don't even need to be enrolled in his school to be a representative apostle of Robert's Rules of Order. But apparently the amount of bleach ordered off Amazon and sent directly to their million-dollar family house is fucking hilarious, and the scary part for DJ's Dad is that Charlene hasn't called him a single fucking time since the story broke. He tried to call her three times from the office before Senator Baetz himself ripped the phone away from him and told him not to tank his personal life and also his career in the same double-fucked reaction. Donger Pony replica sales are completely exploding, too, and since we didn't have to go through TSA to use this plane, the pony's sitting on a satin cushion as though a sultan of scrotum thrusting, as evidenced by the memes they've made of DJ Daddy using the donger pony to fuck the girl next door while his underage son watches the same type of shit that turns him on using his internet. However, instead of completely banning the prickly plastic poner sculpture from the place, Dickson County High School is starting a petition to adopt the holy thing as it's official mascot. The supporters for Senator Baetz, who has publicly distanced himself from the tape but who said he doesn't envy DJ Daddy's positions, is now sitting across the table from us with his head cocked out the window to his left, watching as each of the fluffy, passing clouds remind him of phallic shapes and simpler days.

"You know," he says, the flight attendants dressed in scanty bikinis with the campaign's colors on them worse than the dumb owls on Hooters waitresses. "I can't help but say I empathize with the man." There's a snow globe the size of an industrial fishbowl mounted to a series of strobe lights in the corner, like some sort of Christmas decoration if the colors were white snow and red, male blood. Instead of snow, however, the cocaine gets dispensed from the snowglobe and replaced by more, funneled in by an imaginary source like the porn parodies that are already popping up in the minds of lord knows how many studios. A congressman fucking a barely legal neighbor's daughter. Oh, and that woman has decided to drop out of high school and accept one of the multi-million dollar offers from the same places who made the names for the others who were really rich and copulated on a video camera. She described DJ Daddy's dick as "basically like a needle in a rabbithole" and said that she was surprised his wife actually agreed to have her tunnels wrecked for this flagrant ass-hole. However, other people have reacted to DJ Daddy by saying that they, as well, have moments behind the doors they don't want to share, but that there have been plenty of men who've cheated on their wives and at least not killed their paramours by turning their Oldsmobiles into submarines. This is one of the justifications Senator Calhoun, who himself has three children with a woman he met at his teenage church who called him the Mozart of the debate team, gave as he had leaned over and stroked DJ Daddy's hand in consolation: he probably wouldn't have to pay for an abortion, and if he did, there's a stupendous amount of people who would pay for a literal fetus from a politician, if you knew how to get it out of the morgue or the trash can depending on the United State.

"Or maybe from a Kohl's," The Donger Pony suggested, rubbing his rounded hooves smoothly through the dangling threads of his special pillow. Now, here we are drinking alcohol and riding in the lap of luxury as though we'd been redirected like funds to the Massachusetts Institute of Technology. This plane is probably worth a staggering, exponential function of one of his intern's salaries, but since people like Senator Baetz are able to be tuned into the mustard-gas arithmetic of imaginary capital and how it goes boom and bust and bongripped based on the feelings of a bunch of dicks, we'll only be able to calculate his lack of generosity when we overhaul the curriculum at the school like we've been planning to. Now we're returning our focus to the school board, our clout successfully collected from the Senator's adventures – THE DAFT ONE's rising like a peak on the Dow Jones, DJ Daddy's going sideways and generally increasing in investors, and DJ's still stuck as being the kid who couldn't fire a good gun to protect his own father.

Successful in our goals, the oversight committee is delighted to see how our research develops, now that the man sitting across from us has ordered three cocktails due to the fact we are flying higher than the law, my good friends. We clink our glasses, the Senator turning his bushy eyebrows to the in-flight bathroom and asking one of the stripper assistants straight out of the 1970's to please knock on the door and make sure the man hasn't committed seppuku by shoving toilet paper up his ass until he shits backwards. We toast our glasses, take a good drink while eye-fucking each other in the proper manner of these degenerate, hierarchical apes, and then the Senator shares one of the best pieces of wisdom uttered in the history of cosplaying American political founding daddies.

"The only way my wife can turn me on anymore is if she tries to hang me from a sycamore!" The Senator says, causing the owl to roll his eyes so hard he pulls a muscle alongside each of them.

I make a concerned face at DJ, who has been reticent as hell the whole way back while googling emancipation laws.

"But Senator," I ask Baetz, daftly. "You're not Black!"

He takes a sip of his boulevardier and then raises it at DJ and I, the ice cubes clinking together. "Not because I'm Black, dear boy – because of states' rights!"

It's at this point DJ Daddy emerges from the bathroom with his pants stained by some unidentifiable substance that we're hoping is water but know isn't by the odor lingering in the air. If anything, those poor pants are the same ones that were the star in the feature presentation of this man's whole inner life, so he should be feeling like a million dollars for making anyone unable to look at a stainless steel grin again with any kind of sincerity. Instead, he comes on over to the four seater, motions for a cocktail of his own, to go along with the three empty glasses remaining atop the table, and I imagine whatever emotions are making him break out in red right now around his neck are actually just scrapes from the socks on the chandelier.

"So," Senator Baetz asks the table, tapping his own glass as the stewardess sets down one for DJ Daddy and another fruit bowl of cocaine in front of Baetz's cufflinked wrists. "How about them Florida Gators? Did you hear I'm getting sued by Abby's family?"

DMDMDMDMDMDMDM

By the time the limousine pulls up in front of DJ's family home, the fire company was already there and had managed to contain Charlene in something resembling a bear trap right around her ankle. She'd set the bedroom on fire and burned the utter shit out of their wedding pictures, throwing Clorox across the entirety of the basement and the first and second floors, including on DJ Daddy's prized collection of pornographic magazines, and she'd dyed her hair the same shade of blonde we saw on the woman now known as Hannah Baetzman professionally. Similarly, Charlene has decided to not only strap the divorce papers to their original wedding vows they'd preserved in the closet, but she's also going to go into politics herself using the same last name while she still can. She told this to the officers dressed in guinea pig COVID masks from the new church that's starting up the street, a faction of Guinea Piggers radically inspired by our own orchestration of events the same as it was when we planted those words into Dalton's dumb brain. I suppose, had they let her lunge towards the shell-shocked DJ Daddy with his bags in his hands and his eyes off the ground, she would've probably used the blender in her hand to grind his balls into paste and make him anally inhale them, but instead, there was simply just a really sad moment where DJ looked on at his mother and father and the Uber driver recording video of the whole thing behind us, and seemed to slouch a little bit under his preppy sweater despite swearing to us he was about to become a Platty in reality.

"Guess I'm a child of a broken home, then," DJ said, the fumigation teams on the Hazmat squad beginning to enter through the front door and unbleach the house.

"Don't worry, my friend," I say, clapping him on the shoulder trying not to seem mechanical. "You have to split to be an ´atoms family´ nowadays!"

PART III: FORCE MEJORA (OR HOW TO BEND THE LAW)

TWENTY

This woman who dresses like she's just got done helping Mussolini is about to try to get us to invest in Bisects Leather; she's the kind of woman who would fuck Marilyn Manson consensually. Those stilettos could kill a man in at least six different ways, and those are just from the holes that are already there. But instead of trying to have sex with the assistant principal, who himself is trying to fuck at least a third of the students in the tenth grade, she's here with her black and blue and white and red striped American flag pin on her leather Stasi-chique blazer about to teach us History class after DJ and I blazed a joint bigger than her speared stilettos right beforehand. The pony is so high other people can almost hear his footsteps across these sticky, bullshit tiles.

"WHOEVER DREW THESE SWASTIKAS INTO THE BRUTALLY CHIPPED DESK ON WHICH IM PONING IS WISHING THEY GET BONED BY THIS FRANCO-PHONE-A-FRIEND," the pony rattles, causing the obscenely bored teenager right behind me to think maybe the town greenery's been laced with crop duster. Instead, they start doodling dongers in their notebook; we've also seen them all over the bathroom walls and spraycanned into the bricks next to the shooting range and the practice combat arena. If there were a surface at the end of the world as the last monument to humanity's creation and destruction, they'll paint a fucking cock on it, as evidenced by the fact DJ is trying to hide the fact the thoughts in his head right now are imitating his father. And that's just because Ms. Herr is fully one of those equally responsible for adolescent dreams and fantasies and nightmares, depending on which color of American flag you pray to and which ones blow you away; this one combines the love for cops with the love of country, and I love the fact she's got a guinea pig bobblehead on her desk branded in the school's new style, too. Her face looks like it might've been stung on both cheeks by some really large bees, and her mouth looks like a horse so much I think the donger pony noiselessly neighed at her. She's sorta like Sarah Palin but in a tanner Tina Fey sorta way, I suppose, and the thing about her is that I can imagine her screamingly insane eyes flaring brighter than the flashing muzzle of her assault rifle, themed to look like a musket but with the power to kill everyone in class about ten times over. I would never expect a student to challenge her to any type of duel, not with the way she's talking about what happened when the Libtards started the war on Christmas.

"They've wanted to crucify Santa since I was a girl!" Ms. Herr says, laying an elbow on the podium and batting her thick eyelids. She reminds me of a blow up doll that doesn't believe in taxes, which is ironic considering the fact we're learning about how Real Americans started getting attacked in this class under the new curriculum. Apparently, there was a time they persecuted the sweet, innocent Ryle Littenhouse after he heroically defended his local Publix from a horde of homeless people with an AK-47 he bought off the internet. Amazingly, the protesters were found to be equally guilty of emotionally intimidating him, so their families had to pay damages for false prosecution. Meanwhile, after becoming a senatorial intern, right, there was actually a Christmas shoot done with him posing with some of the people who supported his defense campaign at last year's CPAC, and if we don't identify how history happens, Ms. Herr says, they're going to kill three birds with one stone and throw you into the dark waters of how Christianity is so persecuted in this country. "Cancel culture runs deep when you look underneath it: they're fine with slavery when it's about fucking elves!"

Thankfully, this prestigious secondary institution – to which THE WISE OWL is wearing a gorgeous, feather-tight tuxedo and the Donger Pone is fully charged back to proper angles and areas after our trip to D.C. – models itself after the enlightened philosophy of the classic American universities, and we're allowed to disagree with each other in here so vehemently due to our parents' advanced pocketbooks and our own legalities, so one of the endangered liberal kids puts up her hand and asks, "Teacher, did you ever consider evolution to be a communist theory?"

"Of course it is!" The teacher says, the question triggering three rapid blinks and turning on the crazy in her eyes. The Owl flaps his wings nervously, cranes his neck, and wrinkles his birdly nostrils in my direction at the smell of human ovulation. He whispers in my ear, his little voice terrified:

THE WISE OWL:
Daft One, I'm afraid we've entered a warp,
Where this woman's some kind of natural force,
I think she's about to kill us inside of this course,
And she'll feed us to history with no remorse!

She manages to get back to the point of the lesson after the rather liberal aside, in which she explains the connection between natural selection needing to be prioritized through individuality, saying survival of the fittest has been co-opted by the communists who want to control every aspect of American lives by claiming there's only one true way to do things. "Basically, the liberals want you to believe that America is a bunch of racist, sexist, homophobic, transphobic, agoraphobic, xenophobic, blah blah blah words when the only real people who hate other people just for being other people are the ones who are like the congressional towel-head parade who frighten every cop in a five mile radius!"

"This woman needs drugs," I whisper to DJ. She's showing us a slide with pictures from the textbook talking about the aggression of the north leading to the civil war, saying the civil war generals had been destroyed and that the loss of their statues shows how much people want to forget the true story of the schism. Thankfully, we saw the ad for Monument Memorial Services, and the Watergate isn't pressing charges or seeking damages for the statue we completely destroyed in the melee. This woman is wearing the guinea pig pin too, and thankfully has followed the school's policy that we cannot be vaccinated nor masked nor too far apart from one another, or else we'll lose our sense of community that had been stripped from us by the Democrats. We were introduced to these protocols upon our entry into the school and our ability to demonstrate outstanding intelligence on all their silly aptitude tests. Just wait until we plug into the school server behind us and navigate to the center of this woman's private drive.

Meanwhile, we're being told about a project wherein we need to make a presentation featuring one of the worst persecutions in American history, those false, Salem-inspired political gold-star-giving things like asking people to vaccinate in a place where the needles run free and rampant and the fucking guns gallop through crisscrossing hands worse than death's white horse through this whole countryside. There's so many to choose from when it comes to the unreal way in which these people hound each other, and I think the one that DJ and I are going to have to choose to do by obligation is a report on the legal trial for Senator Baetz, since we can take them from current times. Ms. Herr's got a banner across the top of the chalkboard that says, in the same letters that are supposed to be there for the calendar, HISTORY IS HAPPENING EVEN AS WE MAKE IT with a picture of a man who looks suspiciously like a cross between the orange man and Ronald Reagan next to a full-sized Governor Mercantis poster. Everyone's allowed to be political at schools like these - come on, when you've got constituents who are kids of politicians ranked in popularity the exact same way as DJ is on CS:GO? Our collective heads are buzzing with ideas about how to translate this absurdity to a form understandable by these kids, but according to DJ, the next class – English class, with the woman who howls like a velociraptor but with a hugely different predisposition nowadays – is going to be even worse, especially since we're due to see a teacher shooting drill this class.

TWENTY-ONE

Mrs. Becker's English class has changed a bit since last Friday: the Barnes and Noble posters have been crossed out in huge x's, with fire added behind them and an official firepit in the corner of the room next to the three filing cabinets that's used for destroying "intellectual paraphernalia." Yes. This is what the people who find heroin needles and crack bowls scattered in the bathroom stalls like candy in a plastic jack O' Lantern like to do; we received an email with the school board's justification for every book removed from the curriculum in concurrence with the new Truly Constitutional Curriculum (TCC) they've installed, the same guiding document and canon law guiding Ms. Herr's promotion to not-so Gestapo as witnessed last period, except the kids aren't allowed to wear Nazi memorabilia, they're only allowed to burn books. There is a document that outlines the differences on these, but thankfully, nobody's read it. Instead, every single kid of the thirty sitting in this class (except for DJ, whose mailbox was destroyed by the end of the chemical romance back at home) got a letter written by Principal Dale McDonahough, who looks like he'd play the mid-30s balding cuckold if he weren't already fulfilling every Free Thinker's dream with what he's turned this private, 'prestitigious' school into now that the school board is the most powerful political force from here to the fuckin' panhandle, friend. And this letter the man sent, copies of which we had to pose with in three different ways to make our celestial Supervisors think it was real and not just us trolling them through the photosphere, outlines INTELLECTUAL PARAPHANALIA as different books for specific reasons. Here's just a short sampling of the books Mrs. Becker had abandoned like a believer turning away from her withered, aging gods:

How to Be an Anti-Racist by Dr. Ibrim X. Kendee – The most racist book ever written in history. Why can't we just have kids all be kids instead of being defined by their race, especially in a place like a school where everyone has always been welcome? The parents who love this are the same parents who want to ban the pledge of allegiance in class, but while we still can't put God back in the classroom where he belongs, we can absolutely keep this demonic trash outside!

Harry Potter Series – encourages ideas of witchcraft.

"Yes," The Pony says, wearing his DCSD cheerleader outfit and clacking against the tiles while Mrs. Becker drones on and on about Senator Baetz's new book, How to Survive as a Real American Man, which we've been assigned to read following the new Proper Education Ordinances of Pensacola County. "The people who run their world based on invisible money are accusing these kids of witchcraft!"

The Haindsmaid's Tale – atrocious example of a fictional society that has been co-opted by the left's political assassins to destroy the character of the country where women are the freest they've been in human history.

Watching Ms. Becker, who is dressed in a t-shirt with a picture of Bill Shakespeare painted into the fabric, with her school-colored, red and white and blue and black, echoing the colors of Ms. Herr's Near American flag, sorry, it's taking me a second to comprehend they have school-themed glocks here, but watching her slightly rotate her gratuitous, jean-covered hips while talking about the power of Othello's cock with a strange lust in her eyes and tone in her voice is making me think I should highlight the school's production of The Passion of the Christ that they're doing for theatre this quarter by killing myself in front of everyone. This way, I'll fulfill the strange suicidality these people seem to possess, and I can see why DJ has it as he prepared his presentation for the National Rifle Association. He's got some freshly smelted, high velocity ammunition for everyone in class (since you have to bring enough for everyone!) and is basically reacting like a kid who just got into football and is buying every bobblehead and NFT card modeled after his favorite players from the new team. Word around the school's spread that he's trying out for the militia games, and researching the bravery of those who founded the NRA shooting elephants in African jungles lit a special kind of fire inside young DJ's dick, a particular burning sensation that probably matches the aftermath of bleach. His mother's completely supporting him in the matter, even buying him the hand-cannon that's resting across his right breast, with a bullet big enough to punch a hole through a saferoom door at half the distance of this classroom. However, before DJ can serenade us with the special demonstration of the gun's powers he's arranged as part of his musical act, one of his classmates, who survives on a combination of cigarettes and Red Bull and parental anxiety, offers to energize the class first.

Since Mrs. Becker is grading us based on enthusiasm, empathy, and entrepreneurial spirit when showcasing our love songs for corporations, appealing to the humanity inside of them and their kindness and generosity and ingenuity and opportunity, well, we decided that today's the perfect day to make our plastic horse cocks do tricks. First, though, we get this woman, who is the daughter of a professor and a high-ranking, internet celebrity plastic surgeon who teaches people the amount of money they have translates to health points in the real world. She's the kind who makes DJ roll his eyes and repeat a phrase deemed unto him back when his father was still a low-profile, sorta-wise man instead of the laughingstock of the known world: don't stick your cock in crazy. There's a belief among the straight males of this species that when one of the women, be them young or older or old-maided, as in feudal times, is crazy to the point of allowing her own father to inject her barely-maturing body with his miraculous gel, the same one lining the ribcages and front teeth and scarring the underarms of so many of these fellow students mothers, sisters, aunts, cousins, these fellow children of god. Instead, this woman could be the brunette cross between Courtney Stodden and Joan Rivers with the waistline of someone who may have breakdowns over answering a question wrong on a quiz and failing to live up to their full potential. And she's brought in a motherfucking subwoofer with a backing track that sounds like someone ripped the vocals off of "Like a Virgin" and fed them to this star student, who is smiling from ear to ear with the unnatural straightness that most of this sunburnt society sees as true beauty, according both to the paystub and the command she's got from in front of that dusty chalkboard. Three seconds of speaker-buzzing anticipation, then the music starts thumping, and she starts to bob her Botox breasts and pump a fist in the air like she's raising her microphone towards the ceiling at the Grammy's:

I was beautiful the day I was born,
But my father said there was something more
He could give me to make me a success,
More than a bunch of money and a blue dress.

He told me, if I want to be an actress,
Everything operates on a different axis:
One where my cheeks don't move when smiling,
And my brand new breasts have these bitches crying:
The beat climbs, and she gets ready to slam that invisible micro-
phone right down on top of us.
God bless the excess that we all need:
Hot breasts, round hips and bleached teeth.
If there's one place you want to learn the truth:
The Friendly Needles are the fountain of youth!

She goes on for two more minutes of the 3:05-style banger by serenading the women who have bravely undertaken investing in their images until the end of time, the ones who smile the same and who make THE DONGER PONE afraid for its life when smelling through those surgical bags. There was a 14 year old with implants who almost made the pony go DEFENSE MODE in the airport when she went through the metal detector and made them perform an integrity check to make sure she wasn't storing anything bad bad in there. Anyway, the class claps; Mrs. Becker's delighted because it's clear the woman's got a bright, brick-hard future in front of her.

"What an amazing story of a father's love!" Mrs. Becker says to the dying applause, even from those who think the first girl's a grade-obsessed bitch. "He gave you such gorgeous features, and you gave him an amazing song!"

"I'm still his little girl," The young woman says, sitting down back at her seat, something unidentifiable squeaking when she does so. I believe this student's father looks at her the same way the orange man they all love so much in the orange state looked at his contestants at that really young show for beauty queens. Not the ones they plastered across the home screens of every computer and tablet and man taking a shit while jerking off to something while shitting to make himself feel alive again, but the one where he was doing integrity checks and supervising things with women some one sixth of his age.

Peculiarly, it seems like everyone throughout this species' history, especially the white males with money, have a pension for incestuous behavior. I'm not sure if such a combination is what produced some of the people in this room, as has been propagated by every stereotypical depiction of the people who line the shores of New Smyrna beach and who plant their confederate bikini and hat and truck-decal'd asses in these plastic seats, but by the way DJ's dressed today you'd think he was running for a full seat on the school board, not us! He's got his trucker hat with its embroidered plastic crows, a guitar that has Moby Leith, the famous All-American star who wrote "Kick 'Em Up the Cunt" about the pussy, coward sand (you know the word) terrorists whose outlines grace the targets of the shooting ranges down here, in these roads with stop signs riddled with bullet holes and the lingering scent of gunpowder mixing with the wet heat, heavy in the lungs, whether greeting a friend or killing an enemy for stepping on one's hydrangeas in the front yard garden. Especially if they're darker skinned. This is a golden rule that DJ's told me, as he was gun-shopping at Publix: here, kids like us are encouraged to carry as many guns as we can. Shooting down at the range is the peewee football version of the militia games, and right now, with the maroon and cream stitched trucker's cap with the clay-light brim, the beard he's managed to grow, the dirt underneath the same short nails now about to slide up and down the neck of that guitar, he looks like the kind of dude who would kick the ass of the nerd who serenaded Gaben just the other afternoon. Now, he's successfully shown his fellow people that he's learning to love the gun in a way he couldn't when letting us pop the kid in front of his father.

"The irony," The first girl says, quietly enough to where only we three can hear it. "Looks like he learned it's okay to get triggered sometimes."

THE WISE OWL turns its head completely around, the only smart thing in this entire asbestos-tiled house of "book smarts," and stares straight into teenage Karen's 80s'mascara laden eyes with the intensity of a jeep headlight boring into the corneas of an alpine deer.

THE WISE OWL:

I've never seen an abyss quite as black,
As the words of a teenage kid talking smack.
However, I must ask the first performer, so kind,
If she thinks she's out of her inflated fucking mind?

"Deep breaths," Her friend, dressed in a Tractor Supply gymnast's attire and with a routine planned that involves at least three John Deere's and a few buckets of homemade fireworks. She pats the back of her friend's head, the Owl's question making her think she's about to faint after the stress of the presentation. Luckily, before she can attempt to answer, DJ drags a pick across the acoustic's six strings and prepares to serenade us like he's about to take us to the Grand Old Opry. As the notes ring out into the muggy classroom air, I sense a change in things, like we're moving on the z-axis again …

TWENTY-FUN

In the middle of a wheatfield, a bonfire rages on a funeral pyre that says GUN CONTROL LAWS in columns of burning books. DJ stands in front of it with his trucker hat twisted backwards, his cowboy boots bouncing with jingles of the stirrups, as though he's riding on an invisible donger pony across the wide-open landscape one could find in however many states exist between despair and irrelevance. He's wearing a flannel along with a Gucci belt, the buckle shaped like a target hanging halfway down his lap. His guitar at the ready, this is a music video of devotion to the NRA, where there are guns-girls ready to dance to the beat of the click-click boom gunshots this drummer's about to drop into the crisp fall air to the echoing sounds of tractors plowing through these very fields. DJ winks into the camera, says, this one's for my dad, and then prepares to strum a moderate country jingle, the kind of which you'd hear playing in a bar where you have to remove your mask in order to get service.

DJ sings,
I played war as a boy, making toy guns
Out of my three big fingers having so much fun
Pulling that trigger at my best friend's face,
Front yard, back porch, all over the place!
I played COD in middle school, started in 6th grade
After three years of gaming, I established my aim:

To scare the shit out of nerds using only my screen name,
For all of this who do I lift up in praise?

Pictures of Moe Wyden getting burnt, slapped, ripped in half, and chopped by katanas flash by in rapid motion before the chorus explodes into a country-rock hellhole-jingle straight out of Santa doing a verse on the new Big and Rich

Good guys with guns make everything safe,
I take my dad's m60 all over the place!
For your protecting arms across god's nation,
God bless the national association!

Now the kid's yodeling worse than that screaming cowboy at sunset, and the women who are dressed like little pistols ready to fire dance around the burning legislation, stories, and former dreams with their shadows cast at unreal angles, like barbie dolls being tossed around a campfire by unseen hands. They're basically if Laura Croft were chrome and shaped like the pistols you always see her with, next to those conical tits faker than the smile on the shit-talker's face. Painting them chrome in this way and making them each wear anklets and bracelets and necklaces made of bullets would turn them into androids, but thanks to the steady hum of industrial revolution farm equipment underneath the beating drums and guitar strumming, we should take it as a blessing that they aren't in Daisy Dukes rubbing their bodies across cars the same way those masked fuckers wiped that fucking grill!

Anyway, DJ's back with another verse to fire:
John Wayne, Arnold, the critic in the theatre,
Nothing in the world strikes me as sweeter,
Than a man who has what it takes in the wild,
Needs the arms of Stallone and the eyes of Chris Kyle!
Luckily, when I'm shopping I will never go,

Without my anti-aircraft gun in tow!
When I can bring my Panzer to the bank,
I know exactly who we've all got to thank!

The anti-aircraft shells tear through the Publix roof, penetrate the night sky right underneath the stars, and strike down a series of biplanes with metal skin the color of the women with their faces painted around the propellors. Then, DJ's inside a tank in the drive-through ATM at the local One Florida Bank, the tan armor's camouflage clashing mightily with the orange bank's plating. Next, DJ's rocking on a stage shaped like a bullet, with an entire crowd in front of him lifting rifles and uzis and machine guns and AK-47s and AR-15s and pump action and automatic shotguns, glocks and .38s and desert eagles, long guns and blunderbusses and at least three bazookas out there, a fucking cannon that shoots cannonballs with the 45th president's face on them that tear right through a castle built to look like the face of Moe Wyden and have cartoonish cloud exclamations that say OWNED! on them, there's a military turret in the middle of the throbbing mob that smells of country sweat, so much stained flannel writhing like a tarp in hurricane winds, god damn, as the country breakdown goes yee-haws to the absolute maximum. The action breaks, to where its just the drums counting one two three four while DJ claps his hands above the neck of his acoustic guitar.

"READY?" He shouts.

Everyone raises their weapon of choice towards the sky.

"AIM!" He shouts, louder, forcing the microphone near his teeth.

He inhales as the mic crackles so loudly it nearly pops the pony's eardrums.

"FIIIIIIIIIIIIIIIIIIIRE!!!!!" He howls. The words GUN

CONTROL, made of blue concrete, appear atop the stage. Everyone shoots them, then they clap, then the bullets rain down and around and up and over as DJ, with the gun control argument obviously falling to the stage around him in shards, the hearts of his classmates firmly in his hand after not pulling the trigger for his father's sake, goes back in for one more Chorus to make us all feel twanged 'til the end of time:

The NRA in the USA is the godly, chosen way,
To those who oppose our rights all I've gotta say:
You had better come and take em', and when you do,
I'll say I'm proud to love my country and show you my proof!

The entire class claps louder than the award show audiences did for Sacha Baron Cohen, a rare member of this species able to replicate the kind of absurdity we just saw on display in front of us, everyone clapping decently, respectfully for the kid's time and space twisting display of dedication to country music as projected on the blackboard at the front of the room. Thankfully, for our demonstration, we're prepared to showcase something somehow more destructive than the death of gun control by fire – and I think Mrs. Becker, as an enthusiast of language and firearms and patriotism herself, is going to utterly love the way we put a little bend to things in Florida ...

TWENTY FUN (2)

The Dickson County High School cafeteria has been professionally outfitted to withstand both a school shooting and a nuclear bomb, according to the designers wishes from the Nixon administration and the refurbishing people who bought the bulletproof cafeteria tables the kids can flip up and hide behind like huge shields with wheels. From the research we conducted prior to this demented excursion, we daft three were picturing a cantina where children amble around aimlessly tossing jacks in corners, reeking of cigarettes while laughing, maybe playing cards that will get them called virgins for all eternity, etcetera. But no. No, this place is much much different, since we forgot the golden rule of American society as sacred as the golden arches spiking like cholesterol in someone's blood: food is the center of everything, thus accounting for not only the cafeteria's centralized position in the school but for the fact the massive-ass budget these parents pay through voluntary will in a place that hates paying for anything has been obviously injected into this eatery. From the moment you step through the state of the art sliding doors into the food court, with the buffets overflowing with lava-like mac and cheese, molten and golden and making every weed-stained mouth water in a three mile radius, you are transported into a cornucopia of picnic shit, Stouffer's stuffed patrons grasping bowls of baked beans and potato salad and 'Amish' macaroni salad, the presence of these culinary delicacies a retroactive fuck you to Michele Obama just by the amount of grease oozing out of one of those meat-fucked, guttural Nagasaki pieces of meat lover's pizzas, enough to pool at the corner of one of the trays inscribed with the caricature of the LAND O PLENTY white overalled farmer man gleaming back up at us with dead eyes while we shuffle behind DJ, THE WISE OWL's flapping presence on my shoulder not a violation of any rule in a place where the kids are seated by clique as easily as a clip slid into one of the automatic machine guns and MONSTER-sponsored cases the kids who are part of the Dickson County High School shooting teams have resting against the legs of their still-shitty silver chairs, the burgers chomping between their jowls and staining the hillbilly-Hitler beards and moustaches they're rockin'. Unfortunately for DJ, with his MEAT THE PRESS hotdogs covered in chili sauce and cheese boiling on his plate like a fresh abortion, we aren't going to sit up at the high point in the cafeteria, the metaphorical Eagles' nest for freedom, where sits the militia game favorites and their glorious, sexy weapons – we're lucky we just dropped the NRA-praising single since that's allowing DJ and the rest of us to join his usual loose group of real-life friends at the sorta-nerd table amidst the howling ruckus of slurping, chomping, chewing. Fortunately, we're positioned far away enough from the Guinea Pig People kids – also known as the DCHS Young Republicans – who are gnawing at their carrots and have carried aquariums of woodchips with them to school, which they threaten to throw at the eyes of any administrator or staff member who asks them to wear a mask and infringe their sacred constitutional rights. Their section of the room smells like absolute dogshit, too, like the aftermath of horse de-wormer lingering in the air, and they're also taking pipettes full of disinfectant themed with the newest superstar in cleaning in the United States since Mr. Clean was fired for his baldness: Charlene herself, who is running with her husband's last name faster than an Olympic sprinter and is gleefully telling people exactly like these pantsuit and collared shirt wearing white-ass teens that their daily dose of cleaning products will purify their nostrils of all diseases. And she has the septum(s) to prove it!

Luckily, like I said, we're far away from those scurrying, gnawing offspring, and we take our seat next to DJ, who is still drenched in sweat from the NRA performance and glowing in the fact he's been allowed back here instead of forced by the administration to sit in the gym and eat tons of protein powder along with fresh alligator to become more of a man. One of the kids at the table, one of those who is so into MOBAs he's trying to get a scholarship for it, mentions offhand that the alligator's family is suing Senator Baetz. We tell him we were there, we already know, and he goes on to detail the ways in which the media, "twists everything around in brutally predictable ways."

Peering over the tower of onion rings we procured from the deep fryer, which the Pony is trying to drape around one of his spherical appendages, I tell the acne-faced, Axe Fresh teenage boy that if he thinks the media is good at twisting words, just wait until he sees what we've got planned for our presentation in English class!

ECKSDEE

"The school," The Donger Pony says to me, its football pads successfully affixed to its shoulders and the helmet to its head. "Is the place where everyone laughs and nobody smiles."

The class is chit-chattering away at their desks as Mrs. Becker, as a battle in her perpetual war against 20th century technology, is trying to get the PowerPoint to download from the internet. Luckily for her, we're both inside of it and its inside of us, now. There's no separating the two. She might as well have shoved that cold war extension cord right up her own spinal column until it broke through the soft part of her skull behind her brain and coiled around the shriveled thing like a python around a newborn toddler. Oh yeah, there are some kids in the class who are on the side of the alligator's family, the true environmentalists who will throw blood on anything that disrespects animals, so if not for THE WISE OWL serving as my Kevlar against their projectiles, those "libby kiddies," as DJ Daddy calls them, can only scowl at me and hope its possible to hate me for a reason as easily as making a country-rock song about the power of guns and ammunition. Luckily for all of them, as Mrs. Becker googles gmail and finally allows us to switch back to DJ's account, where we've also sent the presentation in all its mixed-up glory, we're about to present something so mindfuckingly insane to how these people interpret understanding, we're going to take them back to the times of kings and knights and witches faster than having a percentage of them hold an obscenely high percentage of the wealth. Alas, this is not math class, and so as the class dies down, they look up at me with glassy, commercial-eyed gazes through their smiles and their reptilian minds, mascots and Mickey Mouse lookalikes operating casinos for children before they learn how daddy spends his dollars. Yes, for the homage we are about to explain comes from words and their power to bend when you stare into them hard enough. I tell them this, in effect, and then show them the first example from the modern-standard presentation we've so lovingly prepared:

PLAYING WITH WORDS TO OWN THE LIBS

(A demonstration for barely-literate, Gucci-wearing high schoolers who
think their Spotify-Wrapped being 95% black means they can say the n-
word so long as they have a pass from the one black kid in their
grade/school/district)

"Hey!" One woman says, the glasses and piercings and colored hair the kind you'd expect to appear in a liberal ownage LOOOOL video made by Republican student groups at the most expensive Universities in the world of men. Her corporation she chose to cosplay was Starbucks, with the wig and the cup and the green and white face paint and pom-poms and teabags hanging threaded round her neck. "There's three black kids in the high school, not one!"

"My apologies," I tell her. "Congratulations on your exemplary progress and inclusion of diversity in your academic lifestyle and curriculum."

Everyone claps, and after we share the warm moment of feeling really good about doing almost nothing, both them and I for different reasons, we are able to continue in our presentation. We tell them really look at the word, say it like you're tasting each slimy, reptilian syllable, like you're a codebreaker in the second world war instead of someone wearing a gold star to protest vaccination during a time of utter plague, intentionally and incentivized:

DEMOCRA(P)

DEMO:
DEMON
DEMOLISH
DEMOTE
DEMORALIZE

CRA:
CRAP

"As you can see by dissecting their name and how it sounds," I explain, gesturing my lilywhite, young man's hands at their faces like wheeling in a fishing rod. "The Democrats are very obviously at least half demon."

"Who else would intentionally kill children?" Hoffs a student in the back looking like she just walked out of a Manger Scene at a backwoods Christmas market in order to honor the Heritage Foundation. Luckily, before the class can devolve into an argument over aborted fetuses while homeless individuals curl themselves up to cold deaths in the city streets far away from sight and far, far out of mind, we show them one of the incredible images we found expressing their thought patterns:

50% DEMON

HUGE-ASS IMAGE OF MOE WYDEN OR LOOKALIKE, IN THE SAME ART YOU SEE FOR COURTROOM SCENES, HOLDING AN OVERALLED CHILD BY THE ANKLES IN A BLACK, BOILING POT LABELED LIBERAL TEARS IN BLOOD ON THE SIDE SO DARK YOU ALMOST CAN'T READ IT. WYDEN'S FORKED TONGUE SHOOTS BETWEEN HIS LIPS LIKE A MADAME TUSSAUD'S VERSION OF LAW SCHOOL LUCIFER, AND HIS EYES ARE REPTILION DIAMONDS WITH EDGES SHARP ENOUGH TO SLICE VEINS.

"Holy candle-stick jumping Jesus Christ!" Some kid cosplaying a farmer with a corn stalk stuck in his front teeth shouts. "I've seen footage of this on the internet!"

"It's all in the name!" I tell him, continuing before their clearly panicked eyes can spiral deeper into the known truth of their supreme leaders' pedophilic cannibalism.

TIC:

TIC TAC TOE
TICTAK CANDY
TICTOK TIME
TICTOK APPLICATION

"I always knew the Democrats were controlling the time," one of the guinea pig loving kids says, sitting nearest to the cage where the class one is crawling around on his American flag covered woodchips, his needles scraping along all fifty stars and thirteen stripes covering his little shitpellets. This girl's the kind who looks like she's late to the My Chemical Romance scene in more ways than music, but she's wearing a Baetz Lives Matter pin right on her hoodie that has a picture of Mr. Jimmy himself with the thug life sunglasses and lit joint hanging out of his mouth like he's the white Snoop Dogg in a timeless music video. "That's why 2020 and 2021 have felt so much longer, so they can have more time!"

click

Democratic Brainwashing via TicTok

Large percentage of TicTok users are young and not pale skinned, meaning they are most likely to be children of demonRATS!

Shows many vulgar dances, including twerking, dougie'ing, twisting, shouting

Provides access to medical and therapeutic and educational resources **without payment** !!!!!

Allows women to speak when they have not been spoken to, miscalibrating the relationship between man to woman to be something different than the relationship of man to god.

"Social media is the DEVIL!" Mrs. Becker says, her DCHS shotgun draped over her knees with her pink crocs tapping fast. "This is why I only use Foyer to hear the truth without any manipulation!"

"Exactly," I say to her, appreciating her enthusiastic interruption with a friendly smirk. "And actually, Mrs. Becker, my dear velociraptor queen, I'm so glad you brought up how the evil government is manipulating the truth through twisting our words around." For emphasis, I spin the donger pony like a top on the floor, watching as their eyes glue to its twirling cylindrical extremities like shell casings to an industrial magnet. I know that, with one push of this mouse, I'm going to blow their minds in the exact same way researching their beliefs impacted ours, and I suppose, in the equation of everything, all of this really is just a balancing act. In the buzz of the midday mosquitos and the hushed anticipation of the humid air, I click the button and essentially have dropped napalm on the everglades thanks to one word in their flat, shitty, star-spangled language:

"WOAH WOAH WOAH WOAH WOAH!" Mrs. Becker screams, brandishing the school-issued teal and white shotgun straight at the chick who did the presentation on her dad's plastic surgery. The very act of witnessing the word, in its sharp red, made her grab a pair of safety scissors while howling like a coyote and try to puncture her own eyes with the neon yellow and lavender plastic, but thankfully, Mrs. Becker's successful cocking of the weapon allowed for a sense of order to be restored, bringing back amazing thoughts of her childhood when she dreamed of having needles planted into her skin instead of suffering a near breakdown at the sight of the word. Three of the starting shooters in the militia games – kids who are dead eyes and steady shots and have killer, apex instincts – have their assault rifles trained on us, the wireless mouse held in one hand, the pony in the other, and THE WISE OWL trying not to burst out laughing at the idea of us being blown to feathers over something that would save their lives.

"Now, hold on, fellow Floridians," I say to them, trying to sound like I'm talking to delinquent children who I don't want to make mad mads before food time. "I'm not here to promote the vaccine …"

"Show us your upper arms!" One of the kids with Trevor Lawrence's hairstyle and a real weapon modeled after Master Chief's orders me. I oblige, raising my sleeves so they can successfully run the classroom handheld metal detector over my skin without interference from the cloth. Then, I tell them to allow me to demonstrate what Mrs. Becker meant when she interjected with twisting words around:

VAC = VALVE ANTI-CHEAT

"Now," I say, noticing the befuddlement in their narrowed eyes and scrunched foreheads. "As some of you may know, dear Dylan James here and I," I gesture at DJ with an open palm. "Are professional e-sports gamers in addition to being national heroes."

"I heard AOC plays League of Legends," the homeboy with the largest biceps and the shortest gun in the back says. "You sure you ain't a libtard?"

"EXCUSE me," Mrs. Becker says, brandishing her shotgun in his direction and shaking her ass like she has an invisible, coiled velociraptor tail. "Do NOT use such impolite language in this well-mannered English class!"

"Sorry, Mrs. B," The kid says, saluting her fast and turning back to me. ""You sure you is not a libtard, buddy?""

"Saw him wearing that mask all the time, too," the young lady who had the conniption fit with the parentally-endorsed fake tits says, her eyes and her brow and her armpits still moist. "I'm thinking we have a rare breed here, boys."

"Alright, alright," I say, patting the donger pony sculpture's head at her amazingly kind compliment of my kiln-fired horse-shaped friend. "Here, I'll show you what DJ and I learned having to play against terrorists all day on the internet. Do you know what it's like to shoot somebody who you absolutely know is doing something wrong?"

"I admire you for your trigger finger, slimjim," The third of the stand your ground advertisements says to me. "But you better show us what you're on about right now, with your gaming and your mentioning the devil in here and all."

"You need to be careful," Mrs. Becker says, explaining this to me in the same tone of voice she uses talking to students who still don't know how to read. "Words are the most powerful things we have on the face of the planet, Johnny!"

"Exactly," I say to her, steeling myself for the absurdity that's about to blast through this humid apocalypse den where the desks are from the days people were told to hide behind inches of plywood to survive the bomb. "And here's how we knew we were fighting the communist Democratic Chinese, where everything became clear as day:"

ANTI-CHEAT = ANTI-HACKERS

"Alright," the captain says, among murmurs in the room, as if their voiceboxes and bobbing chins were tied together by invisible wires. "I might see where you're going."

ANTI

"Anti, like in Anti-racist?" The young woman asks, her tone a genuine question.

"Close," I say. "You're in the right section of the books we've banned."

AUNTIE

"Oh my lord GOD," A different student screams, this one dressed like a fluffy pillow with the picture of that one suited, white male election memelord's face displayed like a sleepwalking billboard. "He's talking about the Democrat party!"

AUNTIE MAXINE

At the mere mention of the name of one of the nation's longest serving elected representatives, the young white people in this class recoil and gasp, bang their desks and even raise their guns at the whiteboard behind me, above me now, having turned into another messenger just trying to avoid being shot into pieces. I've just revealed to them the same things they see in triangles in traffic ads and immortalized in cement pyramids built alongside their highways, which are supposed to be temples for something according to my species' research the same way these science classrooms have told them the vaccines don't only cause autism, but are actually releasing tons of little trojan robots into their blood.

Therefore:

MAXINE = ANTIFA

"Amen!" a few of them say, their tide turning with me as if pulled by a slow-moving hurricane.

ANTIFA-HACKERS

"YES!" The plastic surgeon's daughter says, her palms open towards the asbestos-tiled, hole-riddled ceiling.

"Finally," I tell them, holding up my right index finger. "You all know what witchcraft is, have I read about your homeland right?"

"You don't need to read about Florida," the Abercrombie model-looking one of the three combat sportsmen tells me. "Florida is a lifestyle, my man. My main man Mejora!"

"Well," I say, bashfully, THE WISE OWL's chest so inflated he's trying not to burst into a green ball of trapped laughter finally igniting. "This is where they use the way the words sound in order to turn our words into weapons."

"Bad weapons," Mrs. Becker reminds me. "Because they're used by bad people."

"I know who the good ones are," I tell her, with a pleasant smile. Then, I proceed to the next slide, and reveal how the liberal media and the coastal elites have successfully infiltrated our everyday language exactly like they did when they had that one guy try to shoot up that pizza shop back in Washington, only to find out it didn't have a basement. The reaction they have to what I show them next is akin to the same one that older, white man gave to the cops, especially since they've been trained to read liminal signals in the positions of hands, Qs, and storm clouds:

TO HACK: : to cough in a short dry manner

Stunned, holy silence.

TO HACK = TO COUGH

Heads nod.

TO COUGH = POTENTIAL
COVID-19

COVID-19 = CHINESE VIRUS

CHINESE VIRUS = SOFTWARE

"I knew it!" A(nother) white student says while rocketing his hand into the sky with the fury of the WWE whom he's written his corporate love poem homework about. "My cousin told me he got COVID from clicking a link on the internet that was supposed to show him DJ's Daddy's sex tape!"

This turns into a rapid discussion between them about the ways in which the 5G towers outside transmitted the virus, in addition to the more widely-accepted belief that being marked by the vaccine is akin to being labeled a Jew during the Holocaust, as evidenced by the emblems hanging from some of the back-packs in the front row I'm able to examine while Mrs. Becker yells for the class to be quiet and respectful. Once they've agreed on the fact all of this is scientifically reasonable so far (according to the sources they have watched on the Internet, naturally, which means they're true as gospel just by preaching to the choir) I am able to proceed to the second half of the word they hate the same way as some places hate their ugly history:

Cine

Cine = sign

It is at this point, in front of the class, that I realize I've made an error in reading English common to non-native students of the language; however, instead of this being to my detriment, the fact that I've contorted the language in this way has them gripping the sides of their heads with both palms, kicking their chairs across the tile, realizing there's been another way to embed a message inside the physical words. Luckily, I confirm this by the following blindingly white, professional software slides:

signs

Signs (Mel Gibson, 2004)

Mel Gibson = Cancelled

"Wowzers," Mrs. Becker says, through a heavy sigh. "The poor burden placed on your generation with the weight of having to survive in a world of identity politics."

"I agreed with every word the man said, personally," One of the armed jokesters in the back says, causing the class to lightly laugh in disbelief the same way they use humor to protect themselves from true agony or wonder. Despite myself, moving through these slides at the speed of their willingness to believe with tear-filled eyes and wounded hearts flushes my neck red with a sense of power I never understood reading about humanity's empires. Blessedly, we're close enough to nirvana now we can clearly smell the Clorox.

CANCELLED = STOPPED

stop signs

Stop signs are red

Red is the color of
blood

Blood

Where does the
vaccine get injected?

"YOUR BLOOD!" Someone yells.

"ONE HUNDRED PERCENT!" I shout back at them, knowing some will know the saying in a way completely different than the people sitting next to them in a way that's impossible to reconcile.

Your blood!

"Ergo," I say, beckoning for them to solve the problem. "THE VACCINES ARE CHANGING YOUR GENETICS AND GIVING YOU SOMEONE ELSES BLOOD!" Mrs. Becker screams, my use of proper language enrapturing the part of her who knows she would've been a wife to Caesar with clearly Shakespearean lust.

"Almost!" I say. "It's worse!"

Vaccine = Demonrats are putting software in your blood!

"*Eureka!*" Mrs. Becker yells, firing her shotgun directly into the ceiling tiles and causing softly falling dust clouds to not only shimmer like frozen rain in the blinding projector beam, but to also stain the green and yellow snake flag with the black text she's now allowed to hang in the corner of the classroom. The whoops and hollars and yips and yees and haws and bravos being shouted from the cheap desks to the front row have me and DJ beaming, despite me being hotter than the projector's burning bulb at nearly being stoned here in the same fashion as an accused heretic in a not-so-ancient square. In the cheers and adulations shouted around me after, the only thing I can think is that this is what it feels like to be in that same town square, but as the trusted Father, standing amidst those eyes with the lord and all his masters.

The way. The way they laugh the most when things just burn.

TWENTY-TWO

The kids who are the all-stars of the militia games really aren't fans of math class. DJ didn't have to tell me this, its as easy to read on them as wisdom in the eyes of THE WISE OWL that have been orbiting ever since we walked into those cursed school doors earlier today. Except the Owl won't even look in their direction.

THE WISE OWL:
Under numbers, next to future astronauts and engineers,
We sit next to shirts with no sleeves and whale-shirted peers!
These people snort numbers like how their fathers snort coke,
But when it comes to the figures, how does one know?

"It's half math half econ," DJ says, answering the bird's question and using his donger pony Muricuh eraser to cross out some doodles of bombs, guns, and 'terrorists.' Luckily for us, we're in the first row of the three, sitting right in front of the whiteboard which smells of both sharpie and cleaner so strongly we expected to be crossfaded by the time the class bell rang. Towards the back, you see the kids who have been trained by their fathers on the first day of hunting season and long before, the same way other kids were taught to read early or were carried to sense a numeric understanding by the shoulders of the same parents who pay for them to sit in these shitty, plastic theatre seats. These kids are the ones who are the killers. These kids are the ones who are your linebackers and wide receivers, maybe a quarterback or two, but for a calculus class to be a structured requirement in a student's junior year, with their jawlines and their square cheeks and their mannered, southern accented language – think Florida Georgia Line on poppers – well, these boys held triggers right after the time their teeth grabbed their momma's teets. If they'd grown up in the 1960s, dressing in collared shirts and reminiscing about not being able to own slaves like their ancestors, they probably would have been breastfed by a Black woman for free instead of whoever their mothers have hired to nurture them today. Instead, those same Big Daddies who wear the suits and fly in the jets and find new ways to push the understanding of pinkish, screaming flesh are paying for a school that teaches them *practicality* alongside the theory. Thus, they've hired an actual, living Black man to basically be the conservative version of Keegan Michael Key in a parody video, except instead of mispronouncing names, the first thing Mr. Robinson does is place a metal trashcan in the middle of the room with a recycling symbol painted on the sides like Shrek's vomit.

"Good morning, class!"

"Good morning, Mr. Robinson!" We echo, all respectful, remembering the origin of math is also music underneath pictures of Charles Murray, Thomas Sowell, and Friedrich Hiyak cartoonishly laughing at us from behind their laminated walls.

"Thank you all for joining me today," he says, sounding whiter than the board in a way that would make Dave envious. "Are you excited to solve your first problems in the new curriculum?"

"YAAAAAAYYYY!!!" We all say, brandishing our huge, stupid textbooks in one hand, heavy enough to kill a rodent from this height, with our school-themed and freely-distributed Dickson Deagles in the other like roman candles on the fourth in a hospital waiting room. The fact the moniker's the name of the school's militia games team is something that hasn't been lost on THE UNHOLY TRINITY of the Owl, the Pony, and I, but for the love of god, these people will find a reason to clap for literally *anything*. Mr. Robinson holds up his copy of the textbook like its an ancient tablet and we are the Egyptians. Then, he points down the trashcan with his hand wearing the watch and says, "Alright, I want the first row to come up and throw their old textbooks into the trash can." We stay seated, but ask DJ first by whispering to him, "Wait, DJ, what changed about the math between the books?"

"A lot of things," DJ says, allowing the woman seated next to us to squeeze past him. "But the big change is the way we count things."

"What?" I ask him, *hearing* the owl's eyes scrape the sides of its skull like a knife across a razer sharpener at full speed. "What do you mean?"

"I'll tell you in a second," DJ says. Meanwhile, Ainsley Elliot for the common core, wearing two pens in the right breasted pocket that look like sparklers to me under these buzzing lights, floats over to us with a welcoming smile and friendly eyes behind his round-framed glasses.

"Well, howdy there, partner!" He says, gesturing to the donger pony sitting on my desk next to my notebook and my plumed feather pen I picked up when we were all drafting edits to the constitution to propose to Senator Baetz. "I've been seeing this horse everywhere!"

"He's talking about *you*," The Donger Pony says, scraping its unhearable hooves across the chalk-dusted surface, leftover across the plastic like snow atop white granite asphalt.

"I'm sure you've been seeing all of us," I tell him, gesturing to the Owl on my shoulder and DJ, who has returned and is sitting with his hands folded staring straight up at the man. Math has never been the kid's favorite subject, which is weird for how into shooting people on the internet he is, but this new curriculum he's talking about must make about as much sense as trying to constrain the infinite space inside the plastic cock horse into something as feeble as a number. Some of these things, when you turn them around, look like they're smiling at you. See? Kick a 3 on its side and you've got a set of balls, a moustache, and two asscheeks. Therefore, we have found two inside of three, as two must be inside three according to the way they count. I don't know what the fuck DJ's expecting looking up at him, and I don't know what Mr. Robinson is seeing looking back down, but as the inverse to the Donger Pony's words and thoughts and actions are deafened to their ears, I can *hear* what this man is thinking: *they're serving burgers in the cafeteria for lunch today.*

Instead of saying that, he says, "Pleased to meet you, Dylan. I'm a big fan of your father's!"

"Thanks, Mr. Robinson," DJ says, the pain in his voice masked the same way a throat gets masked by leather over years of destressing through cigs. "I was trying to tell my friend John here the new way of counting!"

"That's our first lesson!" The teacher says, waving for the next row to go and throw their books in the trash. He steps over to the whiteboard, picks up a big blue sharpie, uncaps it, wipes a part of the board off with his forearm, and draws what I was just considering in my blasted high, adolescent-impersonating mind:

$$2 + 2 = 4$$

"Do we agree?" He asks us, plus the rest of the first row, the three kids to my right and DJ plus the other table across the midway tiled aisle in the center of the classroom. The chatter dies down and its just the industrial fans in the vomit-painted bricks above us plus the hum of sweet anticipation for how to make numbers feel. I nod my head with the *no shit* speed I thought everyone would at this, ditto for the Donger Pone and the Owl, but this is where DJ's looking at me with a smirk on his barely-facial-haired face with a shine in his glazed, bloodshot eyes. Instead, Mr. Robinson walks back to the board, the third row silently proceeding towards the trashcan with a nod of his chin, and plants the marker directly in the center of the second two. He pushes the marker's tip into the whiteboard so hard it squeaks, and now the **2** is bolder than a thick scar.

"How do we feel about this number?" He asks. Everyone sits back, ponders the second two, considering it the same way that statue thought if that statue were on shrooms in the middle of nightmare math. Then, a kid who looks like he's the captain of the debate team raises his hand straight towards the ceiling with the ferocity of saluting the Fuhrer and says, "I feel like we need to hear both sides of the equation!"

Mr. Robinson walks over to the number 4, squints his brows, and asks the number on the board, "Mr. Fantastic Four, do you feel you're greater than five?"

The woman next to us wearing the choker collar and who has a version of the iPhone I didn't even know existed thanks to our shit research slams her head down on the desk so hard the Donger Pony nearly shits itself as it skitters, and says, "Who are we to tell anybody that they're better or worse than anyone else!"

"Exactly!" Mr. Robinson says, like he just taught her how to multiply. He erases the equation and puts the words THE TOP THREE RULES OF NEW MATH in red marker. Then, he writes below it in the same fresh-cut-on-pale-flesh color:

1.   THERE ARE *NO* LIMITS!

"Absolutely *none*," he says, gesturing up at the visages of Sowell gleaming down on us from above the framed panorama of the stock market adorning the walls. This department's better funded than at least three local, public school districts combined, thus his ability to click a button on a remote to light the ceremonial torches underneath the face of the dude who came up with the Bell Curve. "If someone tells you that you're limited, you tell them we're in America!"

The man turns around and honest to god, stitched in the back of that threadbare shirt, he's got the words AMERICA = FREEDOM plugged between his shoulder blades, bedazzled in red, white, black, and blue. To the cheers and claps and proof from the group of wealthy 17 year olds that they can read and repeat things, he scrolls over and uses the blue marker to write the next textbook commandment even *bolder*:

2.   WE MUST KNOW *SIN*!

"Sin," He says, turning around and dropping his face to be the kind you place atop the pulpit to get people to pay you for healing, his voice echoing and louder than the quick *yeses* and muttered *amens*. "Seeks to nest itself inside our most basic calculations."

On the other side of the board, he writes:

NUMBER OF ABORTIONS IN FLORIDA THREE YEARS AGO = 862,320
COST PER ABORTION IN FLORIDA: $3000
MONEY SPENT SOLELY ON KILLING CHILDREN THREE YEARS AGO = 2,586,960,000

The rest of the class is now weeping as though he's just told the story of a prodigal son who committed suicide from the pulpit – oh, if only these mosquito stained, melting hot windows were stained glass as everyone realizes the terrible truth.

DJ's tearing up too, and I say to him, "So many dead kids, you'd think this were *A Modest Proposal Part Two!*"

"No," DJ says, not getting the reference and shaking his head so hard a couple tears squirt out the corners of his eyes in hot streaks. "Look at how much *money* they lost!"

"Wow," I say, the part of me that's supposed to imitate what we were told human souls were like dead as a big bug in an electric blue zapper. I look around at the women whose mascara bleeds downwards in ash waterfalls towards their trembling lips, the future finance bros and top tier lawyers and general managers, those forever royals and clutch protagonists, and realize the reason Mr. Robinson's nodding so hard is due to the fact *this* is what they meant by how the word is spread, straight from the new textbook's plastic wrapped eyes on its thick, glossy spine looking at us like a predator's through the bushes in the Everglades from Mr. Robinson's teacher-desk. They're aspiring to an advertisement for Prozac. The students nearest to his desk are doing breathing exercises over the thought of that much lovely money, so many Benjamins and Jeffersons and soon to be the tangerine man if things do go that way, never being able to fulfill its purpose of bringing meaning to someone's life instead of taking it away. In this vein, someone bought Mr. Robinson a sculpture of a Black union soldier as a way to welcome him on his first day, yet instead of the Union blue colors, his Killer Angel cap has been overwritten with the words of the 45th guy and his musket has been replaced by a massive broadsword; when I asked DJ why Mr. Robinson's been the *only* teacher without a gun in this entire school, DJ told me, "The school board took their inspiration from former California. If the cops had to come or if one of the other teachers successfully engaged Jason Bourne protocol, he'd be the first person they'd drop to the floor and we all know it."

The sheer toxicity coming from DJ's lips versus the wide smile on Mr. Robinson's face, his own eyes emotional as they mourn the opportunity cost for sinful saving of a mother's life or reversing the course of rape, makes me raise my own hand amidst the sobbing and ask what seems, even to my invasive species, to be a rather simple question of this god-fearing gentleman.

"Yes, Mr. Mejora?"

"Mr. Robinson," I ask him, pointing to the board behind him shining in the sunlit, heavy air. "What about the *other* people included in the equation?"

Gasps. A couple things that sound like books hit the floor. The statue, due to the jutting leg of a sportsman dressed in jeans despite the fact its boiling in here, has fallen from the desk and has clapped the tile floor with the same disruptive power as an old-fashioned record scratch. DJ turns to me with wounded eyes, yet Mr. Robinson shakes his head and raises his palms, already apologizing for my apparent lack of manners.

"It's alright," Mr. Robinson says, pushing his palms downward. "He isn't from around these parts."

"Holy *Jesus*," the girl sitting next to me says, her neon red and orange and blue nails across her bony collarbone. "You almost chose some liberals over *profit!*"

When the fuck did I mention liberal? I ask the Donger Pony. The Owl can no longer turn his eyes because their sides are sore to bleeding. Meanwhile, Mr. Robinson approaches me the way Steve Harvey approaches someone who's fucked up on *Family Feud*, and in the same tone of voice asks me, "Where are you from, Johnathan?"

"I'm from along the coast."

"What state?"

"Florida," I tell him, corroborating with the VPN I used to get into DJ's little circle.

"Are you …" Mr. Robinson asks, hands on his kneecaps, the uncapped marker dangerously close to his corduroys. "Are you one of those *mask* people?"

"I saw him wearing one when he went to meet Senator Baetz," The same trucker-cap-wearing bitch shouts from behind me. If she and her school board representative mother were American babushka dolls, they'd come with toy guns and confederate flag lingerie with smaller versions of the same wailing desire to fuck the senator who voted to restrict their birth canals. And now, to quell the tide of growling, mumbling, and daggered eyes sent in my direction, Mr. Robinson writes the newish rule I unintentionally violated by trying to study this species' ways before entering among them. According to what he writes in the black marker, underneath the red and blue one and two, I was incredibly foolish in my calculation, primarily because

3.   HUMAN LIFE IS NOT AN INCENTIVE.

This restores the class's sense of shared serendipity to the point where it feels like there's been a collective exhalation strong enough to deflate the temperature by a few degrees. With a kind smile and joyous eyes, Mr. Robinson walks back over nodding at me like I'm agreeing with the way my sins must've moved through my confessional.

"In terms of mathematics, money, economics," he says, tapping the ass end of the thick marker right beside the Pony sculpture. "Human life cannot be an incentive. Can you *imagine* how much a doctor would make if the point of medicine was to cure human lives?"

The Wise Owl's desperate cry to recite the Hippocratic oath is drowned out by the disgust the students are making, their reason for competing in the Parentlympics of SAT coaching, logic training, focused reading, essay writing being squashed as easily as a flying cockroach by a sledgehammer when considering what would happen if they *weren't a baker making that bread.* I feel dizzy from the attempt to rationalize their suicidality, but thankfully Mr. Robinson, like the shepherd guiding the sheep back to the flock before pointing them over the cliffside, writes another equation on the board that's supposed to illustrate this to me using another one of his dumb numbers. If I called the numbers Arabic, I feel like the frat bro finance bruh cap wearing fuckers in the back might unload their customized automatics straight into the rules and equations like they were partying on an afternoon down at the shooting range during the last couple wars; instead, though, what he's written this time fucks me so hard I find myself blessed that my nature is better than that of those looking for an excuse to turn him into a threat.

ALL NUMBERS ARE IRRATIONAL IF YOU THINK ABOUT THEM HARD ENOUGH

"Who can give me an example of an irrational number?"

A student in the back raises her hand above her nazi-chique fishing hat and says, "Moe Wyden's electoral votes!"

Everyone in the class goes *OHHHHHHHH* and someone snaps a picture of her with her daddy's little princess smile and posts the caption on Instagram, Democrats DESTROYED by Calculus Student using MATH and LOGIC!!!!!! #youngGOP #racialhealing #theyreafraidofustogether. Apparently, some of them thought this was really fucking funny, and the teacher's laughing so as not to lose his job, but I've gone from puzzled to offended to feeling slightly scared for the integrity of my absurd friends and I, solely because the eyes on the woman who made the joke in the lights of the iphone cameras blaze the same way a bullet does from the open wound of a fired rifle, as they say. They needed cheerleaders to watch the boys shoot each other, and that's why I find it amazing there's such a thing as a person who cheers loudest when someone else is hit. Before we can fall into *her* celebrity and the amazing teamwork as generated by the stupendous Dickson school curriculum, however, the bell rings, leaving us only with the 10 homework questions he's given for us to take home, complete, and then check as a group, where of course the answers can be debated so long as we take into account the feelings and the thoughts we have towards all these numbers. What the fuck do they mean? I think we'll be the last to know.

TWENTY THREE

Even before we get close to the door, I can see the plague doctor mask inside the classroom. After all this shit – being mindfucked by twisting words and having my own calculus exploded by all gas, no breaks, sin limits – I grab DJ by the arm of his fuzzy shirt.

"DJ," I tell him. "I'm not sure if I can go to where this shit is taking me." The pony's dongering exhausted, the owl is staring straight ahead and petrified due to the circumference of his eyeballs feeling like raw, festering meat having spun into ground oblivion.

"Don't worry," he says, in a surprisingly confident tone. "This is actually my *favorite* class." A strange series of guttural noises are bouncing around behind the triple-thick, steel-reinforced door painted to look like the outside of a fallout shelter when you've already lost the game. Sighing, my absurd friends and I share glances and gallops, murmurs and thoughts and prayers, and then attempt to prepare our own selves for the insanity of these people in these times, their gluttony and their lust and their greed, but when DJ spins the handle on the reinforced door like the captain of the Titanic looking at the freezer section in a modern appliance store, instead of going into some post-nuclear world, we find ourselves traveling backwards, into a realm where some have crumbs and others crystals ...

DMDMDMDMDMDMDM

The teacher stands in the front of the classroom, which is being taught in an underground grotto with torches hanging from the wall, the short, dirt steps up the side and out the entrance looking as though we've just entered Bilbo Baggins' wine cellar of a subterranean apartment. The desks aren't desks. They're tree stumps. I'm half expecting a nymph who smells like manic pixie teen spirit to come beeple-bopping out of whatever Alice in Wonderland Tinkerbell bullshit is currently happening in front of our eyes. THE WISE OWL is now fully accepted as being part of my magical wizardry, seeing he's perched on my shoulders and wearing a merchant's cap straight out of a Senatorial power fantasy, the Fandrew Duomo of these Middle America Ages in which we now find ourselves. There's a cauldron burning in the corner with some kind of unidentifiable liquid, but the teacher – behind the plague doctor mask colored like Pinocchio meeting the Phantom of the Opera via Venetian furnaces – looks like she's stepped out of a country western from the waist down and out of the GOP national convention from the mid-baring hot witch costume she's wearing and the black Faustian mask framing her wild, wide brown eyes smacked in the center of her baked-yam-looking skin.

This, as the chalkboard says behind her, is the science classroom of Mrs. Margarine Meme herself: Mrs. Calcutta Chambers. The plastic planetariums containing this puny, putrid universe spinning from the ceiling all have the fucking earth at the center of them. And, next to me, THE DONGER PONY has morphed into his nearly final form: as an eggshell colored stallion with a three yard cock that comes up to my waist and infinitely retracts and expands inside of him like he's straight out of a music video to a song none of these kids would know but have definitely kinda sorta heard before. Just like I've smelled liquid shit festering in the boiling underground of DJ's warped-ass septic field, I've been prepared me for the guttural obliteration known as the smell of sliding, chittering, Abby-gator sized rodents that look as though their laps through what used to be the New York Metro have given them the rights to fight each other to be the rodent Michael Phelps. Holy fuck, *that* one has incisor teeth the size of razors that could rip right through DJ's thigh in half a click, and the *other* one looks like he's the inspiration for that animation with the mouse and the potato knishes. However, instead of putting the rat in control of the food, *these* rats – with their boils and their fleas and their jumping, stinking infestation – are being regarded as though they themselves are some sort of spiritual main-course by the kids who are decked out as knights and warlocks and grand, colorful wizards according to their nomenclature. These rats are in a cage that's elevated off the floor by being placed smack dab in the middle of one of those flame retardant science tables, and the Guinea Pig Kids – with their facemasks echoing the Plague Doctor Chambers vibe and their hypotheses as self-confirming as the kids baptized Catholic in the class – have brought them offerings of niblets and mac and cheese and small, shitty pizzas that these hard-ass fuckers probably carry up the metro stairs after swimming through a turn-style deluge at 3:00am on a Monday night. I tell the Owl to stay perched on my shoulder and for the loyal donger pony steed to simply keep stamping his hooves in the twisted dirt beneath us. If we need to engage DEFENSIVE MANEUVERS and cook these rats back into the last ice age, we fucking shall. DJ and our trinity take our seats as far away from the rats as possible, with us and the other kids – some dressed like witches, others like princesses, maybe a naughty monk or two shoved in the mix somehow – as the discussion returns to the need to defend empirical beliefs about the universe, rooted, Mrs. Chambers says, writing with pink chalk in curly writing on the runic chalkboard, in the persecution of people like her who believe in loving global warming because she "hates cold places."

"God damn," The Donger Pony says to me, in a voice much deeper and with a face more human, almost like a Grecian sculpture weathered white by the besieging nature of time in this plane of existence, and the school board rep, Damon – who himself is dressed like a cross between a knight and the people who want to be white defenders of the m'lady's on the internet across the universe – nearly falls out of his chair like the tin man trying to re-establish gravity while on an acid bender.

"He's *talking* to me again!" He says, his voice quivering and his eyes wide.

"Thank you, Damon," Chambers says, waving the steel-tipped arrow she's been using as an instructional tool at the kid who is now trapped by his own gravity in the dirt like a can tossed beside a highway. "What do you think these rats would *say* if they could defend themselves against the royalty labeling them as plague spreaders?"

She calls on a woman who is dressed like she's a model for Merlin Klan apparel, with stars and military ranks on her fake medals and shit.

"We don't like being told that we can't even cross the ocean!"

"Exactly!" Mrs. Chambers says, as the guinea pig memorabilia kids clap and cheer and hoot. I glance over at DJ, who is looking at me with an apologetic nerd smile but who also compared the people who are getting the COVID vaccine after being infected to pussies and commie sympathizers in a way too clean to be ironic. Due to our failure to understand the utter fucking mystical insanity classified as human emotion, our research department is apologizing to me for their inability to capitulate a scenario where ANY OF THIS MOTHER FUCKING SHIT MAKES SENSE.

We can't. It's not possible. Even our computational prowess couldn't calculate the degree of joy and malice mixed in those bloodshot, Adderall-painted eyelids inside that plague doctor mask, but while I find myself to be something of a pacifist, I must admit that as the applause died down and echoed back to us from the roots of the very planet they love to burn, I imagined our own forces arriving here and burning her in that very costume until the nose melts into her nostrils and she chokes on her own fury.

THE WISE OWL:

The Daft One's true anger only stems from the notion,
That there's something that's healthy inside that brewed potion!
The cauldron is boiling and reeks of sulfuric cures,
I don't know if this species is going to endure!

He's right. In the corner, over a bed of ultrahot coals that would roast these fuckers harder than their own sun exploding, there's a cauldron that's been cited as their reasoning for mandating NO vaccinations for their contact sports teams. They've managed to combine ivermectin with natural remedies, such as spleen of mountain ape with sphincter of rhinoceros, and boil that entire thing down into something you kick back like a triple shot of Everclear at your cousin's third birthday party. It's the *feel good boiler*, as Mrs. Chambers called it, and she's got the same twisted smiley joy she did at the start of the class as she invites us to come to the front of the room.

"Let's get a look at the most famous knight for freedom this very land has to offer!" Her nails are so sharp I think they could pierce Damon's stupid armor. I look at DJ.

I shake my head.

He rolls his eyes.

I tell him no, but now the class is chanting it as though it's my turn to read the book up there in church. I bring the donger pony up with me, along with the Owl, and soon find myself staring down at those big ass, matted fur, visibly dying rats they've got here at the front of the room. Oh.

And she wants me to pick one up???

"Go on!" She says, bashfully placing her hand over her mouth like she's embarrassed. "Wow, a young and *humble* man!"

"No," I say to her, my own hair frizzled by my jester's cap and its jingly bell balls. "I'm not picking it up."

"Johnny," She says, placing her talons on her Daisy Duke hitched hips and tapping her talons on her thighs. "Don't be rude to the rats. How would you like it if I refused to pet your horse?"

"Don't fucking touch me, harpy cunt hands!" The Donger Pony says. I can hear Damon screaming into his armpit from the back of the room trying to contain his eruption for what's about to transpire in front of us.

Mrs. Chambers shakes her blonded head at me, bends down to the cage, and uses her batshit eyes to signal to the rat who looks like he swims in the sewer Olympics. And then she lets the fucking thing literally stick its head inside her mouth as she tongues its fucking matted skull and makes at least three other kids openly vomit onto the ground with the furious speed of *what the fuck why is it making that noise?* The rat turns around and sticks its tail straight up into Mrs. Chamber's lips, and she sucks it like it's a worm entering the ruby-crimson dunghole known as her stupid mouth until the rat's ass is orifice to open lips. Her fanclub in the cheap tree seats here are having a collective orgasm watching her hitting triples off this rodent, and by the time THE WISE OWL has vomited itself straight down my shirt and onto the table, THE DONGER PONY ready to turn this class into revelation by stampeding through these disgusting creatures, she's got the rat extended right over the space in front of me, so close he's able to eye-fuck me with a little smirk on his nose like *I know buddy, these people are a real trip!*

"Mrs. Chambers," I say, trying to get the burning bile out the back of my own throat. "I understand why you wish for me to worship this creature as you do, but you must respect my personal choice as much as I respect yours."

"Alright!" She says, nodding, respectfully, as if whatever that twisting thing felt like down to her esophagus blessed her with wisdom and clean nostril tissue. "The rest of you, come up here and show him how the royalty is lying about these little guys being dangerous! They ran experiments on these guys for *how* many years, and now they want us to believe that these little guys are *diseased*? I know liberals are a hateful, stupid breed, but to try and blame an entire group of something as being the source of all their problems is how they've grouped those opposed to tyrannical vaccines." She holds the rodent's stare for an uncomfortably long time. Then, she actually fucking says, "I see myself reflected in his little beady eyeballs." She snorts like she's just held back a tear, and then lets the students come up and cuddle the little nibblyfucks in a way that makes me and the Owl and the Pone retreat back to the far corner, underneath one of the rotating geocentric planetariums. One of the kids I'm standing near scoffs and points up at it with hands resembling those of a jouster whose pole was ripped from his palms so fast it left scars.

"Insane," he says, shaking his robin-hood-inspired mask at me.

I nearly want to grab him and hug him. Oh my god, there's still HOPE here!

"It isn't even fucking *flat*," he says, reaching his hand up and holding the earth like it's a baseball in his teenaged glove.

I don't know what sound I'm making inside of me, but amidst the chittering and the chattering and the skittering of little *feetsy claws* across portions of people's bodies I never imagined for this purpose, I'm squinting through the torchlight and trying to read the sundial mounted on the wall. If we can just survive one more spell cast by Mrs. Chambers, we might be able to position ourselves in time, before our trip back to Washington as a witness, to blaze with DJ again prior to his shooting activities after school. With the militia games set to become a thing this Friday and with us being called as a witness in the Baetz vs Abby's Family trial, this introduction of the new curriculum shit is only serving to make me want to ascend their silly ladders and call in our dongal cavalry as soon as possible. However, before I can sound the trumpets and send the stampeding stallions all through this place until they're reduced back down to apeshit, blood, and crumpled cancer tiles, there's a howling sound from the front of the room. One of the kids apparently put the thick rat into his mouth and the fucker bit something that he really shouldn't've, so now DJ is cursing and spitting blood and rat hair out onto the murky dirt. People rush to his aid.

The rat's, that is.

They ask if he's okay, if he needs to talk to anyone about the trauma of biting that poor kid, if there's any way they could have his autograph for enacting divine retribution onto the son of the man who defiled the sanctity of marriage on national television by using a condom when he said he was going bareback *oh my god*, etc. etc. Meanwhile, DJ is getting bitched out by Margarine Baylor Meme sqwuaking and with her eyes shining worse than a meteor in the middle of a sea of skin-wrinkles that look like they should smell like burning pigfuck inside the skin cancer microwave tube. Jesus *Christ*. Someone please tell me that, if the earth is at the center of these people's universes, there'd be some kind of compensation for the planet's current state, but as I watch them consoling the rat and castigating DJ for imitating their behavior, they have a particular disdain for him that lilts itself between their sharp curses and plants itself inside their words, one that says he's an unbeliever in a way that's impossible to explain, just like the bond between them and their rodentia brethren despite the disease oozing from their dry, matted fur.

It's in this spirit we ride the donger pony from the room, their glares trailing us and the liberal kids not giving too much of a shit so long as they aren't involved in the confrontation. I've been receiving their sunlight in their geocentric guinea pig universe, and I can't help but feel, by the skin of my neck, like we're burning.

8===== =DHORSE: DMOONFACE: EGGPLANT: ANGRYGUN: WHITEPEOPL E======D

WALKING THROUGH THE LAND KNOWN AS THE AMERICAN WILDS, with the donger pony having successfully matriculated into the stallion on which we ride, its retractable appendage avoiding the shittily painted double yellow lines of the back country highway outside the walled fortress of Pensecola now fully open in the true Florida Badlands, I'm half expecting the fresh scent of blood permeating both holes in DJ's tongue plus painting the sides of his cheeks to attract a gang of roaming Jeep or Chevy *brothers* faster than a prey bird to the fresh, heavy scent of carrion cracked open on the sides of these pothole conveyors. We've passed three different stop signs with faces punctured into them by carbines, as well as at least two of those high-speeding, confederate flag waving trucks we saw parked down in the unholy sands of New Smyrna that have had their own rubber and plastic nutsacks proudly painted the colors of that New American flag, as though they've not masturbated for 13 years and been shoved in an icebox. Well, the kids driving those, what with their rocket launchers and sniper rifles, handheld howitzers and tungsten utensils, they actually fired a few friendly greeting shots up in the air, the opposite of warning shots since their trucker triggers are pulled by nothing but LOVE, baby. Ditto for the fucking life-sized replica of the guinea pigs eating the shit out of the actual president, sculpted in clay, in the back of the trailer they're pulling behind their loser-flag decals and small balls stuck between their driveshafts. Fuck *me*, by the time the smell of barbecue hits my lips and causes the pony to neigh in blissful, nose-twitching delight, DJ's tried to say something while also trying to use a mask to staunch the bleeding from where the rat gave him a piercing that would be considered a holy mark to some chem trail people.

"The hell is this?" I ask DJ, the saddlebags underneath me stocked to the brim with our own ammunition in case we need it. "Are those people wearing *yellow stars*?"

"Mhm," DJ says, tongue out of his mouth, duct tape ripping in a jagged line as he pulls it.

I look around. If my research on this has been correct, those yellow stars signify that some of those palms could actually be secret Nazi outposts. Is that *barbecue* I'm smelling, or-

"Have they started putting people in pens yet?"

"No," DJ manages, a little sluggishly. "Just kids in cages. And not the kind you're thinking about."

"So…" I ask. Even from here, the trucker cap wearing and monster drinking and bath salt snorting white walruses around that fucking firepit have their oversized, bloated chests pinned with labels so starry and bright you'd half expect to find them on a gigantic American flag. "Why the fuck are they wearing them?"

"They don't want the vaccine."

I grab the reins around the donger pony's neck and cause him to whinny while he scrapes his hooves across the asphalt to a grinding halt.

"*Excuse* me?" I ask him. Thinking it's something with the bite holes, he puts his smarting, duct-taped tongue back into his mouth and manages to say, clearly, *it's because the* Dems *are communistic and fascistic and totalitarian.*

"DJ," I say, allowing the pony to trot a bit again on its own towards the smells coming off that grill and the blaring cross-state Militia Games happening in the background on their televisions large enough to give the Terminator a malfunction. "I unfortunately have to tell you I'm becoming more American."

"How's that unfortunate?" DJ asks, taking another huge rip of a joint to try and staunch the pulsing mouth pain.

"Well," I tell him, having made eye contact with the Jabba of the group, who is wearing a confederate flag t-shirt with a massive picture of a guinea pig holding an m-80 and a field of wild donkeys running in the opposite direction on it while the guinea pig's mouth screams up into a godless sky in carnal, tameless bloodlust. "Let's just say these 'human beings' have me feeling as though our research department couldn't prepare us for their kind."

"How's that?"

"They're … *unprecedented*." We're in range of the wal-rus-Hulk Hogan hybrid shimmering like a manatee-sized micro-wave, his nipples blaring proudly through his t-shirt. Behind him, his wife has completely colonized the leather armchair she's sitting in with more waves of fat than the ocean washing up a McDicks cruise liner. And their offspring are basically the equivalent of baby pandas at the zoo if they were bald and fat and playing with real guns in the dirt near the bonfire. From here, I can see the television in the background playing the kid's programming to their little watching eyes and listening ears: a bunch of pillows with dead, googly eyes are dancing cancan and macarena around a golden idol that looks like they dude they call orange Jesus, with the body of a voting machine burning in the center and some demented Hannah Montana-minstrel singing going on that would make me unable to sleep again if I were a citizen of this planet, but instead the kids are laughing and play-ing in joy at blowing up the miniature, Rubbermaid 'Indians' they're slamming with F-16s and Shermans and baby nukes. It's nearly Christmastime, and what better way to engage the holiday season in a place where it never snows than by nuking the den to get a laugh or two? The biggest daddy of them all has success-fully ascended to his decked-out motor scooter, which includes cup holders and a massage chair and a fleshlight and *everything else a working man needs while he's on the move,* and he uses its four wheel, ATV style treads to barrel over the ground and stand in front of our pony, his ass leaking dark smoke and with eyes that compare a life saving needle to suffocation in a fucking gas chamber. *Thank god my full mask is covering my face, he can't see me ready to hiss at him and turn him into pina collateral.*

"Well, howdy there, fellas," he says, speaking like Wilford Brimley after putting his nose in the gas tank because he likes the way it spins his wheels. "Where are y'all headed?" He squints his meaty eyelids. "Say, ain't you the kid who blew a hole in that one pussy kid's brain as he tried to shoot our congressman?"

"That's me!" I say. Growling from her recliner on the floor, which is massaging her and causing her to ripple like one massive cholesterol topographical shitfucking, her voice wobbles back to us, "Hiiii-iii-iiiitler w-w-would be p-proud of M-Moe Wyden!"

"HUH *HUH!*" Her husband says, slapping his gooch with a hearty chuckle. "She even *sounds* like 'em, don't she?" He moves the joystick he uses to drive the apparatus and tilts himself more towards DJ, who has been hiding behind my back as much as possible and keeping THE WISE OWL right in front of his vision.

"Hey there, pussy kid," the dude says. "How's it feel to have a mommy who's both into Downy *and* has one for a son?"

"Oh my *gooosh!*," The wife says, snapping off the vibrating chair and raising herself into an upright position so fast with the lever that the motion leaves her sucking air. "Remmy, get the kids away, they might catch the *gay* from that there beta boy!"

"*Remmy?*" I repeat, the Wise Owl now deciding the blood's worth it to eye-roll on.

"Yeah!" The man says. "Short for *Remington!*" As the FLAK cannon Roomba escorts the children further into the woods and away from our frackas like biped hoglets, their father points at each of them and says, "The little boy's Mar, and the other one's a'Lago."

"How nice!" I say to DJ. "They named their firstborn son after the ocean. In *Spanish!*"

"Sorta," DJ says. "These are the *real* Floridians."

"You're goddamn right!" The woman says, rolling across the uneven ground to me, her BAETZ'S BITCHES BANGERS onesie stained with what has to be crude tobacco and methpipe ash plus what might be actual everclear stains from the smell of them right next to her Star of David. Now that I'm close enough to her, I can see what she's inscribed in the center of hers, customized *exactly* like the way they were able to under the Germans:

I HAVE VAC-SEEN THE TRUTH
MOE WYDEN = HE WHOTH PERSACUTE

I compare this to what I can now see is also stitched into her husband's clothes, as she sewed them herself:

YESTERDAY'S PATS
MOE WYDEN'S JAPS

Yes. Of *course*. The people shouting CHINESE VIRUS and call people "c***ks' and whose family members sock Asian grandmothers in the streets of New York City are the people who are going to be slaughtered because they won't take vaccines. It's true. Except, instead of it being done by the people who claim to lead this demented species, its going to be done by the fact the richest and most powerful nation, the nation for which we are here to harvest their wonderful drugs and fear its terrible people, is about to be completely fucking own-ed by a germ which they have the means to defeat but which their people won't even take. It's at this moment, drawing this analogy, that I finally understand how to communicate in the language of this *republitarded* talking cum colored blubber monkey:

"Dear shotgun," I say to him, tipping my fucking jester cap like I'm having a life crisis in the center of a feudal court. "Have you ever considered *both sides* of this here argument?"

"Both sides of what?" He asks. His wife's, uhm, 'glided' over

216

to us in her fucking ion cannon of a mobile armchair and has shut the fuck up about Chinese communist fascist university professors and ivory towers enough to listen to my logic.

"The virus," I tell him. "We're being unamerican if we don't."

The dude's fucking chair lifts itself off the ground with the strength of Atlas shrugging to elevate him past the gorgeous, muscular shoulders of the donger pony and hold him face to face with me. I can smell the freedom and the liquid cancer through the sticky-hot breeze.

"Listen here, you little masked *fuck*," he says to me, spittle bouncing off the stitched patterns of fire and chaos hiding my simple smile from his bloodshot eyes. "I get that you're an American hero and all that, but if you don't explain what you're talking about, I'm going to think you're telling me there's two sides to both pizza and pedophiles." He clicks a button on his chair. Out of the considerably thick back of it, there's a whir and squeak and then an actual glock pistol finds itself in the dude's hands. It's painted in the colors of the Florida gator football team! "If a liberal thinks they can just wander onto *my* property, I don't care how thick you build your walls, friend, that's fucking *treason*!"

"I'm on my way to court after I take him to the hospital."

"The *hospital*?" The woman says, as if I've just taken Jesus's name and worn it out. "You must be fuckin' plum *crazy* to go down there with that horse!"

I can feel the donger pony tightening. I don't want to have to tell you what it does when it engages full DEFENSE MODE, but it would be worse than genocide and having to hear a fucking song about it. Thankfully, though, I'm able to cut the wires around them like an adult taking the nuclear football from someone trying to throw a bomb pass with it on the playground outside the neo-Stasi rose garden.

"No no, fellow patriot," I tell him. "I'm saying we have to take *both sides*."

"Both sides of *what*, buddy?" The guy asks me, like his shepherd puppy just called him a pancake.

"The country and the virus."

"Hold on, Remmy," the wife says. Her chair lifts her into the sky as though she's a modern day empress being carried to her fried grape feeding session. "This sounds pretty smart. Remember when I told you about the remedy of the printer cleaner stuff as the COVID vaccine?"

:full:moon:with:face

"Yeah!" She says, slapping her husband's arm. This is the most contact they've had in three years, so it causes him to almost cream his jeans right in front of us. "I told Remmy here that you had to follow the logic: it blows dust out of printers, and it blows the bad air that holds the covid back out of your lungs!"

"If you fucking touch me, I'm suing." DJ says.

"Woah woah," I say, holding up a hand, blocking DJ's face from the barrel of the guy's gun. "Allow me to continue, gentleman and lady. I'm simply saying you must consider that the virus has a right to life as well. It's the same size as cells that are joining post conception, and in this particular circumstance we're talking survival of the fittest."

"Alright," the dude says, still sounding skeptical but lowering the gun a tad. "Go on."

"Consider the fact that most of the people overloading the hospitals are unvaccinated patients."

"Exactly," Remmy says. "They're people who were smart enough to not get the vaccine, 'cause fighting COVID's easier than gettin' *chimeras* out your bloodstream."

"*What?*" The Owl screams, its eyes pure white and hot as George Foreman charcoal. "What the mother *fuck* are you talking about!"

"Fuck off, Duel-Lingo!" The woman screams at him. "I would rather die of owl flu than listen to your bullshit!"

"A chimera?" I ask, tilting my head like a confused puppy. "I thought they were hydras?"

"Depends on the type of vax," the man says, taking on the most teacherly tone he'll use in his entire earthly existence. "Some are trojan virus horses, others are all types of Greek, pagan creatures that infiltrate your blood the same way their false idols in-fil-tra-ted ancient democracies, and some are even little Moe Wyden androids that track your movements so they can know when you fuck, shit, piss, and spit!"

His wife hocks a loogie right at him to scold him for his foul language, and that's when we hear the siren coming down the block. It looks like there's an ambulance heading right through woods protected like an ancient caravan from raiders who would hide in the tropical canopies along the road. Before we know it, we've attracted these two people and have formed a type of motorcade of our own, passing through the whooped shouts and echoed hollers of the people racing in their jeeps around the open fields, squealing their rubbers in the baha humidity with the ferocity of a flag-bearing chariot.

We get to the hospital parking lot like we're approaching a motherfucking wrestling ring merged with a monster truck derby, with all the cars encircled around a throng of maskless fucking people who are ready to wrestle to the death with what-ever nurse is facing them with the news their family has died. Now I can see what the walrus was talking about when he told us to walk between these flashing sirens and the ones that don't howl anymore because there's no need for it and nothing else to do: I've brought a motherfucking horse to a place where these people are so obsessed with Ivermectin they're suplexing and duplexing and piledriving health care professionals in the parking lot. This one super-fast collared shirt nerd type with white new balances is boxing the shit out of an Oncologist like he's an alpha joey about to brainfuck a colonial motherfucker for the indigenous residents of the outback. The other guy is literally wielding the equivalent of a lightsaber and is dueling with a nurse who has stacked so many of their unvaccinated bodies the bags under her eyes look like bruises in the daytime light. Meanwhile, there's a group of the same people who are wearing the same warped stars of David who are literally trying to set the hospital on fire, barely being restrained by riot police who are being called the army of the antichrist by people who believe tiny robots are swimming through the veins of people who get shit plugged into their arms. The lights from their torches and the smell of gunpowder popping into the air thanks to the fact gun carrying is now explicitly encouraged by the 68th amendment to the McFuck constitution means that these armed, feral apes are able to clog my lungs while the furnaces burning next to the hospital's industrial brick are literally just churning dead bodies down their large-ass conveyor belts directly into the fire, all protected by a massive metal tube that makes the plumage from the gargantuan concrete furnaces look like a hospital Chernobyl. That's how radioactive the air feels when you're walking among these animals trying to harm the only people this repulsive, shitfuck society has dumped its dumb and dumber dead upon. And now those same people who are sitting here and ready to accuse us and them and everyone of working for the communist Chinese with their very dying breaths are ready to try and suck the donger pony's juices since they believe the 'horse' in 'horse dewormer' means they need to get the dewormer *from* the horse. We're back in the motherfucking comment section, and these ghouls have brought their big weapons out in order to ensure the protest is getting national attention: they're destroying no property, but can we really allow this much attention to be diverted from the economy in the state? Aren't there an infinite amount of grandparents to sacrifice? Those are the kinds of things they're shouting at me as I try to explain to them the substance does *not* come from worms you find inside certain horses with long extremities and appendages. Holy mother of fuck. They legitimately want to take the donger pony and turn him into some kind of liquid glue that their triple-inbred children are going to try and snort off their parents' home school, kitchen table desks at some point in the next thirteen years before they ask the family doctor to get 'em started on the pills-

FUCKING JESUS CHRIST GET YOUR FUCKING DISGUSTING MOUNTAIN DEW AND DORITO CRUSTED FINGERS OFF OF ME YOU FUCKING EVOLUTIONARY ERRORS – I 've noticed that this particular breed of 'person,' who loves to throw out words that strip people all the way down to a point below humanity, really have no issues lobbying those same curses at the professionals they're duking it out with. I've managed to grab DJ and hoist him on top of the donger pony as we navigate the swarms, almost like we're surfing through a volcano of radiation on a surfboard made from a bunker door from a school shooter in a chemistry classroom. I can literally see a person who looks like they belong in an advertisement for a trailer park calling her obviously ridiculously educated Black female surgeon words that are better left in the hot wind and the smell of burning, but before we can attempt to administer any kind of punitive justice through our curses or hooves or extra miles, we reach the line towards the emergency room snaking out the door, around the corner, and going around the back of the building in the opposite direction. There are people in wheelchairs and people holding walkers, people propped up by crutches and hanging on the shoulders of loved ones that feel right now like they were invented just for that sole purpose, there are people whose appendixes are engorged and enraged, there's people whose bones are bent and broken and shattered, knocked loose from their connections like jagged glass rent loose under the skin; and then there are the ones whose chest caverns now better resemble the texture of an underwater cave of some kind, where the four winds loan their time and energy to propel into their logged tissues the gift of life one more time, one more time, at some liminal, misunderstood rhythm that dances at the same rate the ambulance's top light spins in the misty afternoon in the glare of red that means blood. Blood is coming. That's the idea that I get as we're greeted by a man who looks like he and his coat and his stethoscope and his face's years of resistance to these kinds of absurdities has been shaken so fully, he's wearing ripped scrub bottoms and smells like St. Augustine bourbon so loudly the pony actually whinnies when the scent reaches his nostrils.

"What's wrong with you?" He asks us, sighing, shuffling through papers with more names on them than Peter's list at judgment day for the fuckers who helped cause this shit.

"A rat bit my friend's tongue and now it won't stop bleeding."

"Ah great," the doctor says, his hiccup tugging his adam's apple like a bobber caught to the top of a gator in the swamplands. "Whelp, we have 96 hours of people waiting ahead of him. Can I get you any morphine to hold you over?"

"Morphine?" I ask, incredulous, noting the doctor's lids

haven't blinked in the three minutes I've seen his bloodshot, dead-set eyes. "Are you just handing that shit out so easily?"

"Good joke," he says. He hands us a clock that's been running for exactly the time we've been in here: 3 minutes 13 seconds and counting. Meanwhile, there's a shadow starting to form over DJ's head, almost as though a vertically columned cloud has blocked out the bit of sunlight reaching us down in this twisted hell – each second we stand here, the sense of weight on DJ's head and the thickness of the shadow grows.

"Your hospital bill is based on how long you're in the ER." He draws a circle on the waiting area with his DICKSON COUNTY HEALTH SYSTEM pen. "*This* is now the ER."

"How is this the ER?" DJ asks, having replaced the peeling duct tape on his tongue.

"The actual ER is filled with overflowing COVID patients," The surgeon says. "Right now, we're so short-staffed that I'm working both as the surgeon and also as the receptionist. I should really be getting back to the emergency room considering the fact I'm supposed to be delivering a child via cesarian section after clearing *this* backlog a little bit." He hands us a clipboard with a bill for $103,000 dollars based on the automatic estimate for repairing DJ's tongue and giving him a bunch of poisons for which the hospital is currently getting sued as being discriminatory against the rats solely based on who they are *as fellow American citizens who believe in rodents with all their hearts.* I share a look with DJ across the clipboard – he's lucky he's a state congressman's kid, they might waive the fee for the doctor having to leave the other surgery and make him help carry the obscene amount of bodies out of the disinfected, hallowed hallways.

"So I guess this is it?" DJ says, taking the pen in his hand, the weight on his head and the shadows under his eyes both darkening. "This is where you leave me?"

"Leave you?" I ask, tilting my head along with the Owl's and Pony's in synchronicity that makes even the zombie Doctor blink. He's strapping on his boxing gloves to go and tell another family their uncle's not coming back home just in case the wife tells him he's the murderer for not turning the Donger Pony's living ass into a miracle she found on an internet forum somewhere.

"You have to go to the trial," he says, folding his arms after signing. "My dad and mom both aren't going, and you're his true star witness."

"I can leave the pony or the owl here with you," I tell him, sounding more invested than even I could've predicted.

"Nah," he says, finishing the last form, clicking the pen, and handing the clipboard back to the doctor. He's procured a COVID-test from his pocket and is getting ready to place the test up DJ's nostrils when we hear the violent churning of wheels and the sense of gravity in a mile radius around us shifting rapidly with their approach. The anti-vax brigade on their motorized Doorstore scooters has shown up like they're the cavalry for the Facebook comments.

At the sight of the Doctor putting the test in DJ's nose, someone shouts, "THEY'RE GIVING HIM THE VIRUS, RIGHT UP HIS NOSE CANAL!"

It's at that point the doors to the hospital open again, and, blaring an EDM remix of HAIL TO THE CHIEF to start their entrance, we see a squadron of *happy, fulfilled* working professionals pirouette their way out of the working mausoleum halls and into the bedlam of the parking lot ...

TWENTY-FOUR

In the middle of a season of completely unadulterated, violently mundane, actual fucking death – where you can hear the last gasps from patients' whose final acts were just another function of the ventilator cart they're now pushing down the hallway to the next waterlogged lung set – they have the nurses, wearing scrubs bluer than smurfs to represent the Moe Wyden victory flag, with tan skin and darker skin and lighter skin and even some more fit for the outside or inside of a Clorox bottle than the maskless, howling, self-persecuted yellow polygon people treating their arrival like a hostile, hungry crowd. The surgeons under the awning sawing off limbs with woodshop tools, sucking the blood out of snakebites with bare faces, and one holding a bucket with a smiling leech on it while planting three suckers on the balls of a dude who won't stop screaming that the vaccine made his penis into a chode, all pause their miraculous work to behold the spectacle of *joyous employment*. These nurses are *ready* for this shit, too: they smile broad and spotless across chapped lips, holding pom poms that are Democrat colors in their hands, some of their braless chests strapped tight with the cheerleader tops they've managed to match the scrub pants where they meet at the waist. Their midriffs might as well be biohazards, to say nothing of the strange fuckers seated in their moving pavement rovers with half chubs from seeing too many naughty movies where this sort of shit gets scripted. Instead, absolutely no director of any news conglomerate nor pornography studio could have prepared anyone for the lead nurse, the Billie Eilish of radiology, to come stomping over here in her squeaky Nikes like victory's the sound of a sole scraping rain soaked pavement, twist her shower cap backwards over her head, adjust the mask she's worn so long it looks like the tattoo of a facemask over her cheeks when she lifts it up, and say, with the dead monotone that sounds like a pop star in a compassionate conservatorship, "We are *so happy* to see you today!"

The beat that comes blasting from the boombox held by a male nurse dressed in a democratic donkey costume over his hairy chest is a horrendous, Frankenstein IVF bastard child of "All I Want for Christmas is You" by Mariah Carey and the same bullshit country bop that's got every down home listener from here to the Georgia line shouting the n-word after kicking back some brews and getting pumped to fuck their sister. Yes, even if she's a nurse who looks like she just stepped out of the meat locker in Dresden who is now singing words praising the people who hanged the *Dickson General Health System* sign in neon flashing bulbs to rival Hollywood by concrete:

Well hello, future corpses, how do you be?
I am so glad to see you standing here, breathing on me!
Fifteen patients just died from this fucking disease,
And now with you here, maskless, my day is complete!

One of the grandaddy golf-carters bearing signs from an election that happened a long time ago turns to his stroke partner and says, "Man, give her three minutes and she'll have *me* stiff!"

His polo shirted friend who got rich as fuck destroying nature with toxic oils tips back his head and old white guy lols to the rhythm of the lead nurse coming back around with more greetings. "I'll give *her* six feet!"

He strokes his rod whose head is shaped like a metal penis and makes me want to snap it over his OLD WELL PLANTATION cap. Before I can, though, the urban nurse is back, and she's got one of those things humans used to use to stoke fireplaces in her hands, already full of air and ready to breathe.

Would you like a bellow shoved in your windpipe?
Can you tell me more about the rat poison from last night,
You tried to kill the virus by downloading MacAfee
On your pacemakers, but you still aren't happy.
You should be shooting rifles, not Clorox bleach,
It's kinda hard to hear you clearly when you speak
With a tube down your throat, but I'm happy to say:
On behalf of the hospital management …
We made a total fucking killing today!

The nurses tip toe and gently gallop and electric slide their way over to her, smiling under threat of firing, the faceless camera leading straight to the Corporate Management Office twinkling at their backs from its rotating position on the ceiling. Synchronized better than some Janet Jackson level dancers, they swing their arms onto their hips in semicircles and then pump a fist in the air to the Med School Musical, rocky pop beat:

Money gives us life, our fortunes are on the rise,
We can't say how we feel, but we're still alright.
Death is expensive, ain't nobody got time for losses,
We might be broken but we've got smiling bosses!

The fucking people in the crowd are clapping along. Even DJ's got his knees pressed into the donger pony's noble sides and is bobbing his bleeding mouth so close to the back of my shirt I can actually feel the droplets hit the nape of my neck. The Owl and I feel as though we are suddenly adrift, but a male nurse who looks like Latinx Channing Tatum if he dropped out of both acting and math nerd school has now taken center stage next to the patient who is getting leeched (to say nothing of the guy with half his blood now in the squirm bucket). He sings over some muted beepings from the machines the nurses behind him are hitting in rhythm, as though he's Snow Patrol meets the oncology department:

Hello, welcome to Doorstore, would you like some health insurance with your snacks?

It's a pretty decent time to buy. These deals are never coming back.

Hey, there's no need to fight! We'll pay for almost HALF that three hundred dollar test,

And do me a favor, on your way out the door, could you send me whoever's next?

That'll be 30k for entering the tunnel, and leaving makes you one of the million

Dollars your next of kin needs to find if they want to bury you before the time

Your skin gets eaten by the early worms and the birds come to pluck your bones,

If you wanted to save a few extra dollars, well, why the fuck didn't you die at home?

"DEBT IS THE MOST DANGEROUS THING IN THE UNITED STATES OF AMERICA!" Screams a guy hooked up to more tubes coming out of his nose than there are tentacles on the underage octopi the dirty fuck beat off to back when he could suck his own air. Luckily – or unluckily? – a couple nurses from the troupe are able to save the hero who was about to eliminate the greatest danger to the American public right now by ripping out his cords, wrapping them around his throat, and cannonballing him to the paved cement underneath him rather than saddle his family with more bills than *three whole semesters* of private college tuition. Without breaking a beat, they all coalesce back into their line for the most dramatic segment of them all: an older nurse, a Black woman, taking the mic and suddenly morphing into Janelle Monae if she stepped outside the computer and aged like twenty years:

Listen, I know why you might not like the vax.
I've been the rhythm to reverse ten heart attacks.
But I can't defibrillate what we can't debate,
Can't keep talking to the walls if they don't talk back, now
I've been called a murderer, devil mistress
By grandparents whose grandkids they can't even kiss,
Miss me with the sympathy, the pity, and the saving
I've been forgiving all the people who see misbehaving
As simple as dying like civilians in war,
I come back and find I've been here before,
We're running short of air and I'm running short of will
But you know how much we need every single dollar bill …

At this point, she reaches into her scrub, pulls out her hand from her front pouch with a wad of hundreds in it, and, as the music climbs to a staggering height of beeps and boops and whirs and crashes, snaps the rubberbands off them and tosses them onto the wet pavement. There, the preternatural fury of finding free money in America overtakes the nurses, the walruses, even DJ *and* the guy running the mobile Soundsystem hunkered over in the background. On their knees, the nurses scrape across the parking lot with their fingernails sharpened, their teeth baring, and the fury of a black Friday crowd who wasn't allowed to shop for two years properly due to being told to stay home over the coins that are now being thrown into their midst, clinking off the pavement as though reaching the bottom of a dry, barren well.

Once the ER tech with the company sponsored flamethrower shows up, and after a couple pumps of the fire on loan from the crematorium merrily turning bodies into ash in the background for people who will never know what truly hit them, the lead nurse manages to get back to her position as fireworks start popping off from the top of the awning and Democratic party banners unfurl themselves from the windows through which you can see unmoving people, in slightly reclined beds, breathing in their robotic paced, plastic-covered tombs. She sings, over a pumped up version of the four on the floor chorus:

We owe our debt to America for keeping us free,
We're all making shit money and living the dream:
No vacations, no abortions, no maternity leave-
We are the privileged ones, and we feel so lucky.
So keep on shouting, keep on raising your voice,
One of our best achievements versus personal choice?
Really, there's no question other than what will it be:
Hydroxychloroquine, or just somebody's pee?

"*UNLEASH THE PISS MONSTER!*" The OG surgeon who was down here ready to treat DJ with liquid cement yells. Collectively, after withstanding the force of nearly three days straight of not being able to take breaks and pumped up by cocaine, adrenaline, pure rage, and the necessity of feeding their children in the richest country on earth solely by blistering their soles and souls almighty, floodgates of which my species had no prior knowledge burst in a mighty golden river from the water cannons hiding behind the Democratic banners, creating a hydraulic forcefield that provides enough cover to whisk the Donger Pony away from the dewormer obsessed crowd now screaming at the same treatment they used to cure the plague – except, instead of drinking their piss to see if they're infected, the medical professionals are simply trying to cure them by giving piss to replace the infected piss inside them, the same way they believe fucking BLEACH IN THEIR VEINS WOULD KILL THE VIRUS.

"Ka-ching," The Wise Owl says, smiling through the tears of blood around his beak and matted neck feathers. "The virus can't live if you just fucking *die!*"

On this apex of spectacular logic, we left DJ in the care of the attending physicians who will bankrupt his future to save him now. By the next time we see him, there'll be thousands more dead, and people still filling up the empty space with isolated laughter that echoes through these humid waves …

TWENTY-FIVE

"Well, dear friends?" I say to THE WISE OWL and THE DONGER PONE, with the latter having reverted to his statue-esque state so as to please the court of Justice Beauregard Britt. "I dare say we're landing." This time, the ride in Senator Baetz's private jet only took about thirty minutes once we told him where to find us amidst the carnage. The pilot had a little trouble navigating the thickness of the smoke from having, like, 3000 fucking bodies dumped into incinerators, but luckily he was able to find us sonically with how loud they blared the music and everyone danced together saying they were *so glad* the pandemic was over.

THE WISE OWL:
Oh Daft One, I sense your tone's a bit down,
Are you sure you still need to be here on the ground?
We've accomplished our mission, we're known in the land,
Where everyone talks and nobody understands!

For once, the bird speaks the truth: following hours upon hours of consultation paid for by the Senator's own stocks in firearms (and some campaign funds that weren't being used to make aquariums filled with matchstick plantations that rained cotton where white people gawk at the architecture), we've been told we have the chance to be the *star witness*. From my rudimentary comprehension of this country's legal system, here's what they told me we should do: first, we're going to go up there and talk about our feelings and how traumatized we were that Senator Baetz was so *unfortunately forced* to use his Senatorial firearm on the state animal. Second, under cross examination – which we incorrectly assumed involved us getting nailed to the one in the Dickson HS library at the next school board meeting – we're supposed to own the guy who is talking to us the same way they do on AutoAdmit. Luckily for us, our top-tier scouting department allowed me to examine the glorious work of one of the best television news writers this side of the Daily Stormer. I won't name any names, seeing as having to envision a man as fallacy-fucker69 makes me picture a fat, bearded nerd crossing off tally marks on his shitty bachelor's degree where he contrarianated his way to being captain of the debate team solely to call himself a master debater, which means (literally) enjamming the allotted time to speak in the competition by spewing a barrage of fucking useless words and arguments and informatory SKUD missiles rather than claiming realness in anything. But yeah, basically we're at the point where I can no longer identify if we're on the internet, in the real world, or if, as Senator Baetz tells us as we touch down on the tangerine tarmac, we're going to have to participate in NEW ANTI-COVID MEASURES in order to enter the courthouse.

"We're going to need a vaccine? Wear a mask? Don't cough into each other's mouths while making love?"

"Not exactly," Senator Baetz says, dressed in a navy suit and white shirt and wearing a campaign badge for the 2024 election featuring him standing in front of a family terrified by a snarling gator cartoon. "And be careful with the owl. Judge Britt can't stand looking stupid."

They made us drink colloidal silver to enter the courtroom. Luckily, I was able to hide it in a part of my mouth humans don't have, basically a compartment underneath my tongue, and then go to the bathroom and hock that shit straight into the sink. THE WISE OWL isn't so lucky, however: in the lights of the bathroom mirror blinking like Jigsaw's basement in the most prestigious institution of the United States, right before my very eyes, the motherfucker's feathers have gone from foresty green to a hue so sickeningly traumatic and indicative of this 'country's' discourse that he falls straight off my shoulder and slaps into the piss, shit, and vomit stickied floor tiles, the pooled blood from behind his eyeballs now sinking into the calked cracks between them.

"Fuck fucking fuckshit," I say, dropping to the ground, ready to perform the life saving procedure of slamming a needle into his heart to reverse the drugs. I grab the Pony by his conical cranium and place him directly over the owl so that he may shield his twitching, pulsing, bluing body from the accursed fluorescent lights' unholy pounding on my temples. I get my iPhone out and prepare to call star command that we might have accidentally triggered a war with these people, but before my phone can ring through the abysmal, signal-meltingly hot atmosphere these dumb apes have created, the Owl opens its eyes anew to reveal they're more frozen and white than ice.

"Owlish?" I ask, craning my own sweating neck underneath the donger pone's stomach.

"Lol," the Owl says, expressionless, to me.

"... Excuse me?" I ask again.

"LOOOOL," The Owl says, as naturally as calling out at nighttime. "I CAN NO LONGER RHYME!"

"Oh my fucking god," I howl, grabbing at my own hair. "They turned him fucking CHIRP-DUMB!"

"LMAOOOOO" The Owl says, hopping up off the floor

and bending over with a laugh that makes its ass distend and plop to the floor underneath a brush of feathers, before retracting back up so hard it forces him to flap his wings and clap himself right onto the Donger Pony's subliminal saddle. The bathroom door bursts open and Senator Baetz – obviously representing himself due to his extensive legal background prior to entering politics – rushes inside, his elephant skinned shotgun at the ready and his Calhoun doo waving in the wind of the hand dryers so lusciously I'm expecting it to crackle in the bathroom's dead heat.

"What in the name of John Birch is going on in here?" He asks, checking the mirrors and even inspecting his own reflection as though it's an enemy combatant. He looks at the Owl, who is staring up at him with its orange beak cocked open.

"Why are you still wearing a mask?" He asks me. I've expanded the material of my surgical mask to cover my entire face, so as to dodge facial recognition by the deep state *and* to protect my identity as a minor even though everyone already knows who I am. The laws in this country are strange, but what's stranger is the Owl flapping its way right onto the barrel of the sawed off chrome shotty the Senator has and going, "LOL JIM BAETZ GETS MORE BITCHES THAN DOG SHELTERS AFTER NEW YEARS!"

Outside, in the revered courthouse halls, amidst the witnesses awaiting entry to history in Baetz vs State of Florida, which will undoubtedly be called one of the most important cases in the precedent of property destruction based on impact and intent, the BAETZ BITCHES have all shown up wearing cheerleading outfits mixed with funeral garb: we're talking the ancient white people mourning kind of dresses that stretch down to their ankles. They're like if the women who supported Charles

Manson met up with some groupies, and they're crying and wailing and weeping and snorting and snarling and using handkerchiefs to blot both their wet pussies and puffy eyelids over seeing their Hairspray Hercules survive his trials as a member of the "most oppressed and persecuted groups of people in the history: white men from elite universities who are in the same fraternity as the *judge*!"

The Senator shakes the owl off the barrel of his shotgun, but instead of coming back to his usual place on my right shoulder, he's on the left, now, which is more indicative of the fact they've got like thirty minutes before the silver they had us bottle shoot together to defend us against COVID turns them all into Democrats and they start shooting *each other*. Just kidding: they wouldn't turn their skin black or brown or anything other than white. However, the Owl gets crowded as soon as we exit into the maskless, packed, zero vax'd hallway; we lock eyes with the prosecutor who is going to do battle with us, only to find the same fucking bald eagle head atop a Brooks Brothers three piece's shoulders; he's not the cop from DJ Daddy's life-defining sexcapade, but more the kind we fought against in the retweet section back in DC. The Dumb Owl sends a series of laughing and crying and xD emojis in his direction, hacking towards him and going LOOOOL LOOOL BIOLOGICAL WARFARE IN COSTCO BECAUSE FUCK THE LIBS, which causes everyone to happily laugh along and for the eagle-masked attorney to hiss at us as though he's diving for the jugulars of the guinea pig kids behind us. They've managed to wrangle all their asses down to hot as fuck, begotten Florida solely to determine whether or not the Senator *meant* to shoot Abby the alligator while avenging the death of one of his beloved guinea pigs, who are also wearing their own suits and dresses, overalls and plaids, comfortably watching from the woodchipped, fresh cages the Baetz Brigade were allowed to bring inside. And of course, the flight attendants, already bruised and battered and bloodied from the course of duty served in the skies, have come with Abby the Alligator's family and talking to the Pastor in the Guinea Pig mask who will be performing the opening benediction for today's day of judgement –

Right after we are ordered into the courtroom by the bailiff. Apparently, Justice Britt has some pre-trial things he wants to go over with us ...

420xxxxSNIPerhashtag42069:

When we enter the judicial chamber, where the scales of justice hang from the ceiling beneath a literal hammer made for Thor if he were a transformer-sized dildo-shape-shifting metallic motherfucker – that thing could be a wrecking ball for the entirety of the lectern flanked by the witness stands, the industrial lights lining the walls behind him better fit for the inside of the newly christened, multi-use stadium that used to be the home of the local football squad before it got renamed Let's Go Ryland Event Center and Arena Bank by Governor Mercantis. Seriously. This looks like some Mad Max meets Perry Mason bullshit, with the floodlights and the steam machines and the fact the man's name, CHIEF JUSTICE BRITT D. BOUREAGUARD, has been emblazoned in gold right in huge, bold letters. It's planted above and is also thicker than the seal of the state of Florida underneath it. And the man himself greets us right as we pass through the doors and into the fucking cocktail party college pregame these motherfuckers have organized, where everyone's maskless and laughing and on the same sorts of drugs that make Senator Baetz's guiltless, glinting eyes smile with a cheeriness only rivaled by the clink of the FUCK MOE WYDEN inscribed champagne glasses echoing underneath the classic German soundtrack. Mozart, I think his name is, and he's not the only pale skinned papi ready to make my donger pony rock with his suave charm and Hugh Hefner erection: nope, that would be the man of the hour himself, the star of the trial who somehow twinkles brighter in this here state than the Senator reflecting his light off my moon face in Washington: Chief Justice Britt, dressed like an American James Bond if he were Christopher Plummer in his 70s. But instead of wearing a suit that would be sharp enough to hack a razor through the endless credit card of every either perfect-jawed or lard-bellied Limbomber dumbfuck in this room, all of whom have taken their colloidal silver prior to laughing and coughing and spitting and licking and chewing and drinking and farting and soon to be vomiting and shitting, I'm sure, well, the judge is dressed in robes that are white and red exactly like the dress of that one congresswoman who understands the rage of crossteam chat wore when she was calling out the rich. Except, instead of a shitty remix of that, Justice Britt's got *his* outfitted with chocolate and caramel and vanilla-furred guinea pigs wearing sunglasses and smoking joints, with the redrum script saying *WE ARE NOT YOUR GUINEA PIGS* on it like open scars.

"Don't worry," Justice Britt says, clapping the defendant on the back with three hearty slaps and handing him a small, diamond blow case shaped like a glass-blown dick. "I'll be *totally* objective in front of the cameras." He winks up at the incredible apparatus of cords and lenses

hanging like one of those machines you see them think of whenever they imagine alien control, who come from different stars and who have different types of gods. However, I'll say in all my travels, I have never nearly attempted to kill myself by jumping into the ridiculous hammer hanging ready to smash in the name of justice from the ceiling than when these motherfuckers turned to each other, reached out a hand, and stood ready to slap their palms together while a group of attorneys – with this pregame the envy of every lawyer in conservative America and consisting of names from across the high-tier legal spectrum – gather around and chant the lyrics of whatever fraternity breeds some of the most brilliant legal minds of the next three successive generations, those who defend liberty and freedom and personal choice above and beyond the calls they learned while blacked out and fucking bitches.

The male attorneys, barrel-chested, off key, having assembled in a small cluster of navy blues and funeral blacks (WITH NO FUCKING BAIGES LOOOL, The Dumb Owl whispers in my ear), BELLOW the technical term for which I can report to command must now be internally referred to as a dickload of white, golden men:

HAIL OUR HOME FOREVER, ALPHA ALPHA DURR,

I PUT MY COCK INTO MY HANDS THEN PUT IT INTO HER.

PARENTS DON'T FEAR, LEAVE YOUR DAUGHTERS HERE,

WE'LL TREAT HER LIKE A LADY EVEN IF SHE'S 18 YEARS!

As the gilded apes chant this, the defendant and the judge engage in a handshake routine where they slap each other's wrists, cross each other's ankles, sniff each other's asses, pass their tongues lovingly across each other's suited gooches, and eventually end up nearly 69ing before the chanting of keg-fueled rhythmic obscenities has the Dumb Owl about ready to commit seppuku by flying into one of the auxiliary fans, hopefully headbutting the larynx of one of them hard enough to make him die on the way to the blades. Everyone claps. Beers are passed around. Chains with the fraternity symbol, literally just a golden dick cumming what they've told everyone is water from a fountain, are placed around the judge's robed neck and the Senator's shoulders. Each of them are given a pair of aviator sunglasses and cigars that smell like the tailpipe of a truck still trailing after exiting the highway, and they pose for pictures and short clips with the captions LIBERALS DESTROYED IN STYLE, LIBTARDS DESTROYED BY ALPHA ALPHA DURR ALUMS, and just a series of albino eggplant emojis next to dollar signs and rifle toons so real they could be draped over the chests of the military police standing in the corner watching all of this go down, before noticing that *those* are part of the personal security team for the white man with a grandfather's body who I'm now watching suck moonshine shots out of the stomach of a woman dressed like the sexy version of a paralegal intern, before squinting my eyes through the residual cigar smoke plus the shit being pumped from the smokesystems that OH MY FUCKING WHITE JESUS CHRIST

"You see, John?" Senator Baetz says, walking back towards me and the donger pone with his aviators in his hand and the woman running her star spangled fake nails through the dude's luscious, Calhounean mane. "This is what happens when you finally ditch those plebs and ascend yourself to the motherfuckin' *star* side!"

"Oh why *hello* there, Mister Mask man," Miss America says, her voice sultry and sweet and the necessity of human imitation causing my own pants to bulge. "Master *Baetz* has told me so much about your *heroic* efforts!"

"Greetings, Madam," I say, bowing my fully-masked head and thanking the lords this thing has one way eyes to hide my own's wide-open shock. "I am glad to have saved the life of your most passionate lover."

This causes her, the Justice Chief, and the Defendant to all laugh like I've just unleashed a huff of nitrous oxide straight up their raw nasal canals. Through his squinting eyes and the sweat beading down his eyebrows, the room seeming to grow hotter with every manic flick of his eyeballs, Senator Baetz says, "Did you *hear* him?"

"What a poor, innocent mind," Justice Britt says, draping his own sleeved arm around Ms. America and winking at me with a wrinkled eyelid. "Son, you're in the *big leagues* now. Your feelings should have left you a long time ago. Here," he says, as a butlery, young Black man brings over another fresh batch of methamphetamine on a golden platter with silver spoons in a bowl made of straight-cut rubies. "This is what they found in Andrew Gillum's hotel room!"

Like a group of bots with their switches clicked, the entire orange royalty in the party hall atmosphere around us starts laughing violently. An attorney with the face of a disappointed truck driver has his tongue LOLLING out of his mouth, pounding his chest with his fake Rolex and shitty cufflinks, going OWNED, OWNED, OWNED! Another, younger male with potentially representative or senatorial aspirations twinkling in his chestnut eyes is actually salivating and staring directly towards the judge's puckered asshole beneath those billowing guinea pig robes. The bailiff raises his grenade launcher into the air and bellows a war cry behind his pure plastic visor, the albino, hairless, SWAT-armored Wookie yowling into the void with his publicly funded jetpack ready to take him skyward into the hallowed, steepled ceiling boards. By the time I'm finished smoking the meth they shoved into the gilded bong, modeled like some upside-down holy grail, I can honestly say I'm ready to narrate the end of the world and can feel it rising like the dicks of every JD-holding lecher who claps his own hands when Judge Britt slaps his open palm straight onto Ms. America's patriot-laced ass.

"BOOM!" He says, lowering his sunglasses to look into her 'adoring' face looking back up at him in NDA-protected surprise. "*Exactly* like we did in college!"

"FUCK YEAH!!!" Everyone screams, lifting me atop the satin pillow towards the ceiling while the DUMB OWL gets ready to live tweet the trial's happenings. And as I'm getting higher, I'm realizing some things: the dumber I am, the higher I go. Senator Baetz doesn't give a single living *fuck* about DJ, or his family, or even or especially his father. By the time I'm back on the ground, Senator Baetz confirms my revelations as Ms. America floats on to another group of rock stars, wiping his sunglasses with his $300 handkerchief.

"You see her?" Senator Baetz asks, pointing at the woman. "When I first saw the video, I could not *believe* that asses could bounce that way."

"The man you saved's a lucky motherfucker," Judge Britt says, pointing a finger at me around his customized Budweiser can, with his shirtless self staining the steel. "Back in the day, Kennedy was only able to fuck Marilyn Monroe when nobody could see it."

Senator Baetz, mid-sip, points his finger right back at him and raises his bushy caterpillars in agreement. "She's doing the Kardashians in reverse."

"Why is she here?" I ask. She's currently in the middle of a group of three young ish straight white male lawyers or lawyer-looking people, the same who screamed and bellowed and stiffened during the earlier fraternity-legal ritual. She's resting her hip on the shoulder of a dude who is sitting in some sort of mechanized wheelchair, not quite the Walley-Level thing since it seems like its needed via medical necessity vs saving milage at Doorstore.

"She's got a hot new boyfriend," Justice Britt says, picking up another can of cold, golden beer. He holds it in front of his mouth, opens his cracking jaw and yellowed teeth, and flexes a full bone smile at Senator Baetz. "What do we say, fellow Beaureaguard?"

Senator Baetz drops down to one knee, puts his elbow on it, plants his fist into his skull, then opens his lungs up to heaven and screams, "WE'VE GOT OURSELVES A BLUNNNNDERRRRBUSSSSSS!"

Justice Britt chomps right the fuck through the side of the beer car, ripping through the metal like a horse chewing grass. He spits out a couple of the shards through lips and over gums that have been trained in these sorts of ancient rituals, having held the can aloft in his locked jaws while draining the beer down his gullet before tossing the recycling straight onto the ground and stomping on it with his steel-toed boots.

"I'd love to see your old friend's father do *that*," Senator Baetz says, having bit his ringless knuckles in joy at watching the spectacle. "That's how you know he's a beta: he raised a son who can't pull trig!"

Ms. America has kissed her new boyfriend goodbye, and he and his frat bred, steroid bourgeoisie wingboys make their way over to us ready to inform us about Dogecoin and how the stock market capitalization on the death industry has been awesome since cremation went public.

"Well howdy there, partners!" The man in the wheelchair says. He's somehow procured a ten-gallon hat from somewhere framing him as halfway between a young bull and the men who tried to tame them. "I'm so glad I could fly here and join the show today!"

Turns out, this dude is actually *in* college – at once, he's the head of the college republicans at Dickson Florida University, a Guinea Pig Convention co-organizer, *and* a Representative for Florida's 420th district. His name is Baddie Pawhorn, named after his propensity to shoot everything from people who step on his property illegally to the kinds of needles that make you dream of worlds with no vaccines. Proudly unvaccinated, this here gentleman has called the virus an impediment to money and has an anti-faucism button pinned right on his lapel next to his Guinea Pig Big Brother insignia. Oh, and the first thing he tells me when I ask him what he's studying is that he wants to drop out of the school soon, but needed to be there to make sure he got into Alpha Alpha Durr just to reach the level of his inspirations.

Why?

"Because," he says, with the same southern twang. "We're all doing battle against the satanic, f****t libs."

"Hey there!" Judge Britt says, playfully slapping him with his pure metal gavel as a warm-up for the ding ding fight bell mounted to the side of the lectern next to his comfortable, fluffed pillow throne. "I don't want to hear that locker room talk out of good natured, young men like you."

"Speaking of the libs," another lawyer bro says, this one a pale as fuck, sorta buff ginger, wearing a white and red guinea pig tie over a maroon buttoned shirt. "I wonder if the government's going to try to paint the *gator* as the victim again."

"Excuse me," I say, feeling as disoriented as prey in a jungle from the chugging THOMAS TONKA TRAIN in my head from the meth and the batshittery I'm hearing, along with the alcohol and coke. "Aren't we not supposed to be discussing the case in personal terms?"

"WOW!" Senator Baetz says, wrapping his arm around me to the lurid smiles of the men around us. "My witness is an *ethics* person! And at so young an age!"

"John, my boy," Judge Britt says, pitying me like a grandfather peering down at a bad report card. "When I was 14, I was hunting alligators and getting a real education from the hottest teacher in my school." He chuckles. LITERALLY. "By 17, I was hunting in the woods and baha-ing the Florida bayous like I myself was a frontiersman discovering an untapped, untamed universe." He steps closer to me, allowing the skunk of aftershave plus his strong-ass liquor to clog my senseless nostrils –

Wait.

I thought it was the *meth* making me cough.

"Chief of Justice," I say, already interrupting his spiel, the blaring camera lights glaring off my puffy eyelids like we're two teammates about to tangle in confrontation. "I must admit I'm screamingly high off government provided methamphetamines and have noticed I cannot smell what's in my nose. I can feel the thickness of the air, but not its particular sensation."

"A newbie," Justice Britt says, sizing me up and staring down at me with unfixable nose caverns opening like inverse abysses clogged with slick nose hair. "Alright." He claps his hands three times. The music stops. A microphone is rushed to him by the same judicial orderly. They wheel a stage over to him to, the cops both scoffing at me for my potential virality, I'm assuming, as they retreat back to the shadows with the gurney. There, between the tables awaiting the imminent arrival of the prosecution and the defense, we now stand on a stage with the audience of American royalty waiting on the buzzing static of what the man has to say.

"Beloved members of the legal community," he says. "I am pleased to tell you we have a new addition to the highest society in the United States: it is the absolute pleasure of the Guinea Piggers to initiate John Mejora into our midst!"

Everyone cheers and claps, blows horns, the whole nine yards. I can feel the room getting excessively delirious due to the nature of my fevered mind. Motherfucking goddammit. Looks like we're going to need the Owl.

"Now, do we know his test?"

"YES, WE KNOW HIS TEST!"

"ARE YOU READY TO SEE HIM PASS HIS TEST?"

"YES, WE ARE READY TO SEE HIM PASS HIS TEST."

"Excellent!" Justice Britt says. "So, let me ask you all: are we *negative* for *COVID-19?*"

"WHO CARES!" They fucking *howl*. "WE ARE ALPHA ALPHA DURR: POSITIVE FOR *FREEDOM!*"

At this, I allow the fast-moving illness to take me far away from the echoing noise, the sound of them saying nothing stops due to germs, the rest of my senses fading as the Dumb Owl cracks his beak and starts click clacking …

TWENTY SIX

THE DUMB OWL (AKA TDO):

LOOOOOOOOOOOOOOOOOOOOOOOOOOOOOOO
OOOOOOOOOOOOOOOOOOOOOOOLLLLLLLLL
LLLLLLLLLLLLLLLLLLLLLLLLLLLLLLLLL
LLLLLLLLLLLLLLOLOLOLOLOLOLOLOLLM-
FAOOOOOOOOOOOOOOOOOOOOO MAN, THERE'S
NO RHYME OR REASON TO ANY OF THIS SHIT IM
FUCKING SEEING. LET ME TELL YOU RIGHT NOW.
(1/INFUCKINGFINITYTHOUSAND)

Cunt.

CUNT.

These daft CUNTS are LITERALLY making our
UNDERAGE LORD AND SAVIOR, JOHN MEJORA,
GET ON THE WITNESS STAND WITH A 103 DEGREE
FEVER, HIS NOSE FUCKING DESTROYED, AND HIS
BRAIN BOILERING LIKE A FLOCK OF HOPPIN FROGS
IN A CROCKPOT

Jesus CHRIST!

Justice Goddamn Britt is up there showcasing this trial like he's a motherfucking rockstar, too. He's doing his shit in style, gesticulating with the microphone and casting each brow cleanse by either the defense or prosecution team with the intensity of a sports announcer at a fucking grand final. And what a grand finale this is, seeing THE DAFT ONE TAKE HIS STAND!!!

THE DAFT ONE: I can report at this juncture that I am flying through some kind of universal mindfuck. That's the shit of needing to use these inferior craniums: due to their purely cylindrical nature, your backwards species, with your hairy asses and your stupid, girthless chodes … my donger pony's design is infinitely superior to any of your laughable attempts at equestrial engineering.

PROSECUTOR: Sir, I'm going to repeat the question.

TDO: Justice Britt SLAMS his hand down on a big red button next to his desk. An axe sharper than the one that felled the cherry tree for Washington whisks through the air like a medieval carnival trap and almost bisects the Prosecutor, Eagle mask replaced with mid-50s white Alpha Alpha DurrDurr Murderer rouge.

The motherfucker's able to juke out of the way as Justice Baits hollers, his neck blotching red like he used Occam's razer to shave, ASKED AND ANSWERED, MISTER DUBLAUNC, OR HOWEVER THE FUCK YOU SAY IT.

I'VE HAD ENOUGH OF THIS MOTHERFUCKING DISRESPECTFUL SHIT IN *MY* COURTROOM. YOU'RE EMBARASSING THE LAW WITH YOUR REPEATED

INABILITY TO CONSIDER THE MOST IMPORANT
ELEMENT OF THIS TRIAL:

(He says this to the jury, who are sitting six and six in the
cheap pleb section, some pressing their folded hands over their
pantsuited or jacketed stomachs in an attempt to stop their violent acid waves. They're all white people between 20 and 45,
modestly business casual)

THE FEELINGS OF THE DEFENDANT AND ALL
THE WITNESSES TO THIS ALLIGATOR'S VIOLENCE!

PROSECUTER #2: OBBBBJECTION! THE JUDGE
CAN'T OPENLY DECLARE HIS UNDYING LOVE FOR A
WITNESS OFF THE BENCH LIKE *THIS*! YOU AT LEAST
NEED TO BE *STANDING UP*!

JB: This is MY motherfucking courtroom Ms. Van Cocklin.
I have not served nearly 50 years on the bench, to the point
where my ass is sculpted in the wood, to be so INSULTED
by a WOMAN with such a SHRILL VOICE interrupting my
attempt to explain why *both* sides of this are so important!

ProseCUTEST celebritorney Lauren Van Cocklin, the district attorney of all former-cop-porn-parody-hot mayor-fucking
rockstars down here in Florida, known for busting crime and
making stupid socialists do time, is about to OWN this here
judge in a TITANIC argument in the courtroom!!!!

!!!!!!!!!

249

!!!

(BELL EMOJI)
SUBSCRIBE to PRO BONO LEGAL OWNAGE ON YOUTUBE RIGHT NOW!!!

LVC: So let me get this straight, your honor: you're telling me this fevered, drug-addicted, political celeb *in media res* is going to be allowed to preach about his love for a wild animal rather than getting another dose of silver to kill COVID-19?

JB: Yes! That is absolutely what I'm doing, Ms. Van Cocklin: I am following the laws as inscribed in the constitution of the United States of America and the even sexier cousin: the constitution of the great state of FLORIDA!!!!

DAFT MEJORA, MASK BRIMMING WITH SWEAT AND STICKING TO HIS CHEEKS AND CHIN AND FOREHEAD: Listen, alright, if anyone calls my pony a *wild* animal again, I'm going to merk them the exact same way you saw Senator Baetz line up and blast that stupid lizard's brain's *straight* down to the tarmac, bleached Kamala!

PROSECUTOR #1, THE DUDE IN THE WHEELCHAIR WE WERE TALKING SHIT WITH EARLIER WHO WE'VE LEARNED DOESN'T USE THE THING OUT OF NECESSITY, HE USES IT IN HONOR OF HIS FATHER WHO WAS *ACTUALLY* PARALYZED: Your honor, please, this is getting ridiculous. Why did we even have a trial if we all knew how this would be?

SENATOR BAETZ, sitting next to the Donger Pony Sculpture on the defense table next to him: OBJECTION, your honor!

He slams down his hand on the table so hard it bends under the weight of his outraged white guy fist, his hair bobbing in the scent of aerosol sprayed fresh from the can right up his nostrils, too, to help push the virus out. Meanwhile, a younger woman with red hair in the front row of jurors is looking a bit squeamish, and her stomach's making boiling sounds.

TDO: ༻°ༀ°༺ uggggggghhhhh I want mommy van Clarkson to cuck me the same way Moe Wanchin cucked Moe Wyden. Every mother trucker in a 103 mile radius who has ever loved a woman telling him exactly how she wants to peg him is now making a meme about this prosecutor who would look even hotter as my Dommy Mommy tbh.

ANYway…

SENATOR JAMES BAETZ, representing himself, his tangerine and navy blue fusion suit making him look like trustfund Phoenix Wright fused with a dude who bet on "mandingos," opens his mouth and gestures, points, waves his fingers for emphasis, and uses more air than Strom Thurmond ripping lines during a filibuster to present the case for why he's innocent for his unfortunately mortal violence towards Southwest Airlines' property.

BAETZ: HONORABLE Justice Britt Beareaguard, ladies and gentlemen and whatever you want to call yourselves nowadays, you fellow Floridian patriot holy guinea pig god-blessed WARRIORS!

He snares the air with a quick whip of his fist like he's tying the last ropes to fasten a caravan.

BAETZ (CUNT): I am so pleased to be able to, at *this* juncture, tell you exactly why what mister John Mejora's saying through his heroic, mouth of baby Jesus Christmas LIPS represents the best vision of justice in this country we here in Orangeland could ever offer. I –

EVERYBODY GET UP

The jury, the watchers in the galleys, the BAETZ BABES ready to spend their entire life savings on conjugal games of put your rear in gear with the very man they want to bear their children, all of them, stand up as the song plays in the confused, nationally televised air of the muggy, buzzing courtroom.

HEY HEY HEY

HEY HEY HEY

HEY HEY -

The judge mutes the ringtone, raises his Iphone to his smugly smirking face, and nods his head at the camera like he's a complete alpha ready to walk on and blow out the country's biggest football teams!

JB: Hey, Leenie bo Beenie! How are you this fine, de-licious day? *he growls like a feral cat and even curls his upper lip*

JB: Yeah!

JB: Hey, so glad you're watching there at home! *Waves to the big cameras, entire fucking courtroom looks around at each other with a combination of 😊 and mouthing the names of loved ones into the blaring lights towards the living, spectating world.*

JB: Okay, sure, I'll tell him after. Right. Absolutely. I will tell him that he needs to swing his dick onto the table and tell everyone exactly how amazing it is he's been able to be such a *champion* for the people of Florida through this trauma.

The Prosecution team looks at one another, with the dude in the choose-your-own scooter chair basically raising his untrimmed caterpillar eyebrows at the utterly mortified Badass van Shocked-Lin. In their seats, the rapid pulsing of tweeting keys around the courtroom, plus the ca-chings of bets being placed for some of the people raking in the per-clicks from their subscribers to the madness plays as a soundtrack to Marlene's dictations on the shitty, uncapped speakers of Judge Britt's iPhone69.

JB: Perfect. I cannot wait to sniff the revelations of your crotch, my darling. *He licks the phone three times up and down, sighs like he's just finished jerking on the shitter, then places the phone back down into the reaches of his desk as they return from commercial break to watch Senator Baetz and the Daft One dance with violently fevered freedom in these dumb seasons of plague ...*

UNNNNNNNNNNNNNNNHNHNHNHJHJHJHJHJHJJFDS-KAJFGASLDFLAD

DiD yOu EvEr HeaR mE sAy I hATeD GaToRadE?

He's telling me this as though submerged underneath the ground of a mass grave knocked loose by necessity when the monument companies failed to make headstones for people passed away, the entire factory of death spewing its juices out solely to have me sweating my ass off on this stand, sniffing everything, smelling nothing, my disgusting gorgeous mask's rimmed insides ruined by the perspiration of

"Son, are you talking to the aliens again?"

Listen here, motherfucker, I told you once and I'm going to just be saying it again: my donger pony didn't ride across an entire country of death and take my BFF to the hospital solely to die of this coronavirus I caught there right here on the fucking floor. I'm a pediatric citizen of this glorious country and I am a young man who knows my rights, Senator!

The drama's caught the crowd in crazy spouted gasps and whispers, some exclamations as the women recalibrate their polit-ical moistness in comparison to Senator Baetz's collar, since he's sweating his little ass off there right now. I don't remember what a script is but I've shouted I WILL NOT BE PROGRAMMED twice already into the microphone, and then as I holler it another time people are starting to catch on that I'm doing the most American thing I ever could while I can't control my inner troll-dom: I'm doing a both sides INSIDE a both sides, so therefore I can see *all* sides.

Gentlemen, allow me, in my dripping delirium, to remind you of a core tenant of this nation's founding documents: I AM A YOUNG WHITE MALE AND MY FEELINGS ARE

SUPERIOR!

The Alpha Alpha Durr's claps and hoots and hollars in the audience, the patriotic, fatherly, misty-eyed way Senator Baetz has his hand plastered over his heart and probably imagining Calhoun's luscious locks raining down his waxed chest in rivers of body oil and perspiration anticipating the climax of Judge Britt slamming his hammer like a toddler with a toy it wants to use to learn how to break shit, saying, "I have never been more *insulted* in my whole career on this bench!"

Yeah, that's right you're on the bench, I'm the motherfucking starting quarterback, cumhaired knuckledragger.

.

...

OH SHIT, THAT WAS *OUT LOUD.*

Cough. Cough Cough. Sorry, Justice, for that unscrupulous insult.

I point to the donger pony sitting at the defense table.

Baetz sighs, pressing his fingers into his nosebridge, pinching them, casting his eyes straight upwards at the godly hammer, probably wishing the pendulum would unmoor from the industrial bolts in the ceiling and crash him back into 1847 in as many ways.

"Yes," he says, sounding like a defeated dad. "I pone, therefore I yam."

"Give him."

Justice Baetz, the defense attorneys, the cameras, the people, the camerapeople, the courtroom. It's like I've just tried to tell them the alligator had feelings, too.

"Give him to me." I repeat.

"But," Baetz stutters. I hold up a middle finger directly in front of my face, pointing at myself, my arm rigid as can be while shaking from the fever.

Judge Britt, who has been biting the top part of his knuckles and probably imagining fifteen different ways to brain me with that silly little gabblewabble, relents. He motions, approving the motion.

Baetz picks the pony under his arm, makes sure he plants it on the side of the witness stand away from the microphone, and leans into me with a look of malice in his eyes someone like him must've given to a million different 'Indians' when inventing collaterality.

"Kid," he says, whispering into my ear. "You had better have some sort of silver bullet behind your mask, or I'm going to make you feel even worse than that lilywhite, weepy-eyed f****t who couldn't hit the killshot when his daddy's life depended on it."

I lift up my mask, revealing my red, pulsing, sopping face. With the pony in one arm, I raise a finger gun directly at the senator's chest, wink one of my sore eyelids, and tell him, "I don't need a bullet, Senator. Not when I've got this here white donger."

I screw the pony's tail off with three rotations of the top. There, sitting in a bowl the size of a grown person's shoulder circumference, is the best cash crop I've ever tasted from this green and blue and sillywhite planet. With a quick, off-camera suction of my virus corrupted lungs, I exhale into the open, waiting mouths of the defense team, the prosecution, Judge Britt and Lady Justice, spreading my personal choices to mix with theirs in drifting smoke.

"Justice Britt," I ask. "Have you ever tried … *DMT*?"

The moon is full, and my puffy mask is smiling, shining.

"*Excuse* me?" Judge Britt asks. I give an easy smile, nodding at the buffest men sitting in the jury pool to see if they're catching on with my vibes.

"You know, DongerMoxyTriptheFiend."

"Oh yeah," Van Cocklin says. "I've heard Moe Hogan talk about this shit before."

"Brooooo," Baetz says, lighting up a hand-rolled cigar made from a tobacco leaf the size of a tablet. He's got his gold chain draping his neck with a solid 69-karot Calhoun hanging right above his solar plexus. "*Now* I see why he was talking about the *aliens.*"

"What did you call this substance?" Judge Britt asks, waving to one of the studio technicians sitting right in front of the audience. "Hector, can we call Governor Mercantis and see if he has any extra?"

"No, no, *noooo,*" I say, before the tech is even done pulling out his phone. "I was just curious, your honor. You know, I'm the kind of guy who has a lot of *thoughts* about things."

"A student in the tradition of great liberal thinkers," Judge Britt says, his voice reeking with sarcasm worse than a shit bed.

"Close," I tell him, screwing the Pony's donger tail back on and craning my neck towards the jury, my lungs feeling like fire that's been trapped under ice. "I consider myself to be more of an amnesiac: I think about a few things again and again, this 'mortal world' shit I can forget about."

The crowd groans. From the convention center speakers, a *wah wah* sound fills my ears so loudly they might as well be infected, too.

"So you're one of *those* people," Justice Britt says, his delivery evoking the audience's laughter like his forehead says APPLAUSE. "You get any tickets to heaven shoved inside that horse?"

"Nahhhhhh," I say, blowing off his comment and winking at the jury, whose eyes are glued to me like I've got them all at gunpoint. "I'm thinking about the *children.*"

"Oooooookay, *here* we go," Van Cocklin says, her heels clacking on the floor from where she stabs them down getting out of her chair. "Your honor, if I have to hear a liberal tell me to 'think about the children' one more god forsaken time, I'll- "

"Excuse me, Miss CUUUUUUNT!" I howl at her, freezing her halfway to the bench. "Would you PLEASE stop trying to IMPRISON my FREE THINKING?"

The bailiffs dart onto the floor and carefully escort Van Brocklin back to her chair, her profuse apologies spilling her over shoulders worse than her frazzled, frizzly hair.

"I'm thinking about the children *underneath* the Chuck E. Cheese."

My words stop her in her tracks as though there's an invisible wall that's been planted right between the benches and the lectern. The Guinea Piggers in the crowd snap to me as though I've just thrown a wet, crunchy bushel of carrots coated with nutritious lifeblood right down the center aisle. The crackling from the speakers dances across the silence like the electricity in the air, as if another whispered word into the microphone would blow the building down.

"That's *right*," I tell them. "This whole time we've been debating over the actions of Jim Baetz, but I'm here to argue there's *levels* to this shit."

In his now blazing eyes staring back at my blazed own, Justice Britt sits straight up in his chair, the laissez-faire, airy tone to his voice completely gone. "Son, are you meaning to tell me you think the gator was a *plant*?"

Somewhere in the courtroom, the Southwest Airlines people, confident in their government's ability to do whatever the fuck they wanted and make it seem like their idea, are currently spamming so many calls towards the nearest cell tower that the entire network's gonna short well before they all go comatose from 5G.

"Not a plant," I say, flinching at the jury like I'm connecting dots with the power of my forehead right in front of them. "A ... *reptile.*"

The white dude who looks like a pornstar lumberjack, in full flannel, who had been ripping air up his nostrils ever since I mentioned *pizza* vibrates his balding cranium and says *ennnn-nnnnhhhh* softly, but firmly, clearly. The Guinea Pig Priest, who gave a benediction that mentioned not Jesus nor God but tons of ways to find healing through wall-mounted water bottles is standing, his own mask so tightly pressed to his face the wires across the back threaten to burn a scar right into him. Across the audience, the mention of their natural enemy has sparked something those stormtrooper bailiffs could never put down with as many guns as they could hold in *three* sets of eager hands.

"It makes *perfect* sense," I say, directly after having just a kiss of Jimmy B's 'cigar.' "Here we are in Florida, fighting one another, just so they can keep us occupied and miles from the truth!"

"Justice Britt," the wheelchair man says, the glow from beer, babes, and bro songs replaced by the hair on his sculpted neck straight on end from the bristling teeth behind him. "I'd like to argue we could use a recess right 'bout now."

"RECESS?" I say, going *pffffffft* and hacking out a laugh drier than the radius around Jimmy Baetz's petrified hairdo. "So you *are* familiar with kids when they're on the playground."

"ENNNNNNNNHHHHHHH!!!!" The lumberjack guy says, ripping open his flannel and popping buttons on the ground like shells hitting paydirt falling off an automatic. The military police have their bazookas trained on the crowd. The discount tabernacle doors to the hallway shake as whatever the fuck they're using as a do it yourself battering ram causes a guard to go rushing past the frothing, vibrating, yelling crowd, the Southwest Representatives with their attorneys on speakerphone and wads of money clenched in hands sweating so hard, dollar green just bleeding down their forearms. The cameras roll on, the independent journalists in the watchful audience encircling the Guinea Piggers in their wannabee combat stances next to the slinking, hunkered Southwest Reps who the Government's decided it's no longer worth defending.

"It's a sad, sad day," I say, sighing and shaking my head. "When our country's sense of justice gets defined by fucking *demonrats*."

Snarling. Snapping. Bared teeth, lacerating the air, feeling as though those implanted rodent chompers were chiseled for jugular puncturing.

"How do you know they're Democrats?" Justice Britt asks, his gaze as distant as a man whose horizons line with mushroom clouds.

"Common sense," I shrug, pointing over my shoulder towards the jury box. "You can see the blue bloods just by looking at their *skin!*"

The whole courtroom pivots. The three jurors of the twelve who were bent over or burping, gripping tummies or popping tums – a white man in his 30s, a white woman right out of college with blonde hair and mercury irises, go figure, plus an older, white woman who remembers calling this shit under *Clinton* – have since felt their symptoms subside, but now feel the weight of all our eyes pressing on their suntanned skin. The other jurors around them gasp in pure shock, scrambling backwards on hands and knees from their chairs and stools. As they realize they've been marked – or rather, that they've marked themselves – the three jurors begin tearing at their bluing flesh, as though their fingernails could be enough to sheer the organ of its traitorous hue. Alas, the door breaks down and the jury from the outside, the true ones, holding the guns and phones and seismic cross they must've stolen straight from the Dickson County High School library comes ramming through the door as the wave of red and white and blue converges in that jury box with a fury I can't quite tell you about even though I'm sitting close enough, on this witness stand, to get some sort of scorching from it. But that's the issue, or so I think, as they drag the three COWARDLY Chinese agents straight against the bench, Judge Britt having left his post to drag the bluish prosecutor from his wheelchair: I didn't start the fire here, in a foremost prophet's words. I've been burning since I reached this place, and I can see, from the crimson flood delirium of them biting at those fellow people, there comes a point where you inhale the smoke so much, you get kinda proud of pumping it out every exhaust and tailpipe. I guess, in their minds, strapping the prosecutor to the wooden bench while he screams he made a mistake, that he isn't afraid, even as his knees knock and bladder bursts and shit stains his thousand dollar pants, this is the freshest air they've ever tasted, and it's the only one they need.

"Ladies and gentleman of the jury," Judge Britt asks, his gavel resting on his shoulder, stained with things that don't belong outside of *anybody's* cranium. "Have we finally reached a verdict?"

"Yes, your honor," The Guinea Pig Priest says, his arms rubber from the cross's mounting. "*Don't* think of the children, or you'll become a Democrat!"

The crowd claps. Cheers. Sending up that symphony of tongues and flesh I've grown so tired of standing before. As I dismount the witness stand, re-holster the Pone, and plant the Dumb Owl – himself turning back to green from the quick colloidal photosynthesizing from his system – back on my right shoulder, Senator Baetz plants his arm around my other side and squeezes me with the closest thing to hug I think he can rightly manage.

"You're a sick man, Mister Mejora," he says, a glint in his eye I can't reproduce no matter how long or hard I practice. "That's why we fuckin' *love* you here."

"No, Senator Baetz," I tell him, mounting my mask over my face. "This is a *sick* fucking country. I just *had* to love the illness!"

With the weight of history behind his words, Justice Britt makes a big show of winding up his right hand above his shoulders, bringing it level with his chest in front of him, and, with a nod of his head at Hector, sticks his fist right out towards him as though he's looking for a robed brofist to celebrate this here occasion.

"THREE! TWO! ONE!"

Britt flicks his thumb down.

"*JUSTICE!*"

The hummer-sized hammer drops from the ceiling in a smooth, straight line, and for the first time on this disgusting planet, I'm understanding why they start laughing as soon as axes start to fall.

TWENTY SEVEN

Following my successful intervention on behalf of the American people to uncover the Democrats' filthy infiltration of our best protection against COVID-19 – I'm a platty in real life now, not just in *GO* like DJ – I was successfully able to convince the federal forces to not immediately nuke the courthouse and count it as a misclick. The last time I ventured up to DC, it was beside both DJ and his father and the Owl whose wisdom is currently on life support with something they're hoping is just an *avian flu*. Basically, the only thing preventing the state of Florida from buzzsawing itself off the country's southern ass and declaring the official religion to be Rodentia, both in terms of the heavenly Guinea Pigs they're ready to die for and the Demonrats they fight against, as on left, so on right, and so on, is me showing up to Moe Wyden's office and somehow getting him to sign the treaty Britt and Baetz have partially drafted. The sheer joy of combing splinters out of Senator Baetz's hair shared between both he and Marlene following the execution showed in the manic way the greatest legal minds the land has seen since Barbie Galaxy fucked Willy C for getting blown while smoking 'stead of smoking blow successfully produced a draft of what they're calling the 69th Amendment to the Constitution of the United States of America, which, thanks to their billowing brill pens and the friendly rivalry between the lengths of their wobbly things while both hardened and flaccid, reads as such:

The State of Florida hereby reserves the right to do whatever the fuck it wants in whatever manner it so pleases. There is literally, absolutely nothing the federal government could do to stop us from handing out actual rat poison to everyone in the state so long as they themselves want to drink it. Therefore, states will no longer be held liable in the courts of public opinion for the Government's twofold ability to kill children, both aboveground and below, and do declare ourselves to be our own independent monarchy: here, ANYONE can be the Burger King! Also, fuck Roe v Wade!

Basically, if Big Daddy Moe wants to keep Didney Worl from going full EPCOT, he needs to say that all the kids who are dying are the responsibility of the federal government after being so 'brutally exposed' for his subterfuge. Half the talking heads bullshit about how there was no actual connection between the Democrats and the colloidal syrup, and the other half who are also going on Fake Time with Buck Rodd on Sunday mornings are claiming they, too, fell victim to the blue-skinned nature of colloidal silver, but got it from actually – GASP! – TAKING THE VACCINE! That's right: the people whose skin turns blue haven't only been turned into Democrats, but have been *ANTI-BODIED* by the COVERT VACCINES!

WOOOOOOOOOW!

Saving someone's life without their permission is already a felony in at least three fifths of these forsaken, separate states. Precedent indicates stories of people bleeding out on the road who have been so distressed by EMTs trying to hold their disemboweled organs inside of them, they've had nightmares of their parents telling them to not touch the stove for WEEKS! So, to avoid a lawsuit in front of the Supreme Court – sponsored by the tangerine guy! – I'm taking this here document in this here holy, latch-locked folder straight to the desk of the very man who is the most powerful person in the history of this here Union:

Moe Wyden's programmer. The only question is: how *many* different versions of him have they deployed across this nation?

The Donger Pony squeaks across the leather of the military taxi that picked us up right from the courthouse. We're flying so fast we'll be sitting in the Ovular Office faster than a Nordic warrior got to the Capitol on his tour day.

Overdosing on Twitter, he says, in words even their best signal transmitters can't detect. *Do you think he'll ever see again?*

Hm. I'd tear out my eyes as well, I guess, if I were thinking in this place.

DMDMDMDMDMDMDMDM

Interestingly, getting through security only took a few minutes. You'd think, as the de-facto leader of an armed coalition of people who are allowed to carry military grade weapons right around their capitols and courthouses, as encouraged by the YOU PROTECT ME I PROTECT YOU tourist initiative they're launching in DC, there would be some sort of scanning or frisking or cavity searching aside from tying rocks around the pony and trying to drown it in the presidential swimming pool. Thankfully, our superior physics allow the pony to not only hold the three boulders they tried to tie around and convict it with, but the buoyancy of the intergalactic plastic allows me to place a phonecall to DJ while my fellow coneheads' beloved totem dances through their witchcraft:

"Hello?"

"Dylan 'pickle' James!"

"Oh ... hey, John."

"Yes, that's right, it is I! The President-Elect of the Dickson County School board!"

"I saw the news, man. Hey, I'd love to talk, but right now I'm helping my mom sell the bleach around the hospital."

"Ah, yes. I saw your mother's glorious, injectable advertisement for the most secure way to turn COVID white this Christmas!"

"Haha, yeah, I'll let her know you liked it. Oh, actually, one sec, let me just step next to this guy dying, here, uh, my dad has a favor that he'd like me to ask of you."

"Naturally. Anything for those who helped me climb!" I pat the Donger Pony's flat head, as they've placed him back next to me and told me *three minutes*.

"Can you tell Ms. America that he misses her cooking?"

"AHAHAHAHAHA, L M F A O, Dylan. Of course. And *she* wishes you luck in the militia games this evening!"

"I'm ready, man. Have fun being someone important, it's a wild, wild world out there."

"It is, Dear Dylan. That much we can agree upon."

I hang up the phone, even as I see high command is wanting to weigh in on things. We've reached the point in our operation second only to when I sacrificed Dalton to the gods of random chance in terms of intensity and restraint. Thankfully, I'm confident in Dylan James' skill playing both terrorists and counter-terrorists that his superior tactical knowledge will compensate for his obvious physical detriments. When has that law ever been proven farcical by the alpha predators in a realm full of kings, peasants, rats, and wolves?!? THE WART SHALL POP, AND MRS. BECKER'S SHOTGUN BLASTS SHALL NOT HAVE BEEN IN VAIN!

Yeah, who am I kidding, he's gonna get blown to swiss cheese tonight by a chunky guy who masturbates to vegetables decimating orifices. At least on the internet, you respawn faster than reality.

Then, in the time it takes for me to be guided across the Kashmir carpets and through the archway to the oval office, I am transplanted from the Dark Ages of unenlightened thought across the history of this gallant species into the chamber from which the fate of a nation, a planet, and these fucking apes they all call *people* ascend past their tribal certainties into the free realm of reasonable, logical ... oh ... *oh* ... oh my *god*, there's ... *THREE* of him???

"HOWDY THERE, NEIGHBOR!" 'Moe Wyden' number 1 says, the same Madame Tussaud's wax body sewn up and suited, his eyes clicking mechanically every time he blinks, their blue neon as invasive to my eyeballs as those halogen car lights piercing a moonless bayou night. His breathing is the same bellowed beat as the machines lining the hallways of every major hospital in the country, and when he shakes my hand, I can feel the mechanisms crudely crunching with a *weew, weet* grip and release you'd expect to see mounted on the stage with the rest of the band of rats. Over his shoulder, I can see Moe Wyden #2, who is literally just a hologram being projected in the same party blue as on every yard sign and pinned button, each waving banner and #BLACKLIVESMATTER bomber he's flown over every desert possible, foreign and domestic, to *post the message of inclusivity right into the atmosphere*! Truly, his campaign is out of this fucking world, and he'll say shit cornier than the slivers stuck between Pilgrims' teeth at the first Thanksgiving based on whatever the nerd sitting in front of that terminal types into that screen. And lastly, sitting behind the vaunted desk, arms sitting on his chair as though draping a throne, there sits the man who is the leader of the free world, with drool running down his chin, his head lolling on a 45 degree angle, and his skin so perfectly preserved by whatever they put on it, it'd probably feel smoother than the leather seats I scraped the pony 'cross this afternoon. A young, white, male orderly, I guess he must be an intern, guides us to a chair in front of the desk and allows Robot Wyden to keep practicing his self-defense kicks and strikes and pirouettes. Then, he grabs a short stepping stool and approaches the high-backed Presidential seat, the Ouija board-looking thing with the letters and the numbers at the ready for Moe to use. Instead of needing to interpret his spirit, though, I tell the orderly to wait. Finally, I say the incantation that causes his bones to dance like the drumbeat of a necromancer back when those sorts of things had names.

"The ... *constitution.*"

The ancient eyes open, their pallid irises the center of a hurricane of saffron streaks. His throat smelling like an opened crypt, with the funk of 245 years emanating from behind his *perfect* teeth in a gutfucking wave, Moe Wyden raises his skeletal hands. The intern tells me to place the proposed amendment directly in their dusted palms. In a motion slower than dialup, he places the paper right over his face, presses a button to recline his chair, takes a hallowed breath, and ... waits.

And waits.

And fucking ... what? What is he doing? Why are we sitting here?

"Mr. President?" I ask.

"SHHHHHHHHH," The orderly says, as though I'm a child who just screamed FUCK at granddad's casket. "He's *working!*"

In a frail voice spoken through rotting teeth and ancient tongue, the President says:

"I ... AM ... ABSORBING ... THE ... KNOWLEDGE ..."

The color they use for his forehead and skin is seeping through the fucking legal-grade paper. Right when its nearly Mache, Android Wyden robots over to us and instructs the orderly to flip the paper. Grabbing chunks of the paragraphs disintegrating into smearing ink, he picks the globs and goops and turns them just like pancakes on the stove.

"A H H H H H H H H H H H H H H H H H H H H H H H H H H H H H H H H," Moe Wyden says, in his purest exhalation. "BOTH ... SIDES!"

Despite the tears leaking from my eyes, I can feel myself laughing, the crumpled amendment racing past me like melted millennia into the donger pony's splendid, nonsensical attraction.

"I feel it," I whisper into the humid, inky air. "I can feel their meaning."

And to think: I came all this way and expected something different. With images of the boy who finally pulled the trigger surrounding me in the supernovic heat from the rotating, spherical dongulation, my mission is accomplished: by being this absurd, I have become a person, too.

EPILOGUE

'Earth'

The tour guide takes them directly next to the statue that stands where the White House once stood.

"Here stands the first monument erected on these grounds," the tour guide says. The statue is quite strange: his head is *round*, his eyes are *blue*, and his hair is a light color the same shade as human urine. However, in the shadow of THE DAFT ONE, sculpted out of the same material as his beloved Donger Pone, with the Owl mounted on his shoulder in eternal emerald green, the tour guide tells them the legend they've heard since the first time they left their homes. In the hallowed ground, they hear of how the man discovered first the beaches with the cancer trucks, then moved through the ancient, farcical systems of crude technology and love of inanimate dollar bills. However, when the tour guide, speaking in bluster and with the fervor of a man standing in his hero's shadow, gets to the part about how THE DAFT ONE heroically saved the tribal leader from the very little pieces of metal he so loved, a being with her headcone draped in golden ribbons raises her hand politely.

"Yes, my dear?" The tour guide asks.

"Mister tour guide," she says, her voice sweetly lifting. "Did I hear right that John Mejora fell in *love* with these disgusting bipeds?"

Head nods amongst the adults. Knowing grins. Her parents pat her head, accepting kids will ask these silly things.

"He has a complicated history," the tour guide says. "At that time, it was very common for the first of us who came to this place to be ensnared by them, the same way the primates wrote about a siren's call: their drugs, their hearts, their stubborn, shrewd hopes. Proportionally, ridiculous technology available at the counterbalance of their own sanities and atmospheres, the potential to see things that aren't there and still believe in them – trust me, if you weren't careful in those days, losing one of those humans might feel the same as your pet donger pony dying!"

"What an idiot," the little girl says, pulling her living alien cock-shaped lizard horse on a Hello Kitty leash. "*You* would never leave me, right JD?"

The indescribable alien familiar hisses E N N N N N Y Y Y Y H H H H as commanded. The crowd laughs, the sun shines, and in the light of unknown history, the Wise Owl still rhymes, the Dong still Pones, and the Daft One, perfectly preserved, keeps on smiling after time.

"Now, for our next exhibit: this was *actually* a place they used to treat their dead and dying! Yes, they actually stacked them *in their parking lots*! The kids! I know! For those who may be disturbed by the barbaric nature of this exhibit, let me be the one to reassure you: we've come so far since then, and that's why we go backwards!"

AFTERWORD

I've lived in Madrid, Spain, since September of 2021 for all but a wedding weekend back in Pennsylvania in June of 2022, and I've seen my country, America, change completely. From this vantage point, living and working and writing and connecting with persons from across the world, I realized the same thing I did whilst living in the Spanish capitol that I did between September of 2019 and mid-April of 2020, when I lived in Madrid the first time: I have been fortunate enough, due to life and due to circumstance, to bear witness to how current times move to become parts of history. The Coronavirus pandemic, which I saw firsthand in Madrid and then during my time back in the United States by necessity (family, friends, funding, dramatically shifting world dynamics), has been responsible, indirectly or otherwise or by official numbers people stopped counting after a while, for over one million deaths in my home country alone, a number which is debated in some circles (as almost everything that used to constitute agreed upon reality is, to some degree). The way I survived the absolute world-changing advent of the coronavirus pandemic in Madrid was to write fiction, and that's where the idea for *Daft Mejora's Infinite Madness* was originally put on the page for the first time. Never did I think this book would have me compared to Kurt Vonnegut by Thaddeus Gunn, never did I think its ambition, humor, and vision would be noted on wider scales … I was surviving, first, and that's how it started: in reaction to President Trump's daily Coronavirus briefings in April 2020, which I watched from Madrid with a reaction of surreal horror and knowledge that the world has been this way, to an extent, for longer than the virus.

This book began as a piece of short fiction that I submitted to the *New Yorker*, which was not accepted at the time, but which allowed me to crystallize the idea in a way that was radical. Basically, I've seen tons upon tons of books published about the Trump administration for lucrative contracts, in positions supporting the former President (who keeps his title, technically) and basically attempting to use the positive or negative nature of the administration as a personal 'cash cow.' Doing that was never my intention with this book, which is an excoriatingly absurd evolution of what Mejora became: instead of being explicitly tied to the Trump administration, this book demonstrates how American life has become a mix of instantaneous absurdity thanks to the internet mixed with the commonly accepted, mentally numbed daily violence of life's mundanities and curiosities. In Spain, there was a coup attempt that happened in 1981 wherein the then-King of Spain, Juan Carlos I, was instrumental in affirming democratic rule was best for the country at the time, having witnessed the alternative; bullet holes from said coup attempt are still in the ceiling of the Congress of Deputies in Madrid, which has, indeed, even as a country with a functioning monarchy, outranked the United States recently in the world Democracy Index as an ally by a couple slots. I believe, having lived in both countries for stretches of time since 2018, with the majority spent in Spain but with a good year and a half under both the Trump and Biden administrations, that the key reason for this is a lack of collective American memory, wherein some Americans literally do not remember the same physical, actual events in a way that is agreed upon to degrees much higher than normal lapses in historical agreement, and I believe the role of the artist in today's age should be to elucidate the reasons for this in a way that is truthful and as close to objective as possible.

Is this still possible in a country addicted to politics and labels and personal judgments in echo chambers like they're addicted to hardcore drugs? Well, let's recap the events of the week prior to the writing of this afterword, shall we? Currently, former President Trump has become the first President to be charged criminally in a court of law, and his approval rating has soared due to this...

Let's repeat that for future generations: the first President to ever be charged criminally in the United States of America has had his approval rating go straight up, meaning increased, due to what is being perceived by white supremacists and otherwise as political persecution, because frankly, and this is my opinion based on facts, everyone has an opinion but objective scientific fact is not only lacking, it's been overwritten by a religious belief in politics that fills a spiritual void in people both Democratic, Republican, and otherwise. Facts are secondary to opinion, with people who spend their days analyzing and overanalyzing and who are reliant upon any escape from the reality of what's happening and how absurd it has become. Individuals, in general, draw conclusions that are non-sensical in physical reality, and people's addiction to technology (metaversally, personal computer based, social media, etc.) is the only way to escape from the sinking feeling it's all been done before. And in 2016, despite the overwhelming notion that Hillary Clinton would win the election, I felt there was something about Donald Trump that *reflected* a part of America instead of being solely responsible for that part's existence.

On that night in 2016, I remember standing in the first floor of Newman Towers at Loyola Maryland watching the results trickle in; the night prior to voting, I had given a presentation to fellow students as the author of mostly "apolitical," contemporary fiction I already was in undergrad, wherein I said that Trump had a good chance of winning the election because the country itself is what produced him. And here we are, seven years later, with the news cycle still being dominated by everything he does and his historic nature - for better or worse, and its been way worse in some ways even *he* may agree with, although I don't speak for him at all. He's looking to define another election cycle based on celebrity and notoriety and addiction of the American popular conscience to something that is supposed to bring meaning to people but simply leaves them, in an image I saw last fall, tied to invisible wires that move people along that leave a void we fill with separate, simultaneous realities and experiences. While other persons my age were shocked to see Trump win, I had long ago accepted that there were parts of America that saw themselves best reflected in him, and so I was logically unsurprised while emotionally disappointed, at best, at the outcome. And now still, to this day, there are people waiting for the reincarnation of John F. Kennedy Jr. in Dallas, who have paid their life savings against their own family's wishes to believe in a reincarnation of someone who was not Jesus Christ, even, and there are people who literally "bong- ripped" hydrogen peroxide to cure the coronavirus.

Personally, I believe in basic vaccination as the great nephew of a Nobel laureate in Science for the United States of America, but even without stooping into conversations about Pfizer and whatnot, anyone who would inject bleach to cure the Coronavirus, to me, demonstrated a level of detachment from reality readily allowed so long as people's "personal freedoms" to essentially end their own lives were not infringed. To me, *that* is madness, because suicide, to me, is madness, and the point of Daft Mejora in all its forms (with the second project already completed and extending to a level even farther beyond this book) would be to show that there needs to be a return to a world that can be agreed upon by all Americans versus continuing to split ourselves for individual gain, because, from both a human life expectancy standpoint, from a personal profit standpoint, and also from a shared recognition of what is more important than just a payday, America's power has been in being red, white, *and* blue, not one of those three choices. Living abroad, Americans are seen as being collectively American in the places that they visit or inhabit, something I have experienced on many levels with those who agree with President Biden's politics and those who do not, and the fact of the matter is that the wider world is not simply which echo chamber on the internet people decide to live inside: much like the full internet itself, it is a wild, dynamic, and wholly shared experience, which reflects itself in internet culture and has, as we can conclude, begun to refract in the opposite direction with how technology dominates our daily lives with signs of accelerating greatly in the coming years.

Thankfully, for me, I deal with truth and in truth, ultimately, and I am hoping there is a collective push to get back to factual reality without ulterior motives interceding on every relationship we maintain. With the current state of things, what gives me that hope as a human is the fact that Madrid and other areas that are actually in the continental United States have persons who are resilient and who are aware of the farcical nature that is now accepted as everyday society in the popular discourse, and the point of this book is that, if a space alien (which I do believe exist in some form perhaps outside of our daily understanding, because the universe is massive) were to judge the human race based on our worst parts of ourselves which we keep in the shadows and then project online, they would ask whether or not we took inspiration from something like *Dante's Inferno* unironically and tied it to a modem...

Such is why this book is at points ugly, obscene, grotesque, and totally real, because the generation I am part of and the one which follows me have been tied to these wires our entire lives, through gaming and through communication and through social media and through constant connection to something better than surviving the tragedies that have befallen the entire planet. Such is why, despite the nature of these things, I refuse to stop fighting for life, and such is why, as this book has aged following the time I decided to directly publish it through the Internet Archive, it may still be overwhelming to realize these truths from a vantage point of living them, or recently surviving them, but I can say, resolutely, that I strived to witness these days for the betterment, overall, of my country, and to use art for its most essential purpose: translating experience in a world where everyone's reality could be its own separate language if not for the enduring, connecting nature of the human spirit. That, to me, is magic, and it's achievable in a place called America.

Karl M. Dehmelt
April 12th, 2023
Madrid, España
Revised July 18th, 2023
Pennsylvania, USA

About the Author

Karl Michael "K.M." Dehmelt is a writer and a graduate of the Loyola University Maryland Writing program in Baltimore who has lived everywhere from Coopersburg, Pennsylvania to Madrid, Spain. Originally from the East Coast of the United States, his fourth book, and science fiction debut, *Daft Mejora's Infinite Madness (Or How to Travel Near America with Friends)*, has been favorably compared to Kurt Vonnegut. Currently, he is early at work on multiple projects, including more long-form satire, as well a non-fiction project related to his experience as a survivor of a traumatic brain injury and the complexities of navigating the world with a brain he newly learned has been altered from the healing process. He is grateful for his writing, his life, his family, and his true friends.

Apprentice
House Press
Loyola University Maryland

Apprentice House Press is the country's only campus-based, student-staffed book publishing company. Directed by professors and industry professionals, it is a nonprofit activity of the Communication Department at Loyola University Maryland.

Using state-of-the-art technology and an experiential learning model of education, Apprentice House publishes books in untraditional ways. This dual responsibility as publishers and educators creates an unprecedented collaborative environment among faculty and students, while teaching tomorrow's editors, designers, and marketers.

Eclectic and provocative, Apprentice House titles intend to entertain as well as spark dialogue on a variety of topics. Financial contributions to sustain the press's work are welcomed. Contributions are tax deductible to the fullest extent allowed by the IRS.

To learn more about Apprentice House books or to obtain submission guidelines, please visit www.apprenticehouse.com.

Apprentice House Press
Communication Department
Loyola University Maryland
4501 N. Charles Street
Baltimore, MD 21210
Ph: 410-617-5265
info@apprenticehouse.com • www.apprenticehouse.com